LEGACY OF HONOR

THE STRATTON LEGACY ~ BOOK 1

RENAE BRUMBAUGH GREEN

Dear Reader,

I've been writing this book for more than a decade.

In 2008, my dear friend and writing mentor, Chip Ricks, shared a book idea with me. Loosely based on her own family history, she wanted to write a story about two brothers—one who chose to live for Christ, the other who didn't. She wanted to follow that family through the generations, to show the impact of that one choice, on the people who came behind.

She just had one problem. Chip was a brilliant writer, but she wasn't a fiction writer. "Will you help me write this book?"

Now, Chip was in her 80s at the time. She was a mother, a grandmother to me in the faith. If she'd asked me to paint the moon pink, I'd have given it my best shot. For several years, Chip and I worked together on several versions of the book. We only ever got through the first few chapters, and we'd change our minds about the characters or the situations. Finally, one day she smiled at me. She said, "You know, Renae. This is your book. I know I whispered the idea to you, but I always wanted you to be the one to write it. I'm getting too old to work on this…please take it. It's your story."

Soon after, she moved across the country to live with her daughter. We stayed connected via phone calls and Facebook, until eventually, she stopped responding. We lost touch. I continued to write the book—Chip's book. Now my book. I'd work on it a while, then put it away for several months, even a few years at one point. In 2017, I finished what would become the first final draft. I fiddled with it more, here and there, but I hung onto it until I met Misty Beller, my publisher at Wild Heart.

I submitted the book to her, and she accepted it, right away! Then the editor got hold of it. God bless Erin Taylor Young! She was brutal, in the best possible way. I spent weeks (months?) making the suggested changes, and each one made the book so much better. The day I turned in those final edits to my publisher, I opened up Facebook. There, on Chip's FB page, was a note to all her friends.

From one of her children.

She'd gone to see her Heavenly Father.

I sat there, frozen, looking at my screen, big fat tears tracking my cheeks. How was it possible that on the day the book was complete, I learned of her death? She was so instrumental in my walk of faith, and in my path as a writer. It was almost like the Holy Spirit wanted me to know…this particular journey was now complete.

I hope you enjoy this book, book one in a trilogy, for it is very close to my heart. And I hope you learn from the actions of two brothers, so many years ago, that our choices have an impact on our own lives, and on the lives of those who follow us.

Renáe

CHAPTER 1

1882

Lampasas, Texas

Nineteen-year-old Emma Monroe watched the rain, like tears, make tiny splashes on the toe of her boot. Fascinating, wet patterns formed on the leather and offered a welcome distraction from the day's events. At least the February rain hid the fact that she'd shed no tears...not a single one since Ma left them early yesterday morning. If she let one teardrop loose, she'd never stop the torrent that would follow.

The preacher droned words of comfort. Empty, bitter-tasting words, for there was no comfort to be had. Ma was dead.

Yes, she knew Ma was in a better place.

But she didn't want her mother in a better place. She wanted her here. Now.

After several hours or minutes, she really couldn't tell which, the small group of mourners dispersed in a rising flood of black lace veils and good intentions. Emma nodded and thanked each person with duty-bound politeness, but she just wanted them all to go away. To leave her and Pa and Lyndel alone with the mound of dirt under which Ma lay buried.

An expensive-looking pair of shoes stepped in front of her. All this mud would ruin that hand-tooled, imported leather. She knew the owner of those shoes even before looking up into Riley Stratton's warm brown eyes. She'd heard he was back in town.

Instead of taking her hands, though, Riley wrapped his muscular arms around her and drew her into a tight embrace. He didn't say a word, just held her against him, and it felt so good. For just that moment, she didn't have to be the strong one. For just that moment, she could lean the weight of her emotions on someone else.

After a long time, Riley let her go, cupping her face in one hand before stepping away, invoking memories of a school-girl crush that best lay buried with the other dead things in this graveyard.

At last, her wish came true. She and her father and brother were left alone with their raincoats, a shared umbrella, and a muddy mound of grief. But the solitude was only temporary. Back at the house, there'd be church ladies and cigar-smoking men and makeshift tables laden with fried chicken and pie, as if that would somehow make up for the fact that their world had just stopped spinning.

Despite her best efforts, a single tear slipped down her cheek, across her chin and down her neck. She quickly shut the gate on the rest. Not here. Not now. Not with Pa and Lyndel on either side of her. They had enough grief of their own without adding hers.

"I suppose we should go. They'll be waiting." Pa's voice sounded hollow and weak...weaker than normal.

"Who's gonna iron my shirts?" Lyndel dug the toe of his boot into the mud.

Emma pulled him closer against her side. "I'll do it."

"Ma always got the creases just right."

"I know. I won't do it as well as she did, but I'll try."

They stood there, even though they should move toward the wagon. Sugar, their sorrel mare, whinnied, as if to remind them she was standing in the rain with no umbrella. Yet none of them could seem to find the will to put one foot in front of the other, to slosh away from the last remnant of the one person in each of their lives who brought sunshine and light and joy...the one person who made life make sense.

Finally, Pa cleared his throat and pressed his hand to her back, silently urging her forward.

And that was it. They walked away from Ma, or what remained of her, and left her with the skies weeping her passing.

~

*R*iley Stratton had known Emma Monroe since grade school, but he'd never hugged her. Why would he? It wouldn't have been appropriate. But today, he hoped that simple hug said what words could not. He, unlike many of their age group, knew how it felt to lose a mother.

"What's taking them so long?" Allison's voice grated Riley from his thoughts. She strained to see down the road from her seat in the enclosed carriage. "It's raining, for goodness' sake. We gave our condolences at the funeral. Do we really have to wait forever for them to come home? We brought a cake. Isn't that enough?"

You could be in the house with the other ladies, helping prepare the meal. But he didn't dare speak the words. His sister-in-law was unpleasant enough without being challenged.

The fact that her own housekeeper and cook had just died caused Allison an enormous amount of grief, but not because of any sadness over the family's loss. Mainly, she just wondered who would cook and clean for her now. The cake they'd brought was purchased from the Sweet Things Bakery in downtown Lampasas.

"They'll be along soon enough." Colt sat beside his wife and chewed on his pipe. "It's good for us to be seen here. It helps our reputation with the townspeople. And we need all the help we can get, after Donnigan and his stunts."

The tension in Riley's jaw—from holding his tongue—found its way through his neck, across his shoulders, and down into his clenched fists. He had no desire to discuss their wayward brother, either. He'd rather be on the Monroes' front porch with the other men, but since it was pouring rain and there were no more chairs, he was better off waiting in the carriage. He almost would have agreed with Allison and suggested they go on home, but he wanted to check on Emma one more time.

He leaned his head back and closed his eyes. Sally Monroe. His mother's best friend since childhood. The only person Mom had trusted to keep an immaculate house and a silent tongue. When Mom died, Mrs. Monroe stepped up as a surrogate mother, at least when Dad wasn't around. She, more than anyone, made the loss of his mother bearable, the grief passable.

Now she was gone. It was his turn to return the favor by sharing the burden of grief with her family.

A clop-clopping from the road warned them the Monroes were nearly there, and Riley opened the carriage door and stepped onto the rocky path that led to the porch. He didn't bother with Allison—that was Colt's job. Instead, he opened his umbrella in time to assist Emma, then her father and brother.

"Thank you," Emma mumbled before taking her father's arm and guiding him through the maze of men to their front door. Her rigid neck and stiff back reminded him of their school days, when she'd try so hard to act like she didn't care a whit that he'd just pulled her braids or let a mouse loose near her foot. Only today, her stubborn posture didn't bring him any joy.

He rushed ahead of them to get the door, but someone in the crowd beat him to it. Pretty much everybody in town was here today...everybody but Riley's own father, John Stratton. Dad begged off, saying somebody had to stay and take care of the ranch, but Riley knew better. They had plenty of ranch hands. Dad just didn't want to have to be polite to Charlie Monroe.

Riley pushed through, nodding and speaking courteously to neighbors and acquaintances, trying unsuccessfully to avoid all the meaningless small talk that went on at these events. He arrived in the Monroe's parlor just in time to hear Allison, with her tilted-up nose and her simpering voice.

"Oh, Emma, dear. I'm so very sorry for your loss. Is there anything we can do? Anything at all. You just say the word."

"Nothing at the moment. Thank you, Mrs. Stratton."

Allison leaned forward and lowered her voice. If Riley hadn't been close enough to hear, he'd have thought Allison was offering whispered words of prayer and comfort. Instead, she said, "You know, dear. There is just no replacing your mother. But we do have an opening, if you'd like to fill her position."

If ever Riley wanted to wallop a lady, it was now. Good gravy, couldn't Allison wait until the grave was cold? He cleared his throat and stepped forward. "There you are, Allison. I believe Colt needs your assistance in the carriage. Go on. I'll be along shortly."

Allison gave him that you'll-hear-about-this-later look, but didn't say more. Instead, she did as he suggested and exited the crowded room.

"I'm sorry about that," he whispered for Emma's ears only. Her eyes found his, and he saw something both shallow and deep at once, like a boarded-up well of grief.

"You've nothing to be sorry for, Mr. Stratton. Your sister-in-law was just trying to be charitable, I'm sure."

"You're as gracious as ever, Miss Monroe. Please...will you let me know if I can help you or your family in any way?"

She looked to the side, out the window, then down at her gloved hands. "Certainly. You're very kind. Please, have something to eat. I don't know what in the world we'll do with all this food."

Someone pulled her attention away, and he stood there looking after her, helpless to do anything that mattered, knowing all too well the tunnel of grief she must pass through before she found light again.

He felt a warm hand on his back, through his coat. "I appreciate your coming today, son. Sally always thought a lot of you." Charlie Monroe looked small and weak, despite his better-than-six-foot stature.

Riley tried to summon a smile. "She was the best cook this side of the Mississippi. Probably the other side, too."

"Yes, well..." The man's lower lip quivered, and Riley looked away to give him a moment to regain control.

His eyes fell on Lyndel. Poor kid, sitting alone by the window, no longer a boy, not yet a man. Riley wasn't much older when his own mother died. For Riley, this was the second mother he'd lost. But today wasn't his day to mourn, as much as be a comfort to those who mourned more. Mourned deeper. Once again, he said the words...words loaded with sincerity but void of any power to relieve any hurt. "If there's anything I can do, sir."

"Thank you, Riley." Mr. Monroe moved to the next person, and Riley debated whether or not to speak to Lyndel. Instead, he placed a hand on the boy's shoulder and held it there a moment before moving toward the front door. He'd done all he could. It was time to go home.

~

*E*mma pulled the buggy to the side of the road to talk some sense into herself. Pa's words played in her mind. "You don't have to do this. We'll find a way. You should be packing for Baylor Female College. It's what your ma wanted for you."

Yes, it was what Ma wanted...for years they'd talked and schemed and dreamed of the day Emma would become a teacher. They'd finally saved enough for tuition, and Emma was to leave for college this summer and begin classes in the fall.

But Ma *wouldn't* have wanted Pa and Lyndel to be left behind with no one to take care of them. Pa with his bronchitis that seemed worse by the day. Lyndel only twelve years old.

No. Plans changed. She wasn't going away to college and that was that. Where she *was* going, was to the Stratton Ranch. Ma had been gone two weeks now, and the bills weren't going to pay themselves. Allison Stratton had offered her a job, and she was taking it. The wealthy Stratton family could afford to pay twice what Mrs. Wesson could pay at the seamstress shop. She wasn't the cook Ma had been, and though she knew how to keep house, she didn't have a clue about keeping a mansion. But she could learn.

She *would* learn.

She clicked to Sugar, and the buggy moved forward. Soon, she arrived in the big circle drive and stopped in front of the wide porch. As long as Ma had worked here, Emma had never been inside, but the outside always took her breath away. Thick, beveled columns flanked an elegant staircase leading to the front door. On either side of the entrance was a parlor-like grouping of white-painted wicker furniture, and Emma could picture the family gathered, sipping lemonade, laughing and dreaming like families do.

Riley grew up here.

No use entertaining thoughts of Riley Stratton. Hadn't Ma

said as much? Emma would never fit into his world of servants and power and more money than she could imagine. Everyone knew a Stratton would never be interested in a lowly farmer's daughter. Ma had made it clear she and Riley were from two different upbringings.

Besides, charming as he was, he was also a scalawag...probably had a girl or three waiting back in Waco, pining for the day he'd declare his love.

She was only halfway up the steps when the door opened and Allison stepped outside. Her strained features fought with her pasted-on smile. "Emma...hello. May I help you?"

"I... Good morning, Mrs. Stratton. I was wondering if you're still looking for someone to replace my mother. If so, I'm interested in the job."

The transformation was stunning. Like clouds breaking to reveal a shimmery full moon, Allison's eyes took on a glow, and the fakey-sweet smile turned almost genuine. "Really? You want the job? Come in. Can you start today? Let me take your coat."

She led Emma into an elaborate foyer. The marble floors needed mopping, and a layer of dust coated the mahogany stair-rails, but the neglect couldn't hide its grandeur.

A lump of anguish caught in Emma's gut. These were the floors Ma had polished. The neglect...well, that was clearly the reason for Allison's sudden burst of friendliness.

"Come in. Don't mind the mess. I've been doing everything myself since...you know. And with little Davis cutting a tooth...and well, cooking has never been my strong point. I'm so glad you're here!"

Allison chattered as she led Emma through a lavish dining room that still held remnants of last night's meal. And possibly bits of last week's meals, from the looks of the dried-on fragments left on the plates. A faint scent of burned toast lingered as they entered the kitchen, where more dirty dishes covered every flat surface.

"Of course you know, you'll be expected to use the back entrance here." The woman's voice and attitude returned to typical Allison Stratton tone. "The carriage house is out back. Over here is the pantry, and out that door you'll find the meat cellar. The icebox is down there, too.

"We'll pay you a dollar a day, seven days. Please report at six each morning, and we'll expect you to stay until you've cleaned up after dinner, which is served at six in the evening. Somewhere I have a copy of your mother's cleaning schedule, I'll see if I can get that for you. Oh, and I have Temperance Society meetings in town on Tuesdays and Thursdays, so I'll need you to watch Davis for me then, as well as some other times during the week."

Emma's thoughts buzzed like a bee in a trash bin. A dollar a day? Twelve-hour days? Seven days a week...and on top of it all, she was expected to provide childcare?

Her mother made twice that and had Sundays off. And she was home by six each evening. Allison prattled on, and Emma knew she should show polite deference. But she was tired. She hadn't slept. And as much as she needed the work, she wasn't about to let the likes of Allison Stratton treat her like a mindless lackey. Besides, from the looks of the place, Emma was in a pretty good position for negotiating.

"I'm sorry, Mrs. Stratton. I believe you meant to say two dollars a day? I'm just making sure I heard correctly."

The prism of emotions that played across Allison's face might have been entertaining under different circumstances. Shock, then anger, then icy indifference, all in a matter of seconds. "Two dollars a day seems a bit high for your level of experience, Miss Monroe."

"I see. I'm sorry I've wasted your time. Good day, Mrs. Stratton." Emma pulled forth her sweetest smile, nodded graciously, and turned to leave, but not before a flicker of desperation and fear consumed the other woman's features.

"Let's not be hasty. I know you need the work, and as you can see, I need a housekeeper."

Emma paused, schooled her features, and turned back around to face her would-be employer. "I realize I don't have the years of experience my mother had. But her schedule wasn't as demanding as the one you just put forth. *And,* she was only the housekeeper and cook. You're in need of a nanny, as well."

Allison opened and closed her mouth like a startled codfish. Then she tugged at her jacket and patted her hair. "I see. Well, I suppose you have a point. I'll pay your rate. But I'll expect you to earn it."

Allison's attempt at keeping the upper hand was comical, and Emma found she was enjoying herself immensely. She couldn't wait to tell Ma about it.

But she couldn't tell Ma.

"I'll be here by six each morning," Emma agreed, and Allison's smug look of superiority returned. "I'll stay until dinner is served and I've cleaned the cookware, but your meal dishes will have to wait until morning. On Saturdays, I'll prepare a meal for Sunday lunch, but I'll not work on the Lord's Day. As for your son, I'll be happy to watch him while you're at your meetings, but at those times I may not be able to get all my other work done, so I assume you'll be flexible on my duties, on those days."

The glare Allison gave her could melt an Arctic iceberg. But Emma was no pushover, and though she was grateful for the opportunity to work, she could make $1.40 a day at the factory in town—not that she wanted to work in a sweatshop. But if she was going to put up with the likes of Allison Stratton, she would be appropriately compensated.

Davis chose that moment to let out a piercing wail, and Allison looked like she might melt, or explode, or some messy combination of the two. "Oh, all right. But can you please start now?"

Emma smiled in what she hoped was a gracious and humble manner. "Certainly. I'll just need to see to my horse."

With a curt nod, Allison bolted toward the sound of the child's misery. Emma made a note to thank little Davis with an extra cookie, first chance she got.

Lost in waves of immense satisfaction, she turned toward the front entrance, only to run head-on into a wide expanse of chambray fabric, buttoned tightly at the chest. A slight tilt of her head revealed the shirt was attached to Riley Stratton.

"Well done, Miss Monroe. Although I fear you'll be wasting your talents working here. With your bargaining skills, you'd be better off in a boardroom somewhere. Or a courtroom. You could be the town's first lady lawyer."

Emma's face spiked with the heat of humiliation, though she had no reason to be embarrassed. She'd only done what was necessary to make sure she and Pa and Lyndel were properly cared for. Still, the idea that Riley had overheard her being so bold with his sister-in-law made her want to run and hide.

Instead, she took a couple of steps backward. "I'm sorry, Mr. Stratton. I wasn't aware I had an audience. If you'll excuse me, I need to see to Sugar—my horse—so I can get started."

To her mortification, he followed her out the front door like they were old chums. Which they were, sort of. But this wasn't a school spelling contest or a game of stickball. She needed this job.

"I'll take care of your horse and buggy if you'll talk to me for a minute." Riley's voice hummed close behind her.

She lengthened her stride. "Thank you, Mr. Stratton. You're very kind, but I can take care of Sugar myself. I don't want to trouble you."

Riley moved in front of her, blocked her path. "Look, Emma. Can we just lay aside the formalities for a minute? It's me. Riley. The fellow you love to hate."

That brought a little smile to her face, against her will. But she kept her eyes downcast.

"Look at me."

He stood so close now, she could smell his scented shave lotion, and the musky smell made her uncomfortable in a most satisfying way. Tilting her head back, she did as he asked. Or was that a command?

"I just want to know how you are."

She looked down again and moved to the side. She didn't want to tell him how she was. Saying it out loud made it more real. "I'm doing as well as can be expected, I suppose. Breathing in. Breathing out. Then I breathe in again."

"I understand."

Yes, he did understand. She remembered all too well when Mrs. Stratton died. Riley had been just fourteen. Emma was eleven. He didn't smile much for a whole year after it happened. But eventually, he became the same prank-pulling, mischief-making Riley, leaving a string of broken hearts in his wake. More subdued, perhaps...but time had healed his spirit some.

The way Emma felt now, she wasn't sure that would ever happen for her. How could her spirit—shattered in a million pieces, crushed beyond repair—ever recover?

"I appreciate your concern, Mr. Stratton...Riley. And I know that you of all people can appreciate what I'm feeling. But I really do need this job, and if I don't get in there soon, I'll be here all night washing dishes."

He laughed, the deep belly laugh she remembered. The laugh that caused many a wide-eyed, lovestruck girl to make a fool of herself. Good thing Emma had always had the good sense to keep her feelings hidden.

"Yes, I suppose that's true," he said. "We've left quite a mess in there. Well, you held up your end of the bargain by talking to me, so now it's my turn. I'll put your horse and buggy in the carriage house and make sure Sugar is fed and watered. Then I'm off to town. Good day, Miss Monroe."

He bowed an overstated, sweeping dip that was more circus clown than gentleman, and moved toward the buggy.

"Thank you," she whispered, but he probably didn't hear.

She started to return the way she'd come, then thought better of it and walked around the house to the back entrance. She certainly hoped Riley Stratton would stay in town a long time. Because if the feelings churning in her gut were any indication, she'd have a hard time concentrating on any task as long as he was around. She may desperately need this job, but she needed Riley Stratton's flirtations like she needed an abscessed tooth.

~

*R*iley watched Emma until she turned the corner, head up, shoulders back. His heart nearly split in two. Watching her like this brought back all the memories of his own grief, as fresh as if it were yesterday and not nearly eight years ago. He felt that vice on his gut, squeezing away his appetite. That familiar anvil pressed on his chest, making it hard to breathe.

But it was more than that. He wished he could make Emma understand...her mother had been there for him when no one else was. He *grieved* for Sally Monroe. Perhaps his grief wasn't as deep as Emma's, but it was real, just the same.

He'd be there for Emma and her family, just as Mrs. Monroe had been there for him. The fact that Emma's eyes were the color of new spring grass, her hair the shade of sun-kissed wheat, and her dimples could coax a smile out of a bawling calf would only make his job more pleasant.

He climbed onto the buggy and clicked to Sugar, and his eyes fell on a lacey embroidered handkerchief. He picked it up, and the words stitched there caused his chest to tighten. "My daughter, my friend."

She would surely want this. It must have fallen from her pocket, or that bag thing women carried...what was it called? A reticule. He folded it neatly and tucked it into his shirt pocket, then guided the horse into the carriage house.

Ten minutes later, he walked into the kitchen to find Emma elbow-deep in suds, with one corner of one countertop cleared. "You don't waste any time, do you?"

"I thought you were going to town." She pushed a stray strand of hair out of her face, smearing bubbles in the process.

He wanted to reach out and set her hair aright, but he didn't dare. What was his reason for coming here? Oh, the handkerchief. He pulled the cloth from his pocket and held it out. "I found this in the buggy. I thought you might want it with you."

Her eyes grew large, and she reached into her pocket, only to find it empty. "Oh, my. Yes. Thank you." She dried her hands on a nearby rag before taking the cloth and replacing it in her pocket.

"Your mother was always special to me..."

"Riley Stratton, I thought you left an hour ago!" Allison emerged from the shadows, and Emma jumped enough to nearly tip over the wash bucket. How long had Allison been standing there?

"I was detained." Riley started to thrust his hands in his pocket, but instead forced them to his sides and stood a little taller. He would not give Allison the upper hand.

She looked at him, then at Emma, then back at him. "I see. Well, please don't bother the help. We're paying her a small fortune, and I for one want to make sure we get our money's worth."

Riley just stood there, looking at his sister-in-law. What in the name of good sense had Colt ever seen in this woman, beyond a pretty face and form?

Maybe that was the problem. Colt didn't look past the surface. Well, one good thing would come of it. Riley would certainly never make that mistake. Not that Emma didn't fit the bill in face and form. She possessed more elegance wearing an apron than Allison had in all her diamonds.

What did it matter? Emma was a friend. Nothing more. There was no way she could become a Stratton. Emma was pure. Strattons were tainted. Emma was diamond. Strattons were glass. It was the coat he wore, the mold he conformed to, like it or not.

Other than trying to make Emma smile, other than lifting her sorrow a bit, he needed to remove her from his thoughts. A connection between them could never work.

"Go on. Shoo." Allison waved him away like he was a fly at a picnic. Emma went back to washing dishes as if no one else was in the room.

Riley held up his hands in surrender and headed for his office. The trip to town could wait. He had things to do right here, right now. Number one on his list...pay a stack of bills larger than Miss Monroe's one-year salary. Number two...attempt to forget about Miss Monroe.

Number one turned out to be a far easier task.

CHAPTER 2

$\mathcal{B}$y lunchtime, Emma had made a decent dent in the kitchen—at least, she had enough cleared so she could prepare an adequate meal. Boiled potatoes with gravy, sausage, and collard greens. Oh, and a pan of cornbread.

She quickly removed the remaining cups and saucers from the dining room and set them to soak, wiped the table and chairs, and set out fresh plates and flatware. If she'd had more time, she would have relished those dishes...with tiny pink roses and blue hyacinths painted around the border. They were the prettiest she'd ever seen. Would she ever own anything that lovely?

Ma had touched these dishes, had washed and dried them with her own hands. That made them even lovelier. Ma...

No. She couldn't afford to linger in memories right now. Too much to do, and Allison watched her like a circling buzzard, waiting for her next meal.

But Riley's words from earlier niggled at Emma's mind. *Your mother was always special to me...* Of course she would be, though Emma had never thought of it before. Ma and Mrs. Stratton were friends from childhood. During Ma's early years in the

Stratton's employ, she was more than just a servant. She'd been a companion and confidante to Riley's mother. After Mrs. Stratton died, Ma came home in the evenings and talked about Riley. Funny, Riley was the only one of the Strattons she ever spoke of. It was as if the others didn't exist.

But when Ma figured out Emma was sweet on Riley, she wasted no time setting Emma straight. *You and Riley come from two different worlds. Best not go wasting your thoughts on him.*

Ma's warnings hadn't kept Emma from her secret dreams, though. Silly dreams. Now that Emma was older, she could see Riley for exactly who he was—a philanderer and a flirt.

But such a handsome one…

She couldn't let her heart betray her sense of reason. Good-looking or not, she would never subject herself to becoming just another notch on Riley Stratton's belt. Ma had warned her, and she would take heed.

"Smells delicious." Riley's voice pulled her from her reflections.

She pressed a palm to her chest to still her racing heart. "Riley Stratton, if you don't stop spying on me, I'll…"

"You'll what?"

Gracious and mercy. What was she thinking, speaking to him like that in his own home? "I'm sorry, Mr. Stratton. That was out of line. I guess I was just lost in my thoughts, and you startled me."

He leaned against the now-clean counter, then hopped up to take a seat on it. "Would you care to share those thoughts with me?"

"I'm afraid they'd be just as confusing to you as they are to me."

Riley chuckled. "If you're not going to share your thoughts, perhaps you'll share a morsel of whatever smells so amazing. I make a very good taste-tester."

"I'm sure you do, but lunch is ready. I'm not sure how to go about gathering everyone for the meal, though."

"Oh, don't worry about that. They'll be here in about five minutes. Dad and Colt are never late for a meal."

"Promptness is an admirable quality," she said. "So is keeping appropriate boundaries."

Riley, who had leaned closer to her while he spoke, sat back and held up his hands in a sign of surrender. "I'll keep my distance from you, but I make no promises about this cornbread." He grabbed a messy hunk of crumbling bread. She swatted at his hand, but he ducked. "I always was faster than you," he said with a naughty-school-boy expression.

That look. It started a longing in her chest, and she pulled her gaze away from him. Through the window, she noticed several men entering a long, low building about a hundred yards behind the house. "What about all the ranch hands? I didn't prepare for them. I probably should have asked..."

"They live in the bunkhouse, out back. They have their own stove, their own supplies. Those fellas take care of themselves. You'll rarely see any of them up here, unless it's Joe, the foreman. And Joe only comes if he has business to discuss with Dad."

Good thing he was giving her these details. The less she had to ask Allison, the better. "Along those same lines of good boundaries, could you please move aside so I can reach behind you?"

For a moment, Riley's eyes sparked, as if he would challenge her. But just as quickly, he hopped down and stepped to one side. "Pardon me, Miss Monroe."

She moved as far to the opposite side as she could, reached for the pretty bowl of boiled potatoes, and removed the cloth that covered them. Honestly. Was he going to be under her feet every day? Hopefully the novelty would wear off soon.

A man's voice echoed through the hall. "Allison! What are you doing there?"

Allison moved from the shadows in the hallway just off the kitchen. "Not a thing. Just waiting for you..."

A spike of frustration flared in Emma's chest. Didn't that woman have anything better to do than spy on her all day?

John Stratton strode into view, followed by Colt. "It looked like you were...oh. I wasn't aware we had...company." The elder Mr. Stratton removed his hat and smiled, but something in his eyes didn't look pleased. "I take it you've hired a replacement." He looked around the kitchen, then inhaled deeply. "Smells delicious. I'm John Stratton...head of this motley clan."

"Pleased to meet you, Mr. Stratton." Emma wasn't sure whether to bow, curtsy, or just shake the man's hand. It was such an odd introduction, for she knew perfectly well who John Stratton was, and he knew perfectly well who she was. And he'd never given her the time of day before this moment. She nodded, offered the sweetest smile she could muster, then turned toward the gravy boat that still needed to be set out.

"Emma will be taking her mother's place," Allison said in a smirkish tone weighted with false compassion. "Isn't that...wonderful?" Funny. She didn't sound like she thought it was wonderful at all.

"I'll let you know after we eat." Colt barely acknowledged her. Soon, all four adult Strattons were seated at the dining room table, digging into the meal in the most uncivilized civility Emma had ever witnessed.

No prayer. No conversation. Everyone's napkins were in their laps, their forks held just so... But the emptiness in the vast room made Emma squirm with discomfort.

She didn't know what was expected. Should she stay in the room, waiting to serve them? Disappear into the shadows? Maybe that was the reason for their aloof nature. They weren't used to having someone else in the room. Emma slipped into the kitchen where she continued washing dishes as quietly as she could.

"I'm not too happy you took it upon yourself to hire someone without consulting me, Allison." John Stratton spoke in a low tone, but not so low Emma couldn't hear. She made note of the way the sounds bounced off the walls. She needed to be careful with every word she said in this house.

"Especially *that* woman," Mr. Stratton continued. "First Donnigan comes home with all his shameful surprises, and now this."

"What do you mean by *that woman?*" Riley's whispered words sprung off the vaulted ceiling, directly to her ears as clearly as if he'd spoken them inches from her.

"You know what I mean. I only kept Sally Monroe on because your mother loved her. And I figured her presence was a comfort to you after your mother died. But now that the woman's gone, did Allison really need to bring her spawn into this home?"

Emma froze. Had he really just said that?

"I must admit, I can already see I've made a mistake." Allison spoke in a normal tone, not even trying to whisper. "She showed up on the doorstep this morning begging for work. I could hardly turn her away. And now she's done nothing but swoon over Riley since she arrived."

"Well, she sure can cook." Colt sounded like his mouth was full as he spoke. "And from the looks of things, she's done a little more than swoon. This is a different place. You can actually see the tops of the furniture, Al."

"What is that supposed to mean?" Allison hissed.

"It means, she sure has cleaned things up, and this is the best meal I've had in weeks. I say we give her a raise."

Emma didn't know whether to burst into tears or go dump the remainder of the gravy into John Stratton's lap. *That woman? Spawn?* What on earth was he talking about?

No amount of money was worth this kind of treatment. She had her pride, and that was that. She untied her apron, hung it on the hook, and as quietly as she could, exited the back door. She made it all the way to the carriage house and was in the process of hitching Sugar to the buggy when Riley appeared in the doorway.

He studied her for a minute, but she ignored him. "I take it you heard all that?" His voice rumbled across the aisleway.

She sent him a glare. "Lyndel and my pa probably heard it back at my place, Riley."

"Oh, so now I'm Riley? You always did let your defenses down when you were angry."

"Of course I'm angry." She jerked hard on the strap she was buckling. Too bad he knew her so well. "I may be in need of a job, but I'm not that desperate. You can inform your sister-in-law she can send my half-day's wages through the post. Good day, Mr. Stratton."

"Emma, please. I know my family can be difficult. Believe me, I have to live with them. But Pa's always been sensitive when it comes to your family."

She spun to face him. "He called me a spawn!"

"I'm sorry." And he truly did look sorry, with a weary sadness creasing the corners of his eyes.

"What in the world did I ever do to him?" Emma tried to sidestep Riley, but he moved in front of her.

"It's not you—"

"I just want to go home. Please step aside."

"Give us another chance. I put Allison in her place about how you were hired. I told her I'd heard the entire exchange. I think after hearing the story, my father's respect for you raised a couple of notches. He's got a lot on his mind right now."

Emma forced back the burning sensation in her eyes. *Don't cry, don't cry, don't cry.* "I'm sorry. But you haven't told me anything that justifies what I heard in there."

"I know. Please don't go."

"Mr. Stratton—" Her voice cracked. "My mind is made up."

Defeat slumped Riley's shoulders, but he moved out of the way. Under different circumstances, she might have felt sorry for him. He couldn't help who his family was. But right now, she just wanted to get as far away from this God-forsaken place as she could.

CHAPTER 3

*E*mma tapped her foot in a steady rhythm, letting the comforting whir of the machine dull her thoughts. She may be powerless to fix anything about her life, but she could certainly stitch a professional hem. Good thing Mrs. Wesson hadn't hired anyone to take her place by the time she made it back to town Monday afternoon.

Two days had passed since that horrible scene at the Strattons. She'd gone over the events in her mind a hundred times, and for the life of her, she couldn't figure out what in the world would cause John Stratton to hate her so much. His attitude went far beyond the typical animosity between farmers and ranchers.

Allison, she could figure out. She may have been a few years ahead of Emma in school, but she was easy to read. The woman valued coins more than character. Prestige more than personality. She cared more about what others thought of her than about who she really was.

But John Stratton? Other than nodding occasionally when they had to pass each other at church or in the general store, she'd never spoken to the man. She'd considered sharing the story with Pa, but decided against it. He had enough on his mind right now. If he knew how she was treated, he'd feel like he had to go over there and defend her honor. And he was in no shape to defend anyone right now. What he needed was peace and quiet and a lot of rest.

The shop door opened, casting a sliver of sunlight on the worn wooden floor. "I'll be right with you," she called without looking up. She finished her seam, gently cut the thread and tied it off, then draped the dress over the back of her chair before raising her head to the customer.

John Stratton. And behind him was Riley, grinning like a circus monkey with a bag full of peanuts.

Her breath caught, and she dropped her scissors. She resisted the urge to pick them up. Resisted the even stronger urge to flee to the back room. She had plenty she wanted to say to the man, but she was a lady. Like her handiwork with the needle, she knew when to keep her thoughts stitched tight. So instead, she lifted her chin and looked John Stratton directly in the eyes. "How may I help you?"

"Good afternoon, Miss Monroe. I was wondering if I might persuade you to come back and work for us."

Emma worked hard to maintain her composure, but all her nervous energy had to go somewhere. It went to her left foot, which started shaking so hard it caused a thump-thump-thump on the wood floor. The sound hammered like the third woodpecker trying to peck his way into the ark.

She cleared her throat, then licked her lips, which were suddenly very dry. "Why would you want me to do that?"

The man gave her a half smile. Did he think he looked charming? More like a snake. She was surprised he didn't speak with a hiss. "Because I haven't had a decent meal in two days, and before that, it had been weeks. Because there's a foul odor coming from the kitchen, and Allison is helpless when it comes to those things. Because my grandson, Davis, is cutting a tooth and screaming at all hours of the night, and none of us have gotten any sleep. Because no one else in three counties is willing to work for my daughter-in-law. Because my oldest son has come home with a child he can't take care of. Because your mother knew how to keep our family's business private, and didn't wag her tongue all over town. I assume you'll show similar discretion. And because I pay well, and I know you could use the money."

Emma took a moment to process all that. Donnigan had a child? Where was its mother? Poor woman, getting tied up with the Strattons. Poor child, who had no say in the matter. She raised her brows at the man. "And how, exactly, do you expect me to help with your lack of sleep?"

"I'll pay you three dollars a day if you'll move into the guest bedroom. You can cook and clean and take care of Davis, and keep Donnigan's little half-breed when she's around."

Her stomach turned at the term half-breed, especially considering Mr. Stratton spoke of his own grandchild. She hadn't thought she could like the man less.

Given the sensitivity of Indian relations, she could see the Strattons' quandary, their fear of alienation and shame. For a family who prided themselves on being the richest, the most cultured, the most sophisticated, this would certainly cause anxiety. Many in town had lost loved ones in skirmishes with the natives. *Half-breed* was a mild term, compared to some she'd heard.

But people were just people, despite their heritage. Maybe she could do some good for those children. If she couldn't be a teacher, maybe she could earn her living as a nanny. Her foot thumped even louder, though she tried her hardest to make it stop. Three dollars a day. That was a lot of money.

But some things weren't worth the money, no matter how much you needed it. "I'm a little confused, Mr. Stratton." She lifted her chin in a way she hoped showed confidence. "Let's not pretend you didn't say some deplorable things about me the other day. I heard you. And you know I heard you."

The man removed his hat and ran calloused fingers through his graying hair. He looked annoyed that she didn't succumb to his charm. But he seemed to consider his words heavily before he spoke. "Truth is, your father and I don't have the best history. He took something that was rightfully mine. Don't know if I'll ever forgive him. But you're not your Pa, and I ought not hold that against you, I reckon."

The more the man spoke, the faster her anger boiled. "My father is one of the most decent, God-fearing men I've ever met, sir, which quite frankly is more than I can say for you. How dare you come in here making accusations against him? Please explain yourself."

Stratton's countenance remained unmoved except for a flash behind his eyes, like a tiger held back by a mosquito net. Fear stung her gut, but she held his gaze. Had she said too much?

Riley stood like a startled deer, unable to move or speak.

Stratton's ears were the color of a lobster. "I've said my piece. Good day, Miss Monroe." His voice was low and thin, forced. He placed his hat on his head and strode—no, stomped—to the door.

"Dad..." Riley spoke with urgency, but if the man heard, he didn't acknowledge it. He just shut the door behind him in an almost-slam that conveyed his irritation, but wouldn't draw too much attention from passersby.

Riley approached the counter and leaned on it, looking like a deflated rugby ball. His gaze seemed to plead with her as he spoke. "Look, here's what I know. It was years ago. You and I weren't even born yet. My father settled our land more than a decade before your father showed up. Dad staked our property, fair and square. But after he settled, he realized there were several natural springs at the bottom, just outside our borders...good, fertile land, with plenty of water so our cattle would never go hungry or thirsty. Even more land beyond that. But since he'd already laid his claim, he had to go through all kinds of headaches to extend that claim. Paperwork back and forth to Washington. Even after hiring a lawyer, it took years to get everything straightened out. In the meantime, he'd already been using that land. He made improvements and irrigated it, even put up a fence. When he finally had all the papers ready, he had to go to Austin to sign it in person, before the state notary. When he got there, they told him the land had been claimed."

During this soliloquy, the door eased open a crack, and Emma had the sneaking suspicion someone was outside listening to their conversation.

Riley continued. "He thought it must be a mistake. But sure enough, your father had claimed it based on a map. He hadn't even arrived in Texas yet, and he'd already filed paperwork to claim that piece of property. When Dad got back from Austin, your father had just arrived in a covered wagon. Dad said your Pa had a campfire going and was eating beans out of a can. He'd already put up string lines where your house is now."

The door opened all the way, and John Stratton charged forward. His eyes held a blaze fueled by decades of animosity. "Riley, we're leaving. Now. If you don't come, you'll be walking home."

Riley stood up straight and faced his father. "She has a right to know."

John Stratton pierced him with a near-murderous gaze. How could a father look at his own son with such malice? But then he turned to her and continued where Riley left off.

"I thought surely, after realizing the land was ours, he'd leave. But he didn't. I offered him well above market value for the property, but he said no. He wanted to farm that land, and he'd chosen it for the springs and the fertile soil. Never mind there was other fertile soil to be had...he refused to budge." The words were more spat than spoken, his eyes bulged, and the veins on his neck popped out. "So all these years, he's been sitting on *my* property, and I'm landlocked. I can't connect to the acres on the other side, all because he refused to listen to reason." He let out a string of expletives under his breath.

For a long time, the only sound in the room was the tick-ticking of the small mantel clock Mrs. Wesson kept on the counter.

Finally, Emma's pounding heart slowed to a near normal pace, and she felt safe to speak again. "That land is legally ours. And from what you say, my father had no ill intent toward you. He didn't even know of your existence when he claimed our property."

The skin around Mr. Stratton's lips went as white as a pail of fresh milk. "Be that as it may, your father will never be one of my favorite people."

"I'm not sure I can work for you then, Mr. Stratton. Good day." John Stratton may command fear in this town, but Emma refused to cower to a bully. Hopefully, she wouldn't regret the decision later.

The man glared, then nodded and turned to go, but Riley spoke up. "What Dad meant to say is, he's real sorry for the unkind, unnecessary things he said about you, and he promises not to say anything like that again."

Mr. Stratton spun to face his son, and for a moment it looked like they'd have a brawl, right there between the gingham and notions.

"Don't go putting words in my mouth, boy." Then the old rancher let out a low growl and shook his head. "We do need someone." He looked at Emma. "We need someone who knows to keep her mouth shut. Whether it's a family discussion or a lucrative business deal, anyone who works in our home is sure to hear some private conversations from time to time. Your mother knew how to be discreet. I'm inclined to believe you'll be the same way. That said, I'm sure we can find somebody else to do it for three dollars a day."

The last thing in the world Emma wanted to do was go back to work for that awful man and his horrid daughter-in-law. But they did need the money. Pa needed medicine. At that rate, maybe she could set back some for teacher college. She breathed deep through her nose and tried not to show fear. "I'm afraid it's out of the question for me to move into your home. My own father is ill, and my younger brother needs tending."

Both men looked at her, eyebrows lifted, as if in shock that she'd even continue the conversation.

"I'll need to lay some ground rules."

"Look here. You're not in any position to—" Stratton's neck turned an awful shade of red, like he'd burst a vessel.

"Dad!" Riley whispered.

The older man glared at his son, then back at her, and she feared the tiger would claw through the net at any moment. "What kinds of rules?" Mr. Stratton's expression made goose-flesh rise on her arms, but she refused to look away.

"First, the kitchen is my domain. When I'm in the house, the kitchen is off limits, except by my invitation." She flashed a pointed look at Riley as she spoke.

He had the audacity to grin. At least he looked at his feet while he did it.

"Second, I'll need a budget. Since I'll be doing the cooking, I'll need to do the shopping as well."

"That sounds reasonable." The inferno in Stratton's eyes smoldered to a flicker.

"I'll leave when the evening meal is prepared. You'll have to serve yourselves. I'll need to get home to see to my own family's dinner."

Mr. Stratton hesitated, then nodded.

"I won't work Sundays."

"That's fine."

"There will be no more cursing. Whether I'm present or not. There are children in your home, and if I'm to assume partial responsibility for their care, I'll not have their ears tainted with such language."

"I can't promise that, Miss Monroe." John Stratton managed to look offended and amused at the same time. Riley cleared his throat and Stratton cut his eyes to his son, then back to Emma. "But I'll try my best."

"Speaking of the children, I know nothing of Donnigan's child. How old is he? What kind of care will he require, and how often?"

"*She's* around seven years old. I'll have Donnigan bring her by to meet you, should you choose to return."

"Fair enough. And I'll require $2.25 a day."

Mr. Stratton looked out the window, then back at her. "You drive a hard bargain, Miss Monroe. If I agree to your terms, does that mean we'll see you in the morning?"

"No. If you agree to my terms, it means I'll go home and discuss it with my father. You'll have my answer in a couple of days."

During this exchange, Riley's gaze had followed them as if watching a duel, waiting to see who would fire first. But the only dead thing, at this point, was the conversation.

After a long draw, Mr. Stratton spoke. "Two days. Then I'll open the position up to other applicants. Thank you for your time, Miss Monroe." He turned and left the store.

Riley made no move to follow his father. Just eyed Emma as if she'd grown feathers.

"Did you need something else?" She gave him a stare sharper than the needle in her hands.

"Not much." He chuckled. "Except with the way you argue, I'd have asked for $2.50."

She raised her brows at him. "With you barred from the kitchen, I'd be inclined to work for free."

Their eyes locked, and only moved when the bells over the door jangled and Mrs. Wesson returned from her lunch break.

"Hello, dear. Oh, hello, Mr. Stratton. Did I miss anything?"

Emma held Riley's gaze a moment longer before greeting her employer. "Nothing to speak of." If only Riley would stop looking at her like she was some kind of circus freak. "If you'll excuse me, Mr. Stratton, I have work to do." She sat down at her machine and spread the dress in front of her once again. Mrs. Wesson straightened a few things and headed for her office in the back of the store.

When they were alone again, Riley spoke, his voice low. "Few have addressed my father that way and gotten away with it. That was...brilliant."

She ignored him. Tried, unsuccessfully, to thread the needle. Fiddled with the controls. Why wouldn't he just leave? Oh, for goodness' sake. Holding back had never been her strong suit. She sent him a glare. "I think it's best you leave."

He bowed like a servant. "Your wish is my command. Good day, Miss Monroe."

As she focused on her sewing again, his footsteps moved toward the exit. The door opened, then shut. It wasn't until she heard his steps on the boardwalk outside, fading into the distance, that she allowed herself to look at the door.

She was alone at last, and she no longer had to keep a tight rein on her emotions. She cradled her face in her hands and sobbed.

~

*R*iley moved papers back and forth on his desk for the tenth time, at least. He couldn't concentrate on anything except Emma Monroe and her decision. It had taken him the better part of two days to talk Dad into asking her to come back. With all the secret Stratton skeletons lurking in every corner of the house, it was imperative they have someone like Mrs. Monroe, who wasn't a gossip. That's the only reason Dad finally relented.

After all that, if she turned down the job, he didn't know what he'd do. He was determined to take care of the Monroe family one way or other. It sure would be easier if Emma worked here.

Upstairs, Davis screamed. That tooth was taking entirely too long to come in. Dad and Colt could escape all day, but with Riley's office right in the house, he couldn't get anything done. Why in the world did he think he'd be good at bookkeeping? Just because he had a talent with numbers didn't mean that was all he wanted to do for the rest of his life.

His gaze caught on the shotgun mounted over his office door. Dad gave him that gun for his twelfth birthday. Taught him how to hunt with it. He'd killed his first deer with that gun, and he, Dad, and Colt skinned and processed it. Good times. He missed the outdoors. He was of a good mind to pull on his boots and dungarees and go for a ride. The more he thought about it, the more he knew exactly where he'd go.

An hour later, he reined in Medina, his black and white paint horse, and tied her to a tree in a shady copse of oaks to one side of the Monroe home. On the porch, he knocked, then removed his hat while he waited.

"Come in." The invitation was followed by a fit of coughing.

Riley eased the door open. It took a minute for his eyes to adjust from the bright sunlight to the dim interior. "Mr. Monroe?"

"Well, well. Riley Stratton. Come on in, son, and have a seat." The older man's voice was raspy and strained, and it sounded like it took all his energy to speak the words.

Maybe Riley shouldn't have come.

Spying a pitcher of water on a table just inside the door, he picked it up on his way to the parlor. Sure enough, the cup next to Mr. Monroe was empty, so he filled it. "I'm sorry to disturb you, sir. If it's a bad time, I can—"

"Nonsense. I said sit down. With Emma at work, Lyndel at school, and me sick with this croup, I'm glad for the company." He wheezed out the words, but didn't seem to want to stop talking. "I ought not be sittin' here when the crops need planting, but...maybe next week." The man coughed.

Riley sat in the vacant chair. "I'm sorry...about everything. Your wife was a kind woman. I don't know what I would have done without her after my own mother died."

The older man nodded, but didn't respond.

Riley took in the well-kept home. Small, but clean and well kept. Unlike the formal décor in his own home, this place had a homey quality that made him feel like he could settle in, stay a while. Blue floral curtains flanked the windows, and matching pillows graced each of the chairs. Lace doilies covered the flat surfaces. All of it handmade by Mrs. Monroe, he was sure. Or maybe Emma. "I...I was wondering if I might speak to you about your daughter."

Mr. Monroe looked at Riley like he held a secret behind those wrinkled eyes. "You want me to ask her to come back to work for you."

"Well, I..."

"I don't blame you. Emma's a capable young woman. Any employer would be lucky to have her, but I'm afraid you overestimate my influence. She's a strong-headed one, and she makes up her own mind about things."

"Did she tell you...?"

"What your father said? Every word. It was no surprise to me. My Sally confided in me, though she never shared much about your family with Emma."

Riley lowered his head. It was hard to meet the man's gaze.

"Sally also told me you were different. More like your mother. And she sure thought a lot of your mother."

"The feeling was mutual, I assure you."

The two men sat in silence, looking into the fire for a long time. Longer, in fact, than Riley realized. The sound of a horse and buggy pulled him from his thoughts. Was Emma home already? He'd planned to be gone before she arrived.

He'd just stood to his feet when the door banged open. Lyndel ran in, dropped his books on the table, and skidded to a halt when he saw Riley.

"Oh. Didn't know we had company. Howdy, Mr. Stratton. Howdy, Pa. Emma's putting Sugar in the stall, so she'll be in shortly."

"Welcome home, son. How was your day?"

"It was all right." The boy shifted his weight from side to side.

"Come give your pa a hug." Mr. Monroe coughed again, then reached up to embrace the boy when he drew near. "Change your clothes and see to your chores."

"Yes, sir." The boy mumbled the words barely loud enough for Riley to hear, then disappeared down the hallway. His shoulders drooped like an eighty-year-old man, not a young boy with his whole life ahead of him.

A vice-like pinch tightened around Riley's heart. He would help this family if it was the last thing he did.

A feminine shadow darkened the doorway, and Riley turned to see Emma. Her eyes followed her younger brother down the hallway, and sadness etched her brow. She sighed and looked toward her father's chair. That's when she saw Riley and sucked in a sharp breath.

"Mr. Stratton. You seem to be making an occupation of sudden appearances. Perhaps it's time you turned in your book-keeping career for one in apparitions."

"I'm sorry to disturb you again. I—"

Mr. Monroe held up his cup. "He was kind enough to check in on me. Poured me some water."

Emma's gaze locked with her father's as if carrying on a silent conversation with him, as if they had a language all their own, that Riley couldn't understand or be a part of. What would it feel like to be that connected to someone? To be that connected to Emma? "I was just leaving. I didn't realize you'd be home this early."

"Yes, well. Mrs. Wesson lets me leave when the school bell rings so I can drive Lyndel home."

It wasn't *that* long of a walk. Riley had a sneaking suspicion she wanted to check on her father.

Mr. Monroe shifted in his chair. "He wants to know if you're going back to work for him or not."

Riley wanted to crawl through the floorboards. "I...yes. I will admit, I was hoping your father might persuade you. He's corrected my way of thinking, and assured me that you are not able to be persuaded beyond your own will."

"Is that so?" Emma placed her things on the table beside Lyndel's books. "Well, I told you I'd have my answer by tomorrow, and I meant it. But since you're here, I do have another question for you."

Hope burgeoned in his chest. "Yes?"

"Tell me more about Donnigan. I don't know much about him, except that he disappeared years ago. Now he's reappeared with a child? Where is the girl's mother?"

Riley looked at his feet again. How to explain Donnigan?

But before he could answer, Mr. Monroe spoke up. "Don't go botherin' the man about things that aren't his concern. Is he his brother's keeper?"

"It's all right." He looked at Emma, with her hair spilling down her shoulders. There was no doubt she really was one of God's finer pieces of handiwork. Her steely resolve only added to her allure.

Her lips puckered in a stubborn little heart shape. What would it be like to kiss her? He'd likely never find out.

And where did that thought even come from? He forced his focus to her question. "I don't really know how to explain Donnigan. He lives in...another house on our property. I'm sure you'll run into him before long. During his time away, he married an Indian woman—part Comanche, part Coushatta. Neither tribe would have her after she married Donnigan, and with her race, most white people didn't want anything to do with them, either. They had a child...and the woman died. We only know that because my father hired a private investigator. Anyway, Donnigan's had some problems, and now he's back."

Silence stretched like a ball of unrolled yarn, tangling itself around the room. Finally, Emma gave a slight nod. "I see."

More silence.

"Will I be expected to prepare meals for him as well? I need to know, so I can estimate portion sizes."

Did that mean she'd decided to return? Something inside him lightened, something akin to hope. "He won't be eating with us. But if you could prepare a little extra, I'm sure he'd appreciate it."

She nodded, then moved toward the kitchen. "If you'll excuse me, Mr. Stratton, I have two hungry men to feed."

"I must be going, anyway." He scooped his hat off the arm of his chair. "Mr. Monroe, thank you for your time."

"My pleasure, son. Come back any time. Emma, see our guest out." There was a mild censure in his tone when he spoke to his daughter.

Emma speared Riley with a look that sliced away another good chunk of his pride.

He opened the door and stood back for her to exit, then followed her onto the porch. Medina whinnied from his place in the shadows.

They stood there for a moment, a dense reserve between them, weighted with unspoken questions and mute accusations. He hated this. Hated that she had reason to dislike him, to dislike his family. He didn't like them much either most of the time, but what could he do? He was a Stratton, for better or worse.

"Look, Emma," he said, his voice low. "I know you hate me. But—"

"I don't hate you."

"All right. Strong dislike."

She didn't argue.

"I'd like to offer a bit of advice."

Her eyebrows lifted, but other than that she didn't move.

"Let yourself grieve your mother."

She stiffened. "What makes you think I'm not grieving?"

The strength she worked so hard to maintain made his chest ache. "I'm sorry. I know you're grieving. But it seems to me like you're more concerned for your father's loss. For your brother's loss. You're trying so hard to take care of them...and from what I can see, you're doing a great job. But who's taking care of you?"

Her eyes glassed over, but no tears fell. "I'm perfectly capable of taking care of myself, Mr. Stratton." She turned her head and stared at the fields surrounding her home.

He followed her gaze across acres that should be freshly plowed by this time. Instead, dandelion and henbit lay across the land like a plush carpet. Pretty...but not nearly as practical as corn and beans and whatever else should have been growing there.

"I didn't mean to imply otherwise." He placed his hat on his head and descended the stairs.

She cleared her throat. "Thank you for your concern."

He looked at her, and the sun's reflection in her eyes, along with the still-brimming tears, made the green look more like something from a painting—a living, breathing painting that saw right into his soul. On a whim, he bent down and plucked a few of the stray henbit blossoms, forming a small bouquet of the delicate purple flowers, and handed them to her.

She smiled, and a single tear slid down her cheek before she brushed it away and accepted the gift.

Something about Emma Monroe reached in and pinched his soul in a most comfortable, yet most uncomfortable, way. He smiled back...a bittersweet smile that stayed with him all the way home.

CHAPTER 4

The following Monday, the sun yawned, stretched over the horizon, and whispered, "Good morning." Emma clucked to Sugar, then glanced around to take in the scenery. To one side, as far as she could see, was Stratton land. Behind her, neat farms dotted the landscape, all except her own farm. A few men had offered to do some work for them, knowing Pa wasn't able this year, but they had to tend their own land first.

But that was all right. With this job, she'd bring in as much money as Ma had, and with her school savings, they'd be just fine...for a few months, anyway. After that, well. She'd worry about that when the time came.

For now, there was no need for concern. At least, that's what she kept telling herself. But there must be a nest of hornets trapped in her stomach, the way it buzzed and burned. *Ma, I don't want to work for these people. How did you do it all these years?*

A breeze rustled the nearby oak leaves. She pulled her shawl tighter and slapped Sugar's reins with a weak, "Hyah!" Sugar seemed to understand, and plodded forward with more effort than seemed to match her slow pace. A verse from Ma's funeral drifted into her thoughts...from Deuteronomy? Something about God never leaving her, never forsaking her, never failing her. *Fear not, neither be dismayed,* the preacher had said.

Well, she didn't want to argue with a man of the cloth. And she certainly didn't want to argue with the Almighty. But it seemed to her that He'd indeed left her, forsaken her, and yes, even failed her. And considering the circumstances, she had every right to feel dismayed.

Sugar turned into the path leading to the Stratton home. She whickered, as if telling Emma, "It's not too late. I can turn around right now, if you'll just say the word."

But, no. Emma was made of stiffer stuff than that. She would go in there and cook and clean and take care of those children, and she would try her best to stay out of sight and not give anybody a reason to notice her.

All too soon, she pulled into the carriage house, hoping for one last moment of solitude before she had to face the music, or the fire, or the devil himself for that matter. But it wasn't to be.

Riley Stratton rose from a stool in the corner, and another man stood beside him. "There you are. I want to introduce you to Joe Barnes, our ranch foreman. I've asked him to be on hand each morning to assist you with your horse."

"How kind of you." Emma slid down from the wagon seat and handed Joe the reins. "I assure you, however, it's quite unnecessary. I can manage on my own."

~

*R*iley's heart did somersaults when Emma pulled her buggy into the carriage house. But a closer inspection of her face subdued his excitement. The fear in her expression made him want to hold her in his arms and hush her like he would a newborn, bawling calf.

Come to think of it, though, she probably wouldn't appreciate the bovine comparison.

The moment she saw him, though, a shutter slammed on her vulnerability, and her usual ironclad resolve took its place. As much as he hated to be the cause of her discomfort, he was glad he'd caught that glimpse. It told him more about her than he could have learned in a two-hour conversation. And then with her quip about handling things herself… Sugar may not be a wild stallion, but her owner was a different story.

"Pleased to make your acquaintance, Miss Monroe." Joe tipped his hat, and Riley sensed, more than saw, the other man's appreciation of Emma's finer feminine qualities. Perhaps this was a mistake, asking Joe to see to her. Why hadn't he asked Clem or Bob or even Skeeter?

"The pleasure is mine, Mr. Barnes." She reached in her pocket and withdrew several sugar cubes. "Sugar can be cantankerous with strangers. Give her these and she'll warm up to you in no time." She handed Joe the treats, nodded, and turned to leave.

"I'll walk you in," Riley said, wanting to smooth the way, to welcome her back the best way he could, but he had to run to catch up with her. If he was there when she arrived, maybe he could quell Allison's behavior somewhat.

"Thank you for your assistance, Mr. Stratton, but I know the way."

"I know. But I thought, it being your first day back and all…"

She stopped at the back door, and he opened it for her. But once she stepped inside, she reached to shut the door behind her, barring his entrance in the process. "My domain, remember?"

"Uh…yes. Of course. Good day, Miss Monroe." Riley tipped his hat and stepped away. "Please let me know if you need any—"

Click. Riley stood there a moment, looking at the closed

door. He turned just in time to see Joe leaning against the carriage house wall, having a good laugh at his expense.

"Don't you have work to do?"

"Yes, sir." Joe straightened and disappeared back into the carriage house. Riley picked up what was left of his dignity and headed around the house. It would have been closer to get to his office if he used the back entrance, but apparently, that wasn't going to work any more.

~

*E*mma leaned against the doorframe and inhaled deeply. That she'd just shut the door on Riley Stratton, of all people—son of her employer—was rude. But after Allison's comment on Monday about her swooning over him all day, she was afraid to even show common courtesy for fear of being misunderstood.

She was still five minutes early, which meant she could be busy working before Allison made an appearance. If Emma was even ten seconds late, Allison would probably dock her pay.

She looked around the kitchen, and her chest sank to her knees. There was no sign of her work from the previous Monday—the place was disastrous again. If the roof and windows hadn't been intact, Emma would have sworn a tornado hit the place.

Where to begin? She spied the wash bucket, empty and turned on its side as if it had been kicked out of the way. After rolling up her sleeves, she picked up the bucket and headed outside to the pump.

"Here, Miss Monroe. Let me get that for you." Joe took the bucket and fell in easy step with her.

"You don't have to. I'm sure you have your own duties to attend to."

"I was headed toward the pump, anyway, to wash my hands.

It's no trouble at all." Joe looked to be in his late twenties. His casual, friendly tone brought such a warm relief in this forlorn place, she couldn't help but smile.

"I don't recall seeing you around town. Have you worked for the Strattons a long time?"

"About five years, ma'am. Before that, I lived in Oklahoma."

"Is that your home?"

Joe scratched the back of his neck, as if considering the question carefully. "I don't suppose any place is really home to me. Not like you'd think. I don't have any family left, so home is just...me, I suppose. Wherever I am."

How hard that must be. Yes, she'd lost her mother. But she still had Pa and Lyndel. She still had her home and a family. "I think that's a splendid attitude, Mr. Barnes. Home is where you hang your hat, I suppose."

"Yes, ma'am." He pumped the water with ease, then walked her back to the kitchen. "Good day." He tipped his hat once again and strode away on his long cowboy legs.

A new friend, whose last name was, thankfully, not Stratton. She hadn't expected that this morning. She opened the door, set the wash bucket on the counter, and began loading it with kitchen carnage. And though she didn't look forward to one minute of this dreadful day working for these dreadful people, at least she wasn't totally alone on these vast acres. For just a moment, her heart felt just a little bit lighter.

~

*D*ays passed in a haze of activity. Thankfully, for the most part, the Strattons left her to her work. By the time Thursday rolled around, she had the main floor dusted, mopped, and set to rights, and had started on the upper floor. Twice, she'd watched little Davis while Allison went to town, and the child warmed up to her in no time. He was a smart little thing, crawling everywhere, getting into everything. Her time with him provided a welcome respite from cooking and scrubbing. She'd still not seen hide nor hair of Donnigan or his child, though.

It was just after two in the afternoon, and the grandfather clock chimed the time from its place in the parlor. Allison and Davis had gone to visit a friend, Riley was in town on business, and she had the place to herself. She had just finished the last of the dishes from the noon meal and poured herself a cup of tea, when the back door banged open and a man walked—no, stumbled into the kitchen. He had long hair, was dressed in buckskin, and though he looked strangely familiar, he didn't look like anyone she'd seen before.

"Oh, hellllloooo, darlin'. They told me there was a new housssse...keeper. But I didn't know you were such a purdy thang, or I'd've come callin' sooner."

That the man was inebriated, there was no doubt. Though Allison had never witnessed a drunk person before, she'd heard enough to recognize the slurred speech and glazed eyes. Besides, the man reeked of alcohol. Emma stood up, nearly knocking over her teacup in the process, and her heart sped like a hummingbird in flight.

The man looked enough like Riley to be his brother. This must be Donnigan. "Hello, Mr. Stratton. How m-may I help you?'

He appraised her head to toe, in a most inappropriate way, and said, "I can think of quite a few ways you can help me, little lady."

Her entire being pounded with alarm. Should she scream? No one would hear. Run? Perhaps... "I...I've been expecting you, sir. I believe I'm supposed to be introduced to your daughter. Your father mentioned she'd be spending time here, on occasion."

The man continued his leering, so she pressed on. "There are plenty of leftovers on the stove, if you're hungry." She spoke in a steady, soft tone, the way she handled Sugar when she was spooked. At the same time, she inched toward the dining room. She couldn't very well escape through the back door, since he was blocking it. "And there's a pitcher of sweet tea, right there on the counter."

"That soundsss delicious, ma'am. Why don't you come right on over here and pour me a glass." He shuffled forward. Emma looked around for a weapon, praying she wouldn't need one.

"I..." What could she say? Politeness might encourage him. Rudeness anger him.

For the first time in many weeks—the first time since Ma struggled for her last breath—Emma cried out to God. *Help me!*

The door opened behind the man, and Emma gasped. Did he have a friend with him? A young girl entered. She possessed the long, straight nose and wide, almond-shaped eyes common to the Strattons, but her skin was dark. Raven-black hair raggedly parted in the middle and hung over her shoulders in two braids. She wore a soiled, beaded buckskin dress and moccasins.

"Pa?" Her frightened eyes looked from Emma to her father, then back to Emma.

"I told you to stay outside!" Donnigan hissed. "You know better than to follow me in here."

"But you forgot this." She held out a lunch pail. Her voice was so soft, so timid, Emma wanted to take the child in her arms and protect her from this beast.

She had always heard coffee could sober a drunk man, but apparently, a child could do the same. The girl's presence, her frightened voice, caught the man's attention and transformed him somehow. The glaze seemed to pass from his expression, and a flicker of shame flashed before he blinked, then placed one hand behind his neck and hung his head.

"Thank you." He took the pail, then looked at Emma as if seeing her for the first time. "I'm sssorry if I frightened you, ma'am. I usually stop in lllate at night, but last night I...well...I wasn't able to get here."

Emma wasn't sure what to say, so she just nodded.

The girl kept her head down, as if she wanted to disappear into the wall.

The man cleared his throat. "I'm Donnigan Stratton, and thhhis is my daughter, Skye."

His thick speech told Emma the man wasn't completely sober yet, but at least he seemed a little less...dangerous. She focused on the girl.

"What a lovely name that is, Skye. And you're a lovely young lady."

The girl studied her moccasins and mumbled, "Thank you."

"Is everything okay in here?" Riley's voice behind her was one of the most beautiful sounds she'd ever heard, and she wanted to jump into his arms. Despite her feelings about his family, she knew no harm would come to her in Riley's presence.

Donnigan said some things under his breath that both embarrassed and angered Emma—more for the child's sake than for her own. Then he looked at Riley. "Everything's just fine. We were just leavin'. Come on, Skye."

He turned to go, but all Emma could think about was the little girl with the enormous, frightened eyes, who was probably very hungry.

"No, wait. Please. Let me send some of these leftovers home with you. They'll go bad if they don't get eaten." Emma spoke in her practice teacher voice, in a way that was more command than request, and grabbed a chipped platter off the countertop. She had meant to ask Allison what she wished to do with it, but now, it sat there begging to be used. She filled the plate with leftover ham and green beans and sweet potatoes, then covered it with a cloth and placed it beside the lunch pail, which she filled with fluffy dinner rolls, a crock of butter, and a pile of test cookies she'd made that morning, with a new recipe.

Skye watched her with wide eyes and a round mouth, but she didn't say a word. Both Riley and Donnigan stared as well, but she pretended not to notice either of them. Instead, she handed the girl one of the cookies. "I'm not sure about this recipe. You'll have to tell me what you think."

The child looked at the cookie, then at Emma, then at her Pa as if begging permission to take the treat. He nodded, and she reached a tentative hand. Instead of eating it, she slipped the cookie into her pocket and went back to looking at her feet.

"Much obliged, ma'am." Donnigan followed Skye out the back door. On the steps outside, he turned back to her. "I'm sorry if I frightened you."

Emma didn't answer. What could she say? The man's behavior had been deplorable. It was almost as if she'd witnessed, in that short span of time, two men living in the same body. She'd heard alcohol could do such things to people, but now she had seen it with her own eyes.

When the door was shut, Riley closed the distance between them. "Are you all right?"

"I'm fine. Thank you." It was all she could do to keep her voice steady.

"Emma, I'm so sorry. I should have warned you about Donnigan. Should have told you to keep the back door locked, especially when no one else is here."

"Duly noted." She struggled to keep her composure. Part of her wanted to sit down and bawl her eyes out. The other part wanted to scream in outrage over that little girl's plight. Instead, she took a deep breath and asked, "When can I start caring for Skye?"

Riley sat down at the table and gestured for her to do the same. She did, and took a long, calming sip of her now luke-warm tea before offering Riley some.

"No thank you." He leaned forward, rested his arms on the table, and breathed deeply. "Donnigan and Skye showed up here a couple of months ago, and Donnigan's been drinking ever since. He mourns his wife, and he's not handling it well. Problem is, Dad wants nothing to do with either of them. Well...that's not exactly true. He wants Donnigan to get cleaned up and make something of himself, but he refuses to acknowledge Skye as his granddaughter. Says she brings shame on the family name.

"But Donnigan is family, and family is important to my father. He would rather Donnigan be here than hauled in for public intoxication. Reputation and community standing is also important to my father, and he doesn't want some do-gooder gossips getting involved. You know how people are when it comes to Indians. Like it or not, it's the way things are."

John Stratton's concern wasn't for the child, it was for his reputation. Emma knew she had no right to hate anyone, but for the life of her, she didn't know how she was supposed to like that man, even a little. Everything about him made her stomach turn. But this...this rejection of an innocent child. It made her want to kick him. Spit in his food. It made her want to act like the wild savage he made his granddaughter out to be. He deserved it.

Then again, he wasn't wrong about public perception. They were little more than a generation removed from The Webster Massacre of 1839. Sweet Anne Webster, in her 80s, lost nearly her entire family. Hatred for the natives ran deep in these parts. What would they do to little Skye?

"Why isn't she in school?" As soon as she asked the question, she knew how ridiculous it sounded. Would Skye even be safe in school?

Riley looked at her, and she knew his thoughts mirrored her own. "I doubt she's ever had formal schooling. Donnigan's probably never thought of it, to be honest. And with Dad's attitude about her, he'd be furious if she showed up in town wearing the Stratton name like a badge of honor. As I said, they've only been here a few months, and they pretty much keep to themselves."

An idea came to her. "I could use an assistant."

"What?"

"I'd like Skye to be my assistant. She could come each day and help me cook and keep house. And I could teach her some...life skills, that she's probably not getting from her father. Since she's not attending school, I think this is a better alternative than showing up here randomly, when her father is too...uhm...when he's not able to care for her. Can you make that happen?"

Riley looked at her in an odd way that made her want to blush to her toes, but she held his gaze. Lifted her chin. And, she wished he'd stop staring at her like she was the last piece of pie at the buffet.

CHAPTER 5

She must have taken Riley's silence for hesitance. She huffed, stiffened her back, and set her teacup down on the table so hard its contents nearly splashed out. "Riley Stratton, that little girl is frightened half out of her mind. I know I only saw her for a few minutes, but she's lost her mother and there's no telling what she has to put up with from her father. I once had aspirations to become a teacher. And though that will probably never happen now, I would like the opportunity to make a difference in a child's life. Please, Riley. You know she'll be better off here than down in some shack with a drunk father."

A teacher. Riley hadn't known that, though it didn't surprise him. "You'll get no arguments from me. It's my father you'll have to convince. He doesn't exactly want to come in contact with her. The reason he asked you about watching her is because he wants to make sure he doesn't have to lay eyes on her. That will be hard if she's here all day, every day."

Emma's shoulders slumped. "I...maybe you could talk to him?"

Riley chuckled, not because the situation held any humor,

but because the woman before him was the most adorable creature he'd ever observed. Why someone hadn't married her already, he had no idea. If he was the marrying kind, and if she weren't far above his station when it came to goodness and grace, he might be tempted to snag her for himself. But he wasn't the marrying kind, at least not for an innocent. He could never bring someone like her into this family. Why, the Stratton way of life would crush her like a bug. All the lying. Underhanded deals. Blackmail.

Not that Riley had taken part in any of that, though he'd sure watched Dad and Colt bully to get their way. He'd managed to escape most of the nastier stuff, but he knew the day was fast approaching when he'd be expected to do his father's bidding for some sour-tasting business. It was the price they all paid, to have a lot of money. It came with the name. And it nauseated him.

Mom had never approved of Dad's ways. What she ever saw in Dad, Riley wasn't sure. But now that he looked back with adult perspective, he remembered sadness in her eyes. Sorrow. He could hear the arguments that were never intended for his ears, as he sat outside the study door to make sure Mom was all right. He remembered her begging Dad, through tears, not to put this fellow out of business or force that one to sell. The doctor's report said she died of consumption. More likely she'd died of a broken heart.

No, he could never drag an innocent into this mess of a family. If he ever did marry, the best he could hope for was someone who was smart enough to look the other way.

"Please? I know you can figure something out." Emma's eyes peered into his soul.

What were they talking about? Oh. Skye. "I'll see what I can do." And he would.

"I do appreciate it." Emma ran her finger along the handle of her cup. "She's a lovely child, and well, I suppose we both know what it feels like to lose a mother." Emma's voice was hushed, her tone almost reverent.

Shame stung Riley's conscience like vinegar in a wound. Why hadn't he taken more of an interest in the child? Granted, he'd only returned home from university a month ago. Still, that was no excuse to let the girl suffer without trying to soothe her pain.

And why hadn't he thought to warn Emma about Donnigan? Oh, he felt certain his brother wouldn't harm Emma, but she didn't know that. And Donnigan wasn't the same gentle soul when he'd been drinking. "I should have warned you about his drinking."

Emma let the silence grow long and thick between them before she answered. "No harm done."

Riley looked around at the spotless kitchen. Even with Davis to care for on occasion, Emma had brought their home to ship-shape in very little time. It didn't look to him like she needed an assistant.

That Emma cared more for his own flesh and blood than anyone in his family embarrassed him. Sometimes, being a Stratton was a privilege. Other times, it was a curse. But it was his curse to bear, as long as he wore the last name. He reached for his neckpiece and tried to loosen it.

Allison waltzed into the kitchen quite abruptly, as if she'd caught them in something scandalous. "Well, now. Isn't this cozy?" She looked at Emma as if she were some kind of two-bit trollop. "Don't you have work to do?"

Emma's eyes flashed as much kerosene as Allison's voice, but she only said, "Yes, ma'am. I apologize." She took her teacup, still half full, and dumped it in the sink, then grabbed her coat from its peg. "I was just about to head to town for groceries."

"Good. We're having guests next Thursday evening. Would you mind preparing something a little extra special?"

Allison's eyes held a glint that meant she was up to something.

"Certainly, Mrs. Stratton." Emma buttoned her coat as she spoke. "Do you have something specific in mind?"

"Yes. I'd like you to prepare this." She handed Emma a page that looked like it had been ripped from a circular. "And if it's not too much trouble, I'd like you to stay and serve, since it's a special occasion. I'll pay you overtime, of course."

Emma looked at the page, then folded it and placed it in her pocket. "That shouldn't be a problem."

"Good." Allison cast a superior look around the room, paused at Riley a moment as if appraising him for auction, then left the kitchen. "Riley, don't you have work as well?" she called over her shoulder.

She didn't wait for a response, and he didn't give one. Instead, he followed Emma out the back door. "I'll go with you. I have business in town."

"Suit yourself, Mr. Stratton. But I'm driving."

"I was hoping I could persuade you to let me take the surrey. It hasn't been driven in ages."

"Your sister-in-law drove it to town yesterday."

"Oh. So she did. I'd still like to drive you to town." She'd enjoy a ride in a surrey. Didn't all women? Surely that would lift her spirits. He recalled the extra chocolate-chip cookies Mrs. Monroe packed into his lunch every day, just after Mom died. They didn't take away his hurt. But knowing someone cared enough to brighten his day, the way Mom had, did lighten the load.

Emma let out an exasperated sigh, with a slight grin that gave him just the result he hoped for. "Oh, all right. But only if you promise me you'll talk to your father and brother about Skye. Today."

"Deal."

~

*E*mma studied the four-course menu Allison had given her on the way to town, and chewed her lip so much she nearly drew blood. She'd never heard of some of these dishes. And the recipes weren't included, only the names. The page was clearly ripped from a ladies' magazine, but which one?

That Allison wanted to trip her up was obvious, but Emma wouldn't let on that it bothered her a whit. She'd just have to figure this out. At home, she had all of Ma's cookbooks. She'd just have to leaf through them tonight until she found the recipes.

She wished she hadn't agreed to let Riley accompany her. She could have stopped by the house on the way to town to get the books, and referred to them while she shopped. Now she'd have to make another trip to town. Maybe she could send Lyndel with a shopping list. He could drop it off before school and pick up the order at the end of the day. But now that he walked to and from school, he'd have a hard time carrying it all.

"What's that look for?" Riley asked. She'd almost forgotten he was there.

"What look?"

"The one where you're looking at the page Allison handed you like it was written by the devil himself."

"Riley Stratton. What a terrible thing to say." But now that he'd said it, she almost agreed. Perhaps the devil didn't write it, but he'd certainly played a role in handing it to her.

A slight pang of guilt rose in her for thinking such an uncharitable thought about Allison. Yes, the woman was awful. But she wasn't the devil.

At least Emma hoped not.

Riley chuckled, and she realized he was waiting for her answer. "I...I just...I'm not familiar with some of these dishes.

But it will be fine. My mother has several cookbooks at home. I'm sure I'll find the recipes there."

"I wouldn't count on it."

"What do you mean?"

"I mean, I know my sister-in-law. She takes pleasure in making people look foolish. I'm sure she gave you that menu in hopes of watching you fail."

"Failure is not in my vocabulary. Or have you forgotten so quickly?"

He laughed. "Oh, no. I'll never forget how you humiliated me in every last spelling bee we had. A girl. And three years younger than me. I was scarred for life."

"It seems you've recovered."

"Appearances can be misleading."

Emma bit the inside of her cheek to keep from laughing. "If you're expecting an apology, you'll be waiting a long time, Mr. Stratton."

"Oh, I'd never expect that from you, though I'll surely carry the wound with me to my grave."

She cut her eyes at him, then looked back at the road. Why did he have to be so handsome? And so likeable? "Only until then? Not into eternity?"

"Probably into heaven as well, where I'll lay it, weeping, at the good Lord's feet."

"Well I'm glad to hear you have hope of laying it down at some point."

Riley parked the surrey in front of the general store, climbed down, and helped her out. "I'll meet you back here in a half hour?"

Emma looked at the menu again, along with the list she'd made earlier. "Better make it 45 minutes."

He tipped his hat, and she felt him watching as she walked to the door, which she shut behind her. If only she could shut out the feelings she wished she didn't have for him. Because now that she'd seen the Stratton family up close, there was no way she'd want to marry into that group.

"Miss Monroe. I've missed seeing you. Are you enjoying your new position at the Stratton Ranch?" Virginia Smith, proprietress of the general store along with her husband Glyn, came around the counter and offered Emma a warm hug.

Better not to comment on her feelings about her new job. "I didn't realize how much I'd miss seeing everyone in town each day. But I'm here now, and I need a favor." She pulled out the menu. "I've been asked to prepare these dishes for a special dinner Thursday evening, and I'm not familiar with them. Can you help me?"

Virginia took the paper and read the words under her breath. "Veal Collops? Vermicelli Soup? German Trifle? Crullers? Sounds pretty fancy, if you ask me. Glyn prefers good ol' steak and potatoes, so I'm afraid I can't help you. Unless..." She studied the page. "Did Allison Stratton give you this?"

"Yes."

Virginia hurried behind the counter. "She gets several of those hoity-toity women's journals. They come in the mail every month. I'll bet this page is from one of them. Surely they would have included the recipes. I wonder why she didn't give you those, as well."

"Yes, I wonder..." Emma refrained from further comment.

Virginia rifled through a stack of mail. "Sometimes they send an extra copy, hoping we'll carry them in the store. Seems like I saw one just the other day. Here it is! Let's see if this is the one."

They flipped through the pages, and sure enough, the style and typeset matched up. But was it the correct issue?

There, toward the end of the circular, was the very page Emma held in her hand. And the next several pages contained recipes for each dish. *Thank you, God!* Emma realized, even as the short prayer of thanksgiving swept through her thoughts, that she hadn't spoken to God much lately. At least, not until Donnigan nearly scared her witless that morning. How could she, after He took her mother from her? From all of them? Still, she recognized the hand of Providence in this morning's events. *And thank You for rescuing me from Donnigan.* That would have to do for now.

Before long, she and Virginia had accumulated quite a pile on the counter, and she still had to make a stop at the butcher for veal. Good thing she had Riley to help her carry the boxes. Imagine, the Strattons lived on a cattle ranch, with all the fine cuts of steak they could ever want, and Allison chose to serve veal for dinner! Well, if it was veal she wanted, then veal she'd get.

"May I leave these boxes until I finish my other errands?"

"Of course. They'll be right here."

On the sidewalk in front of the General Store, Emma heard her name. She turned to find Clara Bridges. Her dear friend had been at Baylor Female College for the past several months.

"Oh, Emma." The sympathy in Clara's face brought that burning feeling behind Emma's eyes. Why was it that when people were awful to her, she stiffened, but when people showed compassion and kindness, it was nearly her undoing? She'd almost rather folks be rude here in public. At least then she wouldn't have to worry about crying and making a spectacle of herself.

"I'm so sorry I couldn't be here for…" Clara drew Emma into a tight hug, but didn't finish the sentence. "I'm just so sorry."

"Thank you. It's been…difficult. When did you arrive home?" Hopefully a change in subject would save her from becoming a blubbering embarrassment to them both.

"Last Saturday. I was planning to come visit you this week. Do you have any time to get together?"

"Clara. We're late." The mayor's voice didn't sound harsh, but it did sound urgent.

"Coming." Clara turned back to Emma. "I'm so sorry. Papa is running for re-election, and he's filled my schedule with public appearances for the next two weeks. I'll find you soon and we'll make plans." She embraced Emma once more before hurrying toward her father.

Emma nodded and watched her friend bustle into the midday crowd, her tailored violet dress and fashionable plumed hat causing her to stand out in the otherwise drab brown and white scene.

They were to have shared a room next year. *What will my future look like now?*

~

The next morning, Riley paced in front of the carriage house. What was taking Emma so long? He was half tempted to meet her on the road, but he didn't want to appear too excited. She seemed to see him as two parts clown, anyway. Why was that? And why did it matter?

It mattered because for the first time in a long time, he cared what somebody thought. He respected Emma. He wanted her to respect him. Where was she?

He was just about to go against his good sense and saddle Medina when the sound of her buggy drifted from the road. He sat on a stool and examined an old piece of rope as if it was the most interesting thing he'd seen in years.

"Good mornin', Miss Monroe." Joe's voice called from the front drive. Riley had nearly forgotten about Joe meeting her here every morning.

"Good morning to you, Joe. Isn't it a beautiful day?"

Her voice sounded lighter than he'd heard it since their school days. A jealous pang rose in his gut, but he pushed it back down. It was just Joe. Surely she didn't see him as...did she? She was way too good for Joe.

Why did it matter to him, anyway?

It mattered because he was trying his best to take care of her, was all. Joe was a wanderer. He was decent enough, but Emma could do better. If Mrs. Monroe were here, she'd steer her daughter away from a lowly ranch foreman who, at nearly 30, still slept in a bunkhouse with a dozen other men. Emma deserved better.

He should intervene. As her friend.

Her friend. If he kept telling himself that, maybe he'd start to believe it.

He didn't like the turn of his thoughts. What was it about Miss Emma Monroe that made him feel like a kid outside a candy store without a nickel?

He heard the horse and buggy draw to a stop outside the carriage house, and from his vantage point he watched Joe's tall shadowed silhouette assist her slim form to the ground.

"A beautiful day it is, Miss Monroe."

"Here, Joe. I brought you some cookies. I like to try new recipes. There's plenty there for you and all the hands."

"Why, thank you. I know the boys will appreciate it. These will be gone by evening."

"Bring the basket back, and I'll refill it."

"I'll surely do it, ma'am."

Then, gentle footsteps retreated in the direction of the house, while Joe climbed aboard and drove Sugar through the wide carriage house doors. He spotted Riley first thing, and cast him a cat-ate-the-canary grin.

"Waiting for me?" Joe asked.

Riley stood up and gathered the rope in both hands. "As a matter of fact, I needed some rope. I found some, so...I guess I'll see you later."

"Have a nice day, Mr. Stratton."

Joe chuckled behind him while Riley walked to the kitchen entrance. He didn't see anything funny at all. At the back door, he stashed the rope beside the porch and knocked.

Emma answered. She looked as pretty as the spring flowers, just starting to sprinkle the roadsides. "Good morning, Mr. Stratton."

Her voice didn't sound nearly as song-like as it had with Joe. Well, maybe his news would help.

"Good morning, Miss Monroe. I wanted to speak with you about the project we discussed yesterday."

Just as he'd hoped, her face broke into a sunshine smile and she held open the door for him. "Come in. Did you talk to your father?"

"I did."

"I haven't started the coffee yet. I need to light the stove, if you'll give me just a moment."

"Here, let me help with that." Riley made quick work of adding wood and starting the fire.

"Thank you, Mr. Stratton. That wasn't necessary, but I do appreciate it." After measuring the coffee and setting the pot to boil, she sat down at the kitchen table and gestured for him to sit across from her. "I have some cookies I was planning to serve at lunch. Would you like some now?"

He felt a little better knowing she hadn't given all the cookies to Joe. "I'd love some, thank you."

She placed a large tin in front of him and opened the lid to reveal golden-brown oatmeal raisin cookies.

He tasted one, and it had a hint of cinnamon and something else he couldn't identify. "This is delicious. Any chance I could keep them all for myself?"

"There's always a chance, depending on what you tell me about Skye." She flashed him a sassy grin, and his heart did a little flip. Did she know the effect she had on him? Was she using it to her advantage?

No. Emma Monroe was a lot of things, but manipulative

wasn't one of them. Nor deceptive. And that knowledge only added to her allure. "Then I'll get right to it. Dad thinks it's a good idea for Skye to help you. 'Good training,' he said."

Emma clapped her hands together like a child being offered a pony ride. "I'm so glad! I hardly slept last night, thinking about her."

"There's just one hitch." He hated this part—it only confirmed what he already knew. His family had their priorities all out of order. "He doesn't want to see her. Ever."

"What do you mean? How can she work here without him seeing her?"

"That's the catch. You'll have to keep her out of sight when he's around. It usually won't be a problem, since you only see him at meals. And if she's gone by the time he gets home in the evenings, I figured you could just hide her away when he's around."

Disgust and disapproval soaked into her features, drowning any remnant of the childlike delight. "Mr. Stratton, a child is not an object that can be stowed in a closet when the lord of the manor stops in." With one swift motion, she picked up the lid to the cookie tin and replaced it with a clack.

"I know. But those are his conditions. Take it or leave it."

She drew the tin toward her, as if guarding it from further enjoyment by the enemy. A myriad of emotions played across her face before she spoke again. "I suppose I'll have to take it." Then she removed a corner of the lid, took out one more cookie, and placed it before him. "Thank you for speaking to him about it."

She stood, and with a swish of her skirts, stowed the tin on a high shelf and dusted her hands. "The rest of those will have to wait until lunch. Now, do I need to fetch her myself?"

"I thought we might do that together, after breakfast."

She nodded. Then she retrieved the flour, a bowl, and a few other items and began mixing biscuits, he presumed. He should leave. But she fascinated him. Everything she did, every move she made, had purpose. Her purpose, it seemed, was to take care of others. Her father. Her brother. Now Skye.

Purpose.

What's my purpose? Do I even have one?

After a few moments of him staring at her, Emma stopped her work and gave him a dismissive nod, as if she were the queen of England dismissing a servant.

CHAPTER 6

*E*mma was so anxious to gather her new protégé, she nearly dropped the pan she washed while the Stratton family ate breakfast. Add to that, she'd come dangerously close to spilling coffee on the senior Mr. Stratton's sleeve and had nearly poured gravy on the bowl of blackberry preserves. She'd better just slow down, take some deep breaths, and think about the magnitude of what was to come.

She actually had a chance to teach. One student, yes. But the idea of hiding Skye away during mealtimes was actually becoming more attractive. Why, she could set up a small desk in the massive pantry where Skye could do schoolwork. Surely she wasn't far behind the other children. Perhaps Emma could have her caught up by next school year.

But after the family finished their meal, when Emma thought surely she and Riley would fetch the child, Allison called Emma into the parlor.

"Have a seat," the woman said.

Why did Emma feel like something bad was about to happen?

"How are your plans for Thursday evening coming?"

"I believe I have everything under control, Mrs. Stratton."

"Good. Because this is a very important dinner. I took the liberty of ordering you two work uniforms. I'd like you to start wearing them when you're here. It just seems more...professional."

Work uniforms? What on earth was she talking about?

Allison retrieved a folded stack of clothing from a side table and handed it to Emma. "You can start now."

"You...want me to wear these?"

"Yes. Do you have a problem with that?" Allison's smug look begged for Emma to protest.

"Uh...no, ma'am. I...suppose I can use the privy to change?"

"That will be fine."

Emma resisted the urge to examine the clothes then and there. Instead, she sat in stiff silence, waiting to be dismissed.

"That will be all."

"Yes, ma'am." She gathered the stack of coarse, folded broadcloth and headed for the fancy indoor privy. Though she'd cleaned it many times in the past weeks, she had never allowed herself to actually use the thing. Instead, she headed for the outhouse when she had need.

But this room... It had an engraved porcelain toilet that actually flushed away the waste, and a matching porcelain tub with running water. She couldn't imagine the amount of money it took for such extravagance. And all for human waste! It seemed absurd. Still, a part of her longed to try it for herself.

Not today. For now, this was a dressing room and nothing more. Once the door was secured and locked, she sat on the closed toilet lid and examined her new uniform. It was truly the most hideous thing she'd ever seen.

The black dress was gathered at the neck, but had no defined waist. It looked like a big black potato sack. The white apron had straps at the shoulders which crisscrossed at the back and loosely attached at the hips. Again, no definition or shape. And to top off the ensemble was a white, ruffled mobcap. She'd seen pictures of these caps, worn during Revolutionary times, but in 1880? She'd look ridiculous. Why on earth would Allison require such a thing?

Then it occurred to her. She *wanted* Emma to look ridiculous. It was a challenge...and Emma would take it. What was it to her what she wore while she cooked and cleaned?

But once she changed her clothes and examined her reflection in the full-length mirror, she truly did feel humiliated. Somehow, she'd have to find the courage to walk out that door and show herself to the world. Or at least, to the Strattons.

Something flickered in her memory, and she sat on the toilet once again and recalled her mother's words. "When everything in the world seems terrible, find one flicker of light, one small piece of hope, and focus on that. It might only be a single flower in the midst of a garden full of weeds, but focus on the flower. You'll always find something to be thankful for, if you look hard enough."

She pressed her palms against her eyes to push the tears back in. "Ma, I wish you were here."

Her mother's face faded from her mind's eye, and Skye's came into view. This ugly dress and cap were nothing. She had a student. A child, who needed her. And she still had her father, who never once felt the need to hide her away or humiliate her. And a younger brother who, despite his current aversion to baths, was kindhearted and decent and respectful and intelligent...yes, she had much to be thankful for.

Someone tapped on the door. "Emma? Are you all right? You've been in there a while." Allison's false concern provided just the encouragement Emma needed to hold up her chin and march out of the room.

She gathered her things, put on her most dignified countenance, and opened the door.

~

*R*iley waited twenty minutes before going in search of Emma. What he found was Allison, pacing back and forth in front of the privy as if Santa himself would pop through the door at any moment.

"Where's Emma?"

"Our *maid*," she replied, disdain clinging to her words like foam on a stagnant pond, "is changing into her uniform."

"Uniform?"

"Yes. I thought it would be more appropriate for her to wear a uniform, especially in light of Thursday evening." Allison tilted her head up and back, and he could see her nostril hairs.

"Thursday evening?"

"Don't tell me you've forgotten." She put both hands on her hips. "It's a very important evening. For you, especially."

"For me?" Why did he have the sudden urge to run for the hills?

"Oh, for goodness' sake, Riley. Would you stop responding to everything with a question?"

"I don't know what on earth you're talking about, Allison. Why in the world is Thursday night important for me?"

Allison leered at him, stepped closer, and brushed a bit of imaginary dust off Riley's shoulder. "Let's just say it's time for you to stop being a little boy, and start acting like a man."

"You're not making any sense."

Before Allison could respond, the door opened, and Emma stepped out in the most ridiculous looking get-up he'd seen since P. T. Barnum last brought his travelling circus to these parts. Without thinking, Riley snorted, then let out a guffaw that quickly escalated into a full-fledged attack of hilarity. By the time he realized Emma wasn't smiling, but Allison was, the damage was done.

He should have bolted when he had the urge.

"I hope this is to your liking, Mrs. Stratton," Emma said.

"It's perfect. Please be sure to wear that at all times when you're working. Even when you make trips to town on our behalf. We have a reputation to uphold."

Allison didn't even try to hide the condescension in her attitude.

Suddenly, Allison looked every bit a spider, Emma her prey. He had to do something. Save Emma from...he wasn't sure what. He looked at Allison. "You're joking, right? You're not really going to make her wear that, are you?"

Allison smiled her wicked smile. "Of course she'll wear it. She's a servant. I'd think she'd be grateful not to muss up her everyday things."

"Allison, I hardly think—"

"It's all right, Mr. Stratton." Emma adjusted the ill-fitting sack. "She's right. It will be so much easier not to have to worry about what I'll wear to work. Now if that's all, I have much to do."

Allison nodded curtly and watched Emma retreat to the kitchen.

"Why are you doing this?" Anger bubbled from deep in his bowels.

"I don't know what you're talking about. It's perfectly acceptable for household staff to wear a black and white uniform."

"In London, maybe. Not in Lampasas, Texas."

"We may live in Lampasas, but that doesn't mean we have to be socially backward. It's our duty to set an example for others in the community. Give them something to aspire to."

"You think people around here will aspire to wear that?"

Allison rolled her eyes. "You're a man. You wouldn't under-stand. About Thursday night—you should wear evening apparel."

"You want me to come to dinner in my long johns?"

"Riley Stratton, you're impossible. You know exactly what I meant. Don't you have work to do?" Why was it that every time he annoyed his sister-in-law, she reminded him of his job?

"As a matter of fact, I do." He left her standing in the hallway and exited through the front door. No use in her knowing he was about to go for a short ride with their newly-clad maid.

Emma opened the back door when he knocked and sailed past him with an icy blast that could have frosted over the early spring blooms. She didn't say a word, just made a black-and-white beeline for the carriage house, like some kind of angry flying insect.

"Emma."

She lifted her chin but didn't respond. That's when he saw the moisture in her eyes, the deep red of her neck and cheeks. Was she trying not to cry?

"Emma, I'm sorry."

"You've nothing to be sorry for, Mr. Stratton." Her voice came out thin and tight.

"Yes I do. I shouldn't have laughed." *Why did I laugh? I'm such a baboon.*

"It's your house. You have every right to behave however you please."

"Emma. It's just...the dress. It took me by surprise, is all. I don't claim to understand Allison. She's an imbecile, as far as I'm concerned. But as far as uniforms go, you make that thing look as good as anybody could."

More silence.

He'd better stop talking. Something told him he was only making things worse. *I finally decide to do something a little bit noble, and I end up making the object of that nobility even more miserable.* He could kick himself. Curse himself and his stupid family. He definitely needed more practice at this do-gooder thing. Medina whinnied, as if scolding him for not knowing the right thing to say, and she was right.

How could he fix Emma's day, or at least make it a little better? She deserved more joy in her life.

That gave him an idea. Instead of the buggy....

"What do you say we take Sugar and Medina? Skye can ride back with you on Sugar."

"I'm hardly dressed for horseback riding."

"My mother wore men's dungarees under her skirts when she rode. There's a pair of her old ones in the tack room, if you'd like to try them."

She looked like she wanted to consider it. Her eyes flashed to the house, as if expecting Allison to pounce at any moment.

"Don't worry. Allison's had her fun with you for today. She'll retire to her room and we won't see her for another two hours, at least."

"I look ridiculous enough as it is. Can you imagine all this on horseback?" She gestured to the austere, shapeless garb.

"Who's going to see you? Besides Skye and Donnigan, and, well, it looks like they'll have to get used to that get-up like the rest of us."

She gave a curt nod, and Riley led her to the tack room, removed his mother's dungarees and a pair of her boots from the shelf and placed them on a bench, then shut the door behind him on his way out. Any other time, he'd have taken a little more time with anything that belonged to his mother. But Emma seemed so fragile at the moment, he didn't want to do anything to cause her to change her mind.

He led Sugar out of her stall and found an extra saddle. He'd just readied both horses when she emerged, looking the same except for a light of mischief behind her eyes.

Without comment, he held out his hand to help her onto her horse.

She accepted, but paused before she hiked her skirt up, revealing just enough leather and denim to make him want to see more. He averted his eyes, even though he hadn't seen anything inappropriate, and cleared his throat. This woman sent his emotions on a runaway Ferris wheel ride.

"It is rather ridiculous looking, isn't it?" Emma asked once she was in place. She searched his eyes, as if waiting for validation.

Riley smiled, cherishing her rare, vulnerable expression. He'd best weigh his response carefully. "Trust me, Miss Monroe. Your face makes any dress look like it's fit for a ball at Buckingham Palace."

She burst into a fit of giggles. "As a scullery maid, perhaps."

~

*E*mma knew the Stratton property was vast, but had never guessed it was this expansive. She pushed Sugar to full speed—which wasn't very fast, really—and enjoyed the velvety feel of wind through her hair. They'd been riding maybe ten minutes when Riley drew his horse in, and she followed suit.

He swept his arms to the right and left. "All this is ours."

And your father would begrudge my pa his one-hundred-sixty acres, just because it keeps you from getting what's on the other side of it? Emma bit the words back, knowing they wouldn't serve any purpose. "How much land does your father own, exactly?"

"Four thousand acres, give or take a little. He didn't start out with that much, of course. When he moved here in the early 1850s, Texas granted no more than 640 acres to ranchers. Ten years earlier, and he could have been granted thousands. But he didn't let that stop him. Over the years, people have sold him the adjoining land. Most people, anyway."

Yes, most people bowed to John Stratton's bullying. To be fair, she had to admire the man's business sense. But there was a fine line between being successful and being greedy. And in her mind, John Stratton crossed that line a long time ago.

"Donnigan's cabin is right through here." He guided Medina into a thick, wooded area. Sugar followed as if she already knew the importance of their journey. Not far into the thicket was a simple, rough-hewn structure, camouflaged by the woods around it. She'd have never found it on her own.

A slight movement through one dirt-covered window let them know they'd been seen. Emma held her breath. Surely Donnigan would agree to this opportunity for his daughter. Wouldn't he?

"Wait here." Riley climbed from his horse and handed her the reins, then approached the cabin's door. After knocking three times, he called, "Donnigan. It's me, Riley."

After a few long moments and some scuffling inside, the door opened wide, and Donnigan stepped onto the porch wearing nothing but denim britches, suspenders, and a soiled undershirt. Emma turned her head away, but she felt him looking at her.

"What?" Donnigan asked his brother.

"I've come to talk to you about Skye." Riley's voice was low, and Emma strained to hear.

"What about her?"

"Miss Monroe here would like to take her on as a sort of...protégé."

"You want your maid to teach my daughter how to be a maid?"

"It's not like that. Emma...Miss Monroe...plans to be a teacher one day."

Emma fought not to stare at Riley, slack-jawed. The way he said it, becoming a teacher was still a possibility, but that wasn't true. Why would he mislead his brother like that? Perhaps he'd misunderstood, though she couldn't imagine how he could have.

A movement to her side caught her attention, and she turned her head in time to see Skye, perched on a low branch of a pecan tree, transfixed on the conversation on the porch. Her face was dirty, and her hair fell in a tangled black nest down her back. She wore the same dress she'd worn yesterday, and Emma had a sneaking suspicion she'd worn it for quite sometime.

Emma's heart broke for the girl. It was hard enough at nineteen to lose her mother. But this little one...she had no one to teach her about fixing her hair or ironing a dress or...how to be a lady. *Please, God. I want to help this child. Let this happen.* Emma nearly added, *You owe me that much,* but even in her current state of displeasure with the Almighty, she knew better than to sass God. *Please.*

She perked her ears toward the porch once again, in time to hear Donnigan say some words she'd never repeat, words that a child should never be subjected to. But then, he shook his head, spat into the yard, and said, "All right. Do what you want."

Did that mean yes? Emma wanted to squeal. Instead, she climbed down from the horse, looped Sugar's and Medina's reins around a low branch, and slowly, cautiously approached the young girl in the tree.

"Hello," Emma said, her voice barely above a whisper.

Skye looked at her, but didn't answer.

"Do you remember me? We met yesterday, in your grandfather's kitchen."

Still no response.

"I...asked your Uncle Riley if you might be able to work with me some each day. I'm dreadfully busy, and on top of that, I'm a little lonely. I'd love to have you there...not just for the work, but to keep me company. Would you like that?"

Skye looked at her father, who was still talking to Riley in a low murmur. She returned her gaze to Emma and offered the slightest nod. So slight, in fact, that if Emma hadn't been watching carefully, she would have missed it.

"Wonderful. Would you like to start today?"

Another nod, and the girl cautiously climbed down from the tree and landed on the fallen leaves in a noiseless action.

"Skye! Get over here, girl." Donnigan's voice wasn't harsh, exactly, and the girl didn't act afraid, for which Emma was grateful. He may be a foul-mouthed drunk, but perhaps he wasn't a complete monster.

"You remember your Uncle Riley."

Skye nodded.

"That lady over there is Miss Monroe. You met her yesterday. How would you like to go with her every day and learn to cook and sew and do some other things?"

Another nod.

"Good. Then it's settled."

Riley tenderly placed his hand on the child's back and guided her toward the horses. He had a gentle way with his niece. He'd make a wonderful father someday. Not that it mattered to Emma.

"Would you like to share the saddle with me or Miss Monroe?" he asked the girl.

Skye looked at Emma, and Emma summoned her most welcoming smile. "This is Sugar. Would you like to pet her?"

Skye reached for the mare's muzzle, then pulled back at the last moment. Sugar nodded, as if telling the girl it was okay.

"Here." Emma reached into her pocket. "Her name is Sugar because she has a sweet tooth. Feed her a sugar cube, and she'll love you forever. Like this...hold your hand flat." Emma demonstrated, then placed a cube in Skye's hand.

Sugar licked up the offered treat, and Skye giggled, a soft sound that sent Emma's spirit soaring.

Thank you, God, Emma's heart whispered over and over, as she held the child close in the saddle all the way back to the main house.

CHAPTER 7

*I*t was all Riley could do to stay out of the way and let Emma and Skye do...whatever it was they were doing. Lunch had been simple but delicious. Emma never served anything that wasn't mouth-watering. And Skye was nowhere to be seen during the meal.

He did notice Emma going into the pantry a lot. And he did notice a chair was missing from the kitchen table. The thought of his niece being hidden away in a dark closet was so absurd, so unthinkable that he wondered how the other members of his family could eat their meal as if nothing out of the ordinary was happening.

And yet Emma quietly went about her work—he could see her from his place in the dining room—and hummed softly as she washed dishes and cleaned the countertops. Despite having lost her mother, she had something, some ethereal quality that Riley longed for.

Her mother'd had it too. Come to think of it, so did her father. Sick as he was, there was just something...

Peace. That was it. Though Emma was still clearly distraught over her mother's death—her daily countenance showed as much—she had an inner light. He looked around at each member of his own family and realized that with all their money, all their finery, none of them possessed that intangible characteristic that couldn't be bought, but seemed to be worth more than any amount of riches.

And Riley wanted it.

He wanted it so much that he lingered after the others had finished their meal and returned to whatever it was that pressed them. When Emma entered to clear the table, she started when she saw him.

"Mr. Stratton. Forgive me. I thought everyone had finished. Can I get you anything else?"

"No, thank you. It was delicious. I was just..."

"Yes?" she asked, and the confused expression on her face somehow sucked the courage right out of him. How could he ask a question, when he didn't even know enough to ask?

Instead, he looked toward the pantry. "You put her in the closet?"

She must have thought he disapproved, because she began backing away. "Oh, uhm...yes. I'll find a better place for her as soon as possible, but there wasn't much time today. I..."

"It's all right. What is she doing in there, if you don't mind my asking?"

A smile swept across her face like wind on the prairie, causing her eyes to dance like wildflowers. "Copying her letters."

Her smile was contagious, and it pulled Riley into the moment, though he had no idea what she was talking about. How could anyone copy letters in a dark closet? But he only said, "What a fabulous idea. May I look in on her?"

"Certainly."

She led him through the kitchen and tapped softly on the pantry door before opening it.

What he saw inside was so simple and charming, he wanted

to laugh out loud. But considering he'd already gotten himself in trouble by laughing today, he held his emotions in check.

Inside the pantry, Skye sat on the missing dining room chair. She leaned over a kitchen bench, using it as a makeshift desk. Beside her was an oil lantern, a chipped pitcher filled with pink and blue and yellow flowers from the field out back, a plate of cookies, and a glass of milk. On a high shelf was another lantern, adding its light from above.

On a piece of paper was a simple handwritten alphabet, with space between each letter so Skye could copy each one. The girl moved her arm to the side to show her progress when Emma knelt beside her.

"Excellent work, Skye. You have lovely penmanship. Have you written anything before?"

Skye opened her mouth to answer, but when she noticed Riley, she closed it again.

"I agree with Miss Monroe, Skye. You've done a splendid job. I don't mean to interrupt. I'll let you two get back to your work." Riley left them and headed for his office. It seemed lately, all he did was think about Emma. Like it or not, he had a job to do, bills to pay, and budgets to balance. But despite the to-do list front and center on his desk, his thoughts pulled him to that little make-shift classroom in the pantry.

Ideas flashed through his mind like lightning. There might be a way he could put a window in the pantry.

How long would it take to build Skye a proper desk?

If memory served him correctly, there was a box of primers in the attic.

Mostly, he thought about the question he wanted to ask Emma, but he didn't know how to word it. Something in his spirit cried out for an answer, and suddenly he realized there was someone he might talk to, who might be able to help him even better than Emma.

Riley's job could wait. He'd have to stay up and work by

lamplight tonight. The questions in his heart hounded him, and needed addressing now. Within the hour, he knocked on Charlie Monroe's door again.

The man's face broke into a wide grin when he saw Riley at the door. "I was wondering when you'd be back."

"You were expecting me?"

"Not expecting you, exactly. Just a hunch I hadn't seen the last of you. You're in time for lunch. Emma left me some bread and cheese on a plate in the kitchen. Would you get it? It's covered in a blue cloth. And get yourself a plate, too." The man shuffled back to his chair and pulled a wool blanket over his legs.

Riley didn't comment on the odd statement about his coming today. He wasn't hungry, but he did as he was told and filled two plates with Emma's bread and a few slices of yellow cheese. The man was probably tired of eating alone. Back in the parlor, he set the plates on the table between the two chairs, used the poker to stir the fire, then took the seat opposite Mr. Monroe.

When the man bowed his head, Riley followed suit.

"Dear Father, thank You for this food. And for my guest. Amen."

Short and to the point. Riley liked that.

"What can I do for you, son?"

Riley stretched his legs and tried to find the right words. Suddenly this didn't seem like such a good idea. "I'm not sure, exactly. I just...I suppose I have some questions, and I don't know whom to ask."

The older man took a bite of cheese, then washed it down with his water. "I'm not sure I have any answers for you. But I'll be glad to listen. I'll surely point you in the right direction if I can."

"Your family..." Riley normally didn't struggle with words. But how did one describe something so indescribable?

"What I mean to say is, my family and your family are different."

Mr. Monroe looked at him with keen eyes. "I'd say that's an accurate statement."

"I guess I'd just like to know why."

"Why we're different?"

"Yes, sir." He looked around the small house. The differences in this place and his were vast. So why did this home, with its worn furniture and tight space feel more welcoming than the Texas palace he lived in?

"I suppose that depends on which differences you're referring to. Some of them are quite obvious."

Riley shifted in his chair and busied himself by eating some of the simple meal. This entire conversation made him feel like it was test day, and he hadn't studied. Part of him wanted to make an excuse and leave. But his desire for answers, for understanding, for whatever source of calm tranquility was out there overpowered his discomfort, and he forced himself to continue. "My family has everything money can buy. But we're a miserable bunch. Your family, on the other hand, seems to have this type of...serenity, I guess. And I'd like to know why you all seem so satisfied with...with...I don't know. I'm probably not making any sense."

"You'd like to know why we seem content, when we have so much less than you do."

"Maybe. But I'm not asking about the money or the lack of money. There's just something deep down in you that has, to this point in my life, eluded me. Your wife had that quality, and so does Emma. And so do you."

"I think I understand your question, and the answer is simple. We have God."

Riley let that sink in for a moment. He hadn't come here for a sermon. He hoped he wasn't about to receive one. He weighed his next words carefully in his mind before speaking them. "We go to church every Sunday. Always have."

"That's commendable," Mr. Monroe replied. "Church is a good thing. But church attendance won't give you the peace you long for."

"I don't understand."

The older man turned to face Riley head-on. "I'm no preacher. But as far as I can tell, what God wants with you, with me, is a relationship. He wants us to talk to Him, to listen to Him, to want to please Him. He wants us to think about Him all the time, the way a young man thinks about a pretty girl he's fancied."

Riley had been looking at the fire, but he couldn't help but look at Mr. Monroe at that last line. Did he suspect Riley was sweet on Emma?

If he did, he didn't say more. He just continued. "God loves you, son. And when we love someone, we long for them to love us back."

Riley nodded. He thought he understood, sort of.

"I loved my wife with all my heart, Riley. I miss her more than anything. When she was alive, I looked forward to the time she came home from work each evening. I couldn't wait to tell her about my day, about the crops and which ones were flourishing, which needed coaxing along. I wanted to share with her about which insects threatened, and if the soil was dry or moist.

"I also wanted to hear about her day. I was interested in what she'd fixed all of you to eat, and which rooms in your house she'd cleaned. And of course, we always enjoyed talking about Emma and Lyndel, what they'd said or done.

"But we didn't always have to talk. Sometimes we'd just take care of our evening chores, then sit on the porch and watch the sun go down. Other times we might hold hands and walk our property, taking in God's creation."

Riley pictured Sally and Charlie as young people, madly in

love. As older people, holding hands. He tried to conjure a picture of his own parents doing the same, but he couldn't.

"The point is, we longed to be together because we loved each other. If Sally had come home from work and fixed supper for us, and I'd sat at the table and eaten, but we never talked...if I ignored her except to sit next to her at mealtime...we might have shared a roof. But what kind of relationship would that have been?

"God wants a loving relationship with you. Sitting in church on Sunday doesn't mean much to Him, by itself. He wants your heart."

Riley didn't respond. Couldn't respond. It was like a candle had been lit in his mind. All those Sundays in church, he'd never heard a sermon quite like this one. A relationship? With God? Comparing it to a married couple? The thought made him uncomfortable. Curious. He'd have to think on that some more.

After a few minutes, Riley nodded, thanked the man, filled his water glass for him, returned their dishes to the kitchen, and bid him good day.

Charlie Monroe must think Riley was one strange bird. But that didn't matter right now. He'd given Riley much to consider.

~

*E*mma yawned, even though she felt like her heart had grown wings. It was only three in the afternoon, only a few hours since she'd taken Skye into her charge, and here the girl was, chattering like a magpie. Emma had given Skye's hands and face a quick wipe down, combed the rats out of her hair and pulled it into a single braid down her back. Tonight, she planned to make the child a new dress. Maybe two. When she would sleep, she wasn't sure. But she hadn't slept well since Ma died, anyway. Might as well make use of the time.

They were in the library, dusting the massive shelves. "Skye, what do you like to do when you can do whatever you want?"

"I talk to Mother Earth."

"Mother Earth?"

"Yes. The plants, the trees, the animals. Mother Earth has stories to tell, if we listen. This morning, a squirrel got mad when a bluebird swooped in and stole some of her food. She fussed at that bird for a long time before she finally gave up and looked for more food. I think the squirrel was saving up for a treat for her babies, and the bluebird stole it away. But the bluebird's babies were hungry, and the squirrel had more than enough. The bluebird was only trying to care for her babies."

What perception and imagination this child had.

"When you and Pa's brother came, I was trying to find the bluebird's nest."

"Were you going to climb higher into the tree?" Emma recalled Skye had been on the bottom branch.

"Yes. I'm a good climber."

"Did your father know what you were doing?"

"No, but he doesn't mind. He taught me how to climb."

"I see." Emma wanted to ask about the child's mother, but didn't feel she'd earned the right to pry. For now, she'd let Skye lead the conversation.

She sensed someone watching them and turned toward the door. Sure enough, Riley leaned against the doorframe, a wooden crate tucked under one arm. How long had he been there?

"Mr. Stratton. Did you need in here? We can finish later."

"No, I'm fine. I want to show you something and ask you a couple of quick questions, though, if you don't mind."

Emma instructed Skye to continue the dusting and walked toward him. "Certainly."

Riley moved to the desk and set the crate down, then pulled out a worn *New England Primer*. "I thought you might be able to use these." He laid the book on the desk and pulled out another —*The School and Family Primer*, followed by *A Child's New Plaything, Tom Thumb's Playbook*, and several other letter and number books. Emma recalled using some of these when she was young, but they'd belonged to the school. She'd never dreamed of having actual primers to use with Skye.

She laughed and dropped down in a big leather chair to leaf through the pages of one of them. "Skye, come here!"

The child was at her side in seconds, and Emma showed her the pages and read her a few silly rhymes, which made them both giggle. "I'm going to teach you to read these for yourself. Won't that be fun?"

Skye nodded, but didn't say much. She snuggled close to Emma's side, and Emma realized that Riley's presence must make the child nervous. "Your Uncle Riley brought these for you. Wasn't that nice of him?"

A nod was the child's only response. Emma couldn't blame the girl for being reluctant. She hadn't exactly received a warm welcome from this family of hers, though it looked like Riley was trying to set things right.

Riley knelt beside the chair. "Your father learned to read from those books when he was young. Our mother would sit in a rocking chair in our nursery for hours at a time, rocking us on her lap and reading us stories. She was quite proud that each of her boys could read well before starting our formal education."

In that moment, Riley looked swept away to another time and place. Emma pictured him, sitting on his mother's lap, loved, treasured, safe. How long since he'd truly felt that kind of acceptance? Aside from his mother, did anyone else in his family offer that security?

"And that brings me to my next question, Miss Skye." Riley spoke to the girl as if he were talking to another adult. "May I measure your height? I'd like to make sure you have a desk that fits you. It's important for a scholar to have a proper study area."

After a short hesitation, Skye stood tall, and Riley opened a desk drawer to pull out a folding yardstick. "Four feet, two inches. My, aren't you a tall girl. I thought I might have to build you something, but I believe there's a small desk in the nursery that will work just fine. I'll bring it down and put it in your classroom."

Her classroom? Did he mean the pantry?

As if reading her mind, Riley looked at Emma. "I'd like to add a window to the pantry, up high. Would you mind emptying the shelves on the back wall for a few days, so I can work there?"

For a moment, Emma got lost in the deep waters of his blue eyes. He had the same build, the same height, the same look as the rest of the Stratton men. But his heart? His heart didn't carry a family resemblance at all. In that moment, Emma wanted to hug him.

Instead, she hugged Skye. "Your own classroom, your own books, and your own desk. Isn't that wonderful? Your uncle must think a lot of you." She leaned close to the girl's ear and whispered, "Do you think we should tell him *thank you*?"

Skye nodded, but said nothing until Emma nodded back. Then, as if taking courage from Emma's nod, she looked at her uncle and said "Thank you" in a voice so timid, it almost didn't even seem like the same child who'd babbled away only a few minutes earlier.

"You're welcome. And thank *you*, for agreeing to help Miss Monroe out this way. She was quite lost without you. If you hadn't agreed, I was afraid I'd have to start helping her with the baking, and I assure you, I don't look very good in an apron."

Skye giggled then, and Emma covered the thrill of his teasing by shooting him an offended look. Though *offended* was truly the furthest emotion from her heart, at that moment.

CHAPTER 8

"What are you doing?" Allison blocked the doorway to the nursery so Riley couldn't pass.

"I'm taking this downstairs." He started to set the small desk down, then thought better of it. It might look like he was relinquishing control.

"Why do you need a child's desk downstairs?"

"Davis won't need it for several years."

"You didn't answer my question. Why are you taking it?"

"Allison, this is my home. This was my nursery. I believe I have a right to move the furniture around as I see fit."

"Correction. This *was* your nursery. Now it's Davis's nursery. Why are you taking his furniture?"

"This was in the corner. It's not being used."

"Just answer my question."

"I think you already know the answer. Now if you'll excuse me." He charged forward and hoped Allison would move out of the way.

She didn't.

Instead, she put one hand on her hip and lifted one finger to his face. "You may have gotten your father to agree to let that little half-breed in this house, but she's not going to step in front of Davis as the first grandchild."

So many thoughts went through Riley's mind at that moment. Was her heart made of ice? Was she that greedy, that she'd begrudge a poor, motherless child a little kindness? But he knew voicing them would only make matters worse. "Allison, no one is trying to take Davis's place. She's just a little girl who needs a desk. Now, if you'll excuse me."

Allison stepped aside, probably more out of fear of being trampled than from any acknowledgement or agreement on her part. The contrast between Allison Stratton and Emma Monroe was, in Riley's mind, like the difference between a squirrel and a skunk. Neither was bad to look at. But while one of them was hardworking and resourceful, the other stunk to high heaven.

Downstairs, he found the kitchen empty, though a delicious aroma filled the air. He returned the bench and the dining room chair to their places and set the desk in the small space. Not the ideal classroom, to be sure. But it was kind of cozy. Add a plate of Emma's cookies, and any place felt like home. Come to think of it, with or without baked goods, Emma Monroe did a lot to brighten up any space.

For just a moment, he allowed himself to picture what it might be like to be married to Emma. But the picture was tainted with his father's disapproval, with Allison's sneering judgment, even with Colt's mocking superiority. He really did need to get this infatuation under control. If not for his own sake, then for hers. On the off chance she did return his interest, it wouldn't be fair to subject her to this family's cruelty. She'd never fit in here.

She played tricks on his mind and heart, what with her big, soulful eyes and her smell—like cinnamon and vanilla—and her recent loss that so reminded him of his own journey of grief. He felt compassion for an old friend, and nothing more. Any thoughts of a romantic relationship with Emma Monroe were rubbish. If she weren't in such a vulnerable state, he might consider having a little fun with her, but in her current circumstances, that would be cruel.

Yes. That's all this was. She was pretty. She was here. And his moral compass wouldn't let him pursue her. And that was driving him mad.

The thought both agitated and depressed him.

He forced all thoughts of Emma from his mind and evaluated the space above the top shelf. Just as he thought, he could add a high window for some natural light. He didn't know why no one had thought to do it sooner. It would sure make hunting for a jar of maple syrup or mayhaw jelly a lot easier.

Then, from nowhere, his thoughts changed course, bringing to mind what Charlie Monroe said about having a relationship with God. Riley had been to church nearly every Sunday since he was a child, but he'd never paid much attention to the sermons. When he was a boy, he was too busy examining his pocket treasures to listen to some stodgy, blustery old man talk. And when he got older, well...he got really good at mentally running through his list of chores while watching the preacher move his mouth.

He remembered once, about a year before Ma died, she'd tried to talk to him. "Riley, we've never spoken much about God. But I want you to know God loves you more than anything. And He wants you to love Him back."

"I do," he'd told her, more because he wanted to get out of the odd conversation than anything.

She'd smiled and said, "I'm glad."

Funny. He hadn't thought about that conversation in a long time. But now, it seemed like it might have been one of the most important things his mother had ever said to him. Now she was gone.

Her life was too short. As was Sally Monroe's.

This God thing...maybe he shouldn't put it off. But doggone

if he knew what to do. How to start. He thought about what Mr. Monroe had said, about simply sharing your thoughts. Talking to God, like a friend? The whole idea made him squirm. But since no one was around to judge whether he did it right, he might as well start now.

Hello, God. Uhm...it's me. Riley Stratton. I don't know much about You, though I suppose You know everything there is to know about me. I was just wondering if, maybe, we could be friends.

Uh...that's all. Amen.

He really did need to get some bookwork done. He'd spent this entire day on other matters. But before he did, he thought he remembered seeing an old window propped against the wall in the far corner of the barn.

Feminine voices approached from the back part of the house. Riley shut the pantry doors and tried to slip through the kitchen door before anyone detected his presence, but he wasn't quick enough.

"Oh, hello, Mr. Stratton. We were just coming to check on the peach cobbler. Skye made it herself." Emma smiled at the girl as she spoke.

"Is that what the delicious smell is? It reached out to me, wrapped itself around my neck, and drew me here like a lasso." Riley wrapped his hands around his neck and crossed his eyes as he spoke.

Skye giggled, but didn't say anything. It was a start.

Emma shook her head like a tolerant schoolmarm and looked at Skye. "Should we let him sample it?"

The girl nodded.

"All right, Mr. Stratton. Have a seat. You get a small taste, and that's it. Then you must leave. We have work to do."

Riley did as he was told while Emma pulled the cobbler from the oven and set it on top of the stove. Skye retrieved a small plate and held it while Emma scooped a big dollop, then poured cream over it. It was more than a small taste, but he wasn't about to complain.

Skye handed him the plate, Emma gave him a spoon, and they both watched him like two kittens waiting for the fish bowl to tip over.

He filled his spoon, blew on it, and took a bite.

His taste buds exploded with warm, sweet peaches mixed with a flaky, melt-in-your-mouth crust, and just the right amount of cream to balance it out. Without a word, he took another bite and another until it was all gone. Finally, he looked at Skye and said, "I can't decide if I like it or not. May I have a little more?"

The girl giggled again, but it was Emma who answered. "No, you may not, Mr. Stratton. You've had your taste. Now out with you."

Riley pushed back the bench and stood, an odd sort of warmth filling both his belly and his spirit.

~

"What's this?" Lyndel wrinkled his nose that night at the dinner table.

"It's called Veal Collops. Try it." Emma scruffed his hair before adding some of the entrée to her own plate.

"Why'd ya fix this? We never eat veal."

"Allison Stratton requested it for a special dinner on Thursday, and I wanted to practice. The butcher was kind enough to give me a small portion of veal at his cost, since I also purchased enough for the dinner party. By the way, Pa, I'll be late getting home that evening. I'll put a pot of beans on to simmer, and that can be your dinner that night."

"This is delicious," Pa mumbled around a small mouthful, his voice frail. He coughed. Would he choke? When his breathing settled, he said, "You're almost as good a cook as your mother."

Would he ever get well? She looked at Ma's empty chair, then pushed her own plate away. Would the gaping hole in her heart ever stop hurting? "Thank you, Pa."

There were crullers for dessert. A cruller, she had learned, was simply a deep-fried, braided, or twisted pastry. In reality, none of the recipes were hard, but Emma was glad she'd given them a test-run before the dinner party.

"This girl...you say she's Donnigan's child?" Pa asked after he wiped his mouth and dropped his napkin on his plate.

"Yes. They're living in a shack in the woods—well, it's a little better than a shack—and when I found her today, she was filthy. But she's the sweetest thing, and sharp as a pin."

"And John Stratton doesn't want anything to do with her?"

"No. I want to pity her, but honestly, I pity him more. To have such a dear creature in his family and not even know it."

"She has school in the pantry?" Lyndel asked. "I'd hate that. Unless I could eat while I was in there. Then it might not be so bad."

Emma chuckled. Lyndel was growing so fast she could hardly keep his pants at the right length, and it seemed like all he thought of was food. Would they be able to feed and clothe him after her savings were depleted? Good thing she had a job that paid well. She didn't see how she'd ever be able to quit, to attend teacher college.

After the dishes were washed and put away, Emma got out Ma's old basket of fabric and notions and sat in the chair next to her father's. Lyndel disappeared outside to catch fireflies. It was still early in the season for the little bugs, but she didn't tell him that. He really just wanted an excuse to be outdoors until dark.

"Riley Stratton paid me another visit today," Pa told her.

She nearly dropped her basket. "Really?"

"Yes. Really."

"What did he want? And when did he come?"

"Early afternoon. He just wanted to talk."

She wanted to press further, but she knew better. If Pa wanted her to know more, he'd tell her. If he didn't, wild stallions couldn't pull it from him. Instead, she pulled out several different fabrics from Ma's basket and held each up to the lantern, trying to decide which she had enough of to make a small dress. Which would look nicest on Skye? The dishes still needed doing, but this chore was more fun. She'd cut out the patterns, then tend to the kitchen.

Skye was a lovely child, and in all truth, any of the fabrics would do nicely. After several minutes of deliberation, she decided on the yellow gingham. She had some yellow bric-a-brac for the sleeves and hem, and a set of tiny mother-of-pearl buttons she'd been saving for a special project.

If she had time, she'd make her another dress from the blue calico. If not, she'd get to it later this week. For the first time, she thought of Ma without fighting back tears. Oh, the ache was still there. But as she cut the fabric and pieced together the tiny dress, she almost felt like Ma was right there with her, approving.

What would Ma say if she knew how much time Emma spent thinking about Riley Stratton, or how her stomach flipped like a hot griddlecake when he came near? Emma recalled his flirtations with every pretty face in school, and the stories she'd heard about all the swooning girls while he was away at university, and suddenly those griddlecakes in her belly went flat.

~

The next morning, Skye waited in the kitchen for Emma when she arrived. The little girl sat at the table across from Riley. The oven fire was already started, and the aroma of fresh coffee filled the room.

"Are you trying to steal my job, Mr. Stratton?"

"Not at all. Skye insisted she couldn't start her day without coffee. I didn't have a choice."

Skye giggled.

"Is that true, Skye?" Emma asked.

The girl giggled some more and shook her head.

Emma looked at Riley, who was holding a finger over his lips, telling his niece to "shush."

"It appears that someone else is in need of coffee, and is trying to blame an innocent child. Shame on you."

"I confess. Will you make me write sentences, Teacher?"

Emma tried to keep her face stern, but she couldn't help but laugh. "If you're not careful, I might do exactly that. Now if the coffee is ready, you may pour yourself a cup and skedaddle. Skye and I have important business to conduct, and it doesn't involve you."

Riley feigned a hurt look, poured his coffee, and exited into the hallway, mumbling something about being unappreciated.

When he was well out of hearing distance, Emma looked at Skye. "I have a surprise for you. But first, we have to get you cleaned up. Let's move this washtub into the pantry and fill it halfway with water. I'll boil some more water on the stove to heat it up. Do you have running water at your house?"

"No, but a creek runs behind the house."

"That's nice. When I was your age, I used to love to bathe in the creek in the summertime. But in winter, Ma made us haul water into the house to bathe, so she could heat it. That wasn't nearly as fun. But she made us do it every day."

Skye smiled, grabbed a bucket and slipped out the back door. Emma watched her pump water, and held the door open for her as she carried it to the big tub in the pantry.

The child continued her work in silence, and Emma tried to think of a way to teach Skye about appropriate hygiene without embarrassing the girl. Skye's mother had probably taught those things, but Donnigan clearly didn't know how to address such issues. When the tub was half full, Emma added a big pot of boiling water and stirred it around. Then she pulled out the brown paper package she'd discreetly placed on the counter when she came in.

"I made this for you." She handed Skye the package.

The girl's eyes lit up. She held it in her hands, as if she didn't know what to do with it.

"Aren't you going to open it?"

Skye nodded and sat in the small desk Riley had placed there, which was now scooted to the corner to make room for the tub. Carefully, tenderly she untied the string and set it aside. Then she unfolded the paper as if she wanted to save it to use later. When she saw the dress, her expression held such awe, such wonder, that Emma's chest tightened with emotion.

"Do you like it?" Emma whispered.

Skye nodded. She poised her hand just above the fabric, as if she were afraid to touch it.

"Go ahead. You won't hurt it. That's one of my favorite fabrics. It's cotton, and it's very soft."

With an almost holy reverence, Skye touched the fabric, then picked up the dress and held it to her cheek as if she wanted to remember this moment forever.

Emma cleared her throat. She had to stop being so sentimental. "I'm glad you're pleased. But we never want to wear a new dress unless we're nice and clean." She turned the lantern up as high as it would go, then stepped back into the kitchen. "Off with your dress, and hop in. I'll be back in a few minutes to help you wash your hair."

She was glad Riley had started the fire and made the coffee. Otherwise, she would have been late with breakfast. As it was, she and Skye had breakfast on the table, and Skye was contentedly ensconced in her classroom, looking radiant in her new dress and clean braids, by the time the Strattons were seated.

Hours flew by in a whirl of activity. Emma found a chapter

on table settings in one of Ma's old cookbooks, and she helped Skye practice her numbers as they tried out various designs. "Place four plates, one at each of these places. Now count out four forks, four spoons, four knives...and set them in this pattern, beside each plate." Emma couldn't say for sure, as she didn't have any other students to compare her to, but Skye seemed uncommonly bright for her age.

By the time Thursday rolled around, Emma felt like she could conquer the world. She could certainly conquer this strange cuisine Allison had requested. Everything was ready, and as close to perfect as she could make it. Emma had been given two uniforms, so she brought them both with her and changed into a fresh one twenty minutes before guests were scheduled to arrive.

When she emerged from the privy, Allison waited in the hall. "They'll be here soon. You'll answer the door and escort them into the parlor, where you'll serve hors d'oeuvres. Please give us about twenty minutes, and then call us in for dinner."

Hors d'oeuvres? Oh dear.

Emma refused to let on, refused to show panic. Instead, she simply nodded. "Yes, ma'am."

Then she calmly dismissed herself from the woman's presence and slowly, with as much dignity as she could muster, returned to the kitchen pantry. "Skye, I need you to help me with a project."

"All right."

"See that shelf of pickles and nuts? I want you to choose several things that you think would look nice on a tray. Look for different colors, shapes and sizes, while I look for a serving platter. Can you do that?"

"Yes!" The way Skye said it made it sound like they were playing a game instead of standing on the brink of disaster.

And why not make a game of it? They were in a race with

the clock to create an hors d'oeuvre tray to beat all hors d'oeuvre trays, and they would win. They had to win.

That Allison had set her up again was indisputable...or perhaps not. Emma should have known hors d'oeuvres would be expected.

In the dining room, beneath the large buffet cabinet, Emma knew there was a beautiful silver tray, intricately etched with a floral design, and with ornate handles on each end. She'd just polished the silver last week, and had taken extra time with that tray. But could she remove it without Allison seeing?

Slowly, silently she crept into the dining room. There was Allison, sitting across the way in the parlor, with her back to Emma. If she took extra care, she could retrieve the tray without being detected.

As quietly as possible, she knelt in front of the cabinet, eased open the doors, and found the tray. It took her longer than she wanted to remove the items stacked on top of it, as she had to take her time to avoid any clatter. But at last, she'd replaced the unneeded pieces and shut the door, and was just standing to her feet when a male voice cleared his throat behind her.

Riley.

He was watching her from the foyer, a look of amusement in his eyes like he didn't know whether to laugh or not.

"Riley, is that you?" Allison called from the parlor. "What are you doing?"

He must have read the panic in Emma's face as she held a finger over her mouth and pleaded with her eyes for him not to give away her presence, for he just smiled, but didn't acknowledge her verbally. "I'm coming to join you, Allison. I was hoping to see Davis...is he already down for the night?"

"He was nearly asleep when I left him. I'm about to go check on him once more before..."

Their conversation trailed out of Emma's hearing as she snuck back through the kitchen and into the pantry. She set the large tray on Skye's little desk and gasped in delight at the assortment the child had lined up on the edge of the middle shelf. Pickled okra, pickled olives, pickled carrots. Add to that the practice loaf of bread she and Skye had baked this afternoon, plus some dainty jars of jam, a jar of nuts, and a fresh crock of butter and voila! An hors d'oeuvre tray.

The crack of the giant brass doorknocker echoed, and Emma's heart quickened. "Skye, do you think you can arrange these pickles in a pretty pattern around the edge for me? Leave room in the middle so I can add a few more things."

Skye nodded. She looked like she was having fun. And truly, the child was heaven-sent, especially in this moment when her serenity fell over Emma's anxiety like cold lemonade on a hot day.

After a deep breath and a few pats of her hair and skirt as she approached the foyer, Emma answered the door. Mayor Bridges and his wife stood on the porch. And there, hanging onto his arm and looking like an illustration from a fashion journal, was Clara.

And here she was looking like a cross between a mortician and a lace doily.

"Good evening, Mayor Bridges, Mrs. Bridges, Miss Bridges. Won't you come in?" Emma focused on the mayor, in hopes of bypassing conversation with Clara.

"Why, Emma, I never in a million years expected to see you here. And...dressed like that." Clara giggled, but there was no malice in her tone.

Allison and the Stratton men waited just behind Emma, so Emma didn't respond. She simply held the door open wide and allowed the visitors to enter.

Clara threw Emma a look that was part question, part apology as she swept past.

"Mayor Bridges, I'm delighted you could join us this evening. Mrs. Bridges and Clara, as always, you ladies grace any room with your presence." John Stratton's words felt like a slap to Emma, punctuating even further her own status in the Stratton family.

Though Emma had never spoken of her own feelings for Riley, Clara had whispered and dreamed and hoped for the day she'd one day become Mrs. Riley Stratton. Clara and every other girl in school. Emma silently excused herself from the group, but not before she saw Clara's doe-eyed look in Riley's direction. After all these years, Clara still had feelings for Riley.

Is this whole evening a matchmaking opportunity? A burning sensation pierced Emma like a knife in the gut. In all honesty, the two of them would probably make a very nice match. And what did it matter? She had a job to do.

She stiffened her spine, schooled her features, and put the final touches on the tray.

CHAPTER 9

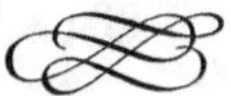

$\mathcal{R}$iley stood as Emma led their guests into the parlor. He hadn't even thought to ask who was coming to dinner, but he shouldn't have been surprised Allison would try to manipulate the mayor's favor. Dad probably put her up to it. Money and power were all they thought of.

Dad took the lead, stepping forward to shake the mayor's hand and complimenting Clara and her mother.

Clara blushed and said "Thank you," while she lowered her eyelashes in that dainty way women do when they're trying to appear modest.

Colt stepped up and shook hands with the mayor, then finally it was Riley's turn.

"Mayor, Mrs. Bridges. Miss Bridges." It was going to be a long evening. Maybe he could escape to take Skye home. He should have taken her home two hours ago, but since Emma was still here, he figured she could use the extra help. Both Skye and Emma seemed to enjoy the new arrangement immensely, and as long as they both stayed busy and out of sight, it seemed to work out well for everyone.

They'd just taken their seats again when Emma entered,

carrying a tray with several small plates and a stack of neatly folded napkins, which she placed on a side table before disappearing again. Soon she returned with an enormous silver tray loaded with all kinds of good things to eat and placed it on a low table in the center of the room.

Everyone ignored her, just continued with their small talk as if she didn't exist. But for Riley, Emma Monroe was a hard person to ignore.

He heard his name and realized Allison had been speaking to him.

"Oh, I'm sorry," he said. "My mind was wandering. Could you repeat the question?"

"I just wondered how many grades you were ahead of Miss Bridges."

Riley looked at Clara, who smiled demurely. She really was a pretty thing, though in school he'd always thought her rather silly. He'd much preferred Emma and her willingness to join in a game of stickball or tree climbing. But several years had passed, and he doubted any of them would be getting up a game of stickball anytime soon. "I believe I was...two years ahead of you. Or was it three?"

"I think it was three," the young woman replied, and did that eyelash thing again.

Emma now held the tray with the dishes, and stopped by each person to silently offer the items. Everyone took a plate and a napkin. She never looked at any of them directly, just kept her head bowed in humble deference.

"Mr. Stratton, I haven't had an opportunity to welcome you home from university," Clara told him.

"I'm sure in this setting it will be fine to call him Riley," Allison interjected in her too-bright voice. "After all, you are schoolmates, and there are three Mr. Strattons here this evening."

"Oh, all right. Riley." Clara smiled, a dazzling smile that was sure to win some poor lout's heart with a single flash. "I'd love to hear all about your time there. Was it truly exciting?"

"I don't know if I'd call it exciting," Riley told her while Emma presented the hors d'oeuvre tray. He didn't want to make Emma nervous by staring. Her being required to serve this way didn't set right with him. But Allison had mentioned extra pay. That was a good thing, wasn't it?

He took some bread and butter, added some pickled carrots and a pile of salted pecans to his plate, and thanked her. She nodded and moved on.

"Oh, I know it must have been. Please tell me some stories." Clara beseeched him with enormous, violet-colored eyes, and he felt like an oaf for putting her off.

"I suppose I might have a story or two."

"Perfect." Allison interrupted again. "You two can sit next to each other at dinner."

Colt, Dad, and Mayor and Mrs. Bridges made small talk, the kind of talk he'd much rather be a part of than stuck trying to entertain a socialite. But good manners dictated his actions.

When Emma entered the room again a few minutes later, she tapped Allison on the shoulder and whispered something. Allison nodded. "Dinner is ready, everyone. Shall we move to the dining room?"

They all stood, and Clara took Riley's arm even before he offered it. They followed the others, and Clara spoke to him in a low voice. "I'm glad we're sitting together, Riley. I've thought about you a lot while you were away."

Really? He hadn't thought of her once since...since... Well, he couldn't remember when he'd ever thought much about her. But he only smiled and held out her chair.

That's when he looked at the dining table, and it looked stunning. That was the only word he could think to describe it, and he wasn't one to notice such things. But each place was set with their finest dishes. In the center of each plate was a napkin, folded like a fan. Where did Emma learn to do that? Had her mother taught her?

Skye probably helped her. The thought of them bent over the table, brows furrowed, trying to get each one just right made him smile. Clara must have thought he was smiling at her, because she grinned back at him like a hound pup eying a rib eye.

Unfortunately, the one he wanted to smile at him, or even look at him, acted like he didn't exist except as a no-name, no-face customer. Emma's performance as a servant was flawless. He couldn't fault her for anything. But for some reason, that bothered him.

A lot.

Emma came around and filled each of their glasses with tea, standing behind and to the left. When she got to Allison, Allison lifted her arm at the last moment as if she had something important to say, and the pitcher spilled all over Emma's apron, soaking through that awful sack of a dress.

"Miss Monroe! Can't you do anything right?" Allison hissed. Then, to the table, "It's so hard to find competent help these days."

Emma apologized several times, then rushed to the kitchen.

After an awkward lull in the conversation, Mayor Bridges said, "Have you heard the railroad will be finished within the year? Possibly sooner."

"That's wonderful news," Dad told him. "It should bring all kinds of business to Lampasas."

"Yes, I hope so. I have a few business ventures I'm looking into that I hope will bring tourists."

"Lampasas, a tourist town?" Colt laughed. "I can't see that we have much to offer tourists."

"Oh, we may have more than you'd think."

Several minutes later Emma appeared again, in a dry dress—how did she do that?—holding a bowl with a lid. Riley thought it was called a soup tureen, though where he'd learned that, he couldn't recall. As if nothing out of the ordinary had happened, she placed the lid on the buffet behind them, then went behind each person, head lowered in serene deference, and ladled something that smelled heavenly into each of their bowls.

He had to speak to her. Had to pull her into the conversation somehow, if only for a moment. "Pardon me, Miss Monroe, but what is this called? It looks delicious."

She stood upright and looked at him for just a moment, then straight ahead as if she were talking to the wall. "This is vermicelli soup, sir. Mrs. Stratton chose the menu. If you enjoy it, the credit goes to her good taste."

Allison cleared her throat, as if in preparation to regain control of the conversation. "Miss Bridges, I understand you've been published? Tell us about that."

Clara did that eyelash thing again. "Oh, it was nothing. I submitted a recipe to the ladies' section of the Herald, and they printed it."

"That's quite impressive. Not many women your age have seen their names in print. Of course, someone of your background and breeding will certainly be a credit to your family. Cream always rises to the top." Allison cooed over Clara like she was a precious doll on Christmas morning. "Speaking of cream, Emma? I believe you added too much cream to this soup. It's quite thick. I do apologize, everyone. If the soup isn't to your liking, we can move to the next course and hope for an improvement."

Everyone shook their heads that no, the soup was fine.

Emma didn't respond. Just continued her service as if she didn't have a thought of her own, other than to see to their comfort and disappear.

He wanted to wipe that smug look off Allison's face. No one else in the room seemed to notice anything at all. They simply dug into their meals and continued the conversation, but it was lost to Riley. For a moment, he was swept back to the simple meal, the simple prayer with Charlie Monroe. He'd rather be sitting in that small house, eating bread and cheese with water, than here with all the finery and shallow conversation.

What was wrong with him?

In his mind, he said a silent, *Thank You, God, for this food. Amen.* Then he leaned forward and sampled a spoonful of the most delicious soup he'd ever tasted.

~

*E*mma's heart pounded like a hummingbird beating to get out of a cage. She felt certain Allison had spilled the tea on her dress on purpose. And that comment about the soup? Allison hadn't even tried the soup when she said it was too thick. Emma had followed the recipe exactly.

As a matter of fact, she'd done everything she could to present a beautiful table, to prepare a savory meal, to make Allison look like the gracious hostess. And yet, the woman seemed set on making her own house staff look incompetent.

Emma tried to remember that her worth was found in God, not in her employer's opinion of her. And she tried to remember to show grace to Allison, who was probably nervous about making a good impression on the mayor. But grace was a hard concept to grasp when she was covered in a cold, sugary drink.

With every ounce of her flesh, Emma wanted to charge in there and dump the remainder of the soup on Allison Stratton's head. She wanted to toss this ugly uniform in the fire and dump the ashes on the Stratton's front porch.

Of course, she'd never actually do any of those things. But she might march out of this place and never look back if it weren't for Skye. Emma didn't know how much difference she could make in Skye's life, but she knew one thing—that child didn't have anybody else in this world looking out for her.

Other than Riley. But who knew how long his interest in the child would last? Emma hoped it was permanent, but she had no way of knowing. If she could help, in even a small way, to make Skye's life better, to coax a smile here and there and prepare her for this cold, harsh life, well, Emma must stay.

For Skye, she'd use every last drop of self-control she could find and continue through the meal like an obedient, whipped puppy. Tail tucked. Eyes to the ground.

But even with her head down, she couldn't miss the way Clara gawped over Riley. Well, good for them. She hoped they were very happy together. Clara would fit right into this bunch, with her fancy clothes and manipulative eyelashes. She and Allison would create quite a force, though against what, she didn't know. Didn't care.

That Clara had done nothing to deserve such harsh thoughts, Emma was perfectly aware. But right now, she was put out with everyone at that table.

Why was she angry with Riley? He hadn't actually done anything other than be a polite dinner guest. Did Emma think Riley would fall for *her?* Even if he did, she wouldn't return his feelings. Not if it meant becoming a part of this crowd of lunatics.

She placed—slammed was a more accurate term—the veal onto yet another tray, one more tray she'd have to wash later. Part of her wanted to spit on Allison's veal. But of course she wouldn't, and was ashamed she'd even have such a thought.

"Miss Emma?" Skye's voice whispered from across the room.

Oh, dear. She didn't know why Riley hadn't taken her home earlier. Poor child shouldn't have to remain in a closet. It was wrong. Perhaps she could sit on the back steps until after dinner. When did Riley plan to take her home, anyway?

"What is it, dear?" Emma whispered back, looking over her shoulder to make sure no one saw.

"I...I need to go..."

"All right," Emma whispered. "Go to the outhouse. You know where it is. Take the lantern with you. It will be dark soon. If you want, you can stay out there and play for a while." She remembered Lyndel's firefly jar, and scooped a mason jar off a shelf. As quickly as she could, she removed the lid and replaced the inner ring with a thin rag. "Why don't you catch some fireflies and put them in here?"

"It's too early for fireflies," Skye told her. Goodness, she was smart.

"You're probably right. A frog, then? Or whatever you want. Why don't you find a treasure, and when I'm done here I'll see what you found. It will give me something to look forward to."

The girl nodded and made a beeline for the outhouse, leaving the lantern behind. Emma set it and the jar on the back steps and rushed to serve the main course. As much as she hated certain aspects of this job, there was too much at stake now to lose it. Some things were worth even more than money.

～

For Riley, the next hour seemed to take four hours to get through. That Clara had taken a shining to him was obvious. That Allison wanted Riley to notice Clara was also quite clear. Honestly, all he wanted to do was check on Emma, but he'd only make things worse for her if he did.

So he sat politely while Clara peppered him with questions about his job and his years at Baylor and his plans for the future. If he hadn't been so preoccupied, he would have been amused at the way she treated each of his short answers as though he'd stated something rare and profound.

He supposed it could have been worse. Clara *was* rather nice to look at. But Emma, even in her shapeless black and white outfit, outshone any woman Riley had ever known. And the knowledge that she would never be accepted by his family grated at him more each day. Not so much because he cared what they thought—though he did. They were his family—but because if he were to pursue her, they'd surely make her life miserable in the process.

Not that he wanted to pursue Emma. *Argh*. That woman enchanted him. He didn't plan to pursue any woman for a good long while, if ever. Right now he had freedom to go and do and dine with whomever he wanted. And he liked it that way. He did. Who did Allison think she was, trying to force him into a relationship with Clara Bridges? Dad too, though Dad had a way of keeping his hands clean in his underhanded schemes. If Riley questioned him, he'd deny any knowledge of a match-making endeavor. Whoever was behind this, they'd just have to whoa their horses. Riley was a bachelor, and he planned to stay one.

When everyone had finished their desserts, Allison suggested they take coffee on the front porch.

Riley reluctantly escorted Clara and somehow managed to seat himself between her and the mayor. Maybe he could ease into some of the conversation with the menfolk now.

"So, Mayor, tell us more about this idea you have to turn Lampasas into a tourist town," Dad said between cigar puffs.

"The springs. Some of our natural springs have healing powers in them."

Colt laughed, really loud. "Healing powers? What do you mean?"

"Perhaps you've heard of Saratoga Springs in New York? Some of the early native tribes swore by its healing powers. Even George Washington claimed the place had restorative powers. He tried to purchase the land with one of the springs for himself. He was unsuccessful, though."

Dad leaned forward. "I've heard of Saratoga Springs."

"Over time, people have continued to make sensational claims about the benefits of this special type of mineral water. Even doctors have recommended taking the waters to cure kidney and liver complaints, rheumatism, diabetes, heartburn, scrofula, dyspepsia, cancer, malaria, hangovers and"—he cleared his throat—"weakness of women."

An awkward silence settled over the group at that declaration. Colt broke it with a laugh. "Are you talkin' about the stinky springs? Why would anyone in their right mind want those?"

"They stink, son, because of the sulphur. Does sulphur have healing properties?" Dad asked.

The mayor nodded. "There's a similar place in West Virginia called Sulphur Springs. About a hundred years ago, a woman claimed her rheumatism symptoms disappeared after bathing in the warm, sulphurous water there. Since that time, people have made the journey from hundreds of miles around, just to bathe in those springs."

That grabbed Riley's full attention. "You said *some* of our springs. How many springs are you talking about?"

"We need to do more testing. I've hired a man to test the waters, but many of the springs are on private property, and we need the owner's permission." Bridges took a sip of his tea.

Riley caught the mayor's vision. "With the railroad coming, we can capitalize on these natural springs and draw people to our town. West Virginia is a long way. New York is even further. If we advertise the same type of healing power, people will come."

The mayor nodded. "My thoughts, exactly."

Riley leaned forward and placed his elbows on his knees. Sulphurous springs? Healing waters? "But like Colt said, most people think the sulphur smells bad. What do they do? Buy bottles of it? Bathe in it? Drink it? Rub it on their ailments?"

"All of those things," Mayor Bridges answered. "I've done my research on this, and I believe Lampasas can become the 'Saratoga of the South.' It's what I'm aiming for, anyway."

Riley tapped his foot in excitement. "That will take a lot of preparation. We only have one inn, and it has four rooms."

"Yes. I'm hoping the people of our community will get behind this. I've drawn up a development plan, and I'm currently looking for investors."

Dad leaned back in his chair, and Riley recognized the look deep behind his eyes, that he wasn't pleased. "Sounds mighty interesting, mayor. But Lampasas is a ranching community. Turning this into a tourist town will cause more industry, more commerce. That could damage the cattle business, encroach on grazing land. Before long, our green pastures will be filled with shops and hotels. I'm not sure you'll be able to drum up the support you're hoping for. Your constituents don't want more industry here. We just want our nice, peaceful community to continue on like it has."

Mayor Bridges, to his credit, looked unaffected by Dad's comment. "I think there's room enough for both. But perhaps you're right. We shall see."

"Oh, Papa. Must we always discuss politics?" Clara fanned herself with an ornate fan. "I'd much rather hear another of Riley's stories about college."

"Well, Clara, if things go as I hope they will, we'll soon have a college right here in Lampasas. And an opera house, and much more."

Dad's eyes took on that glinty look he got when someone dared go against him. Riley felt torn. He wanted to hear more of the mayor's plans. He also wished the man would be quiet. Mayor Bridges didn't know it, but he was entering dangerous territory by going against John Stratton.

Allison snickered. "A college in Lampasas? Why, mayor, I believe that's the funniest thing I've ever heard."

Something darted by, to the left of the porch, and everyone

looked that way. There was Skye, oblivious to them all, holding a jar in one hand and chasing a bullfrog. Her yellow dress stood out against the dusky background, and the effect should have been delightful.

Instead, Dad nearly bit his cigar in two. He looked at Riley, his eyes flashing lightning rods, but didn't say a word.

Riley read the unspoken command and stood. "If you'll excuse me, ladies and gentlemen, I need to see to something inside."

He found Emma in the kitchen, washing the last of the dishes. "Did you know Skye is outside?"

"Yes. I didn't think it fair to keep her in a closet all evening."

"My father saw her."

Her shoulders stiffened in that way he was all too familiar with. "Good for him. I hope he invited her onto his lap like a proper grandpa should."

"Emma..." The shame he felt over his family had become woven into his fiber like strings in a loom. He didn't like it, but it was as much a part of his existence as breathing. "Please believe me when I tell you I don't like the way things are any more than you do. But if my father has to come face to face with her, he'll simply forbid her from coming to the house. You don't want that, do you?"

She set the pan on the stove a little too firmly, creating a loud bang in the quiet kitchen. "Fine. I'm finished here anyway. I was just about to take her home."

"I'll ride along with you. I suppose I made a bad call, not taking her earlier, but I thought...I don't know what I thought. I...kind of like her being here."

Emma's face softened, just a bit, then hardened again. "You have guests. I can find the way."

"But it's dark. You're normally home by this time. I insist—"

"No, *I insist.* Mr. Stratton, I appreciate your concern, but there's no need for you to trouble yourself over a mere servant."

"I don't think of you as a 'mere servant,' as you put it. I thought we were...old friends."

"Perhaps you should adjust your way of thinking. Good evening, Mr. Stratton." Emma grabbed her things off a hook behind the door and shut it behind her.

CHAPTER 10

The sky lay with torn-paper edges across the horizon in diminishing shades of blue and orange and gold, making a great collage of the day's farewell. It almost seemed a misuse of a perfectly lovely sunset to cast it on such a useless family as the Strattons. Honestly. John Stratton was a waste of good oxygen.

A pang of conscience rose up in her at such spiteful thoughts. No one was irredeemable. Who was she to judge another man's heart, when she herself was capable of such unkind reflections?

Still. Knowing that man would pass up the opportunity to love a child—his own flesh and blood—was unthinkable to Emma.

"Skye, it's time to go," she called softly, hoping the girl was nearby.

"I did it, Emma. I caught a frog!"

The thrill in Skye's voice washed over Emma like a spring rain. Even with all the hours they'd spent together the last few days, she hadn't heard that kind of pure, childish joy in her tone until now.

"Really? Let me see." Emma had seen many frogs in her day, and had no real desire to examine another one up close. But for the child's sake she did, pronouncing it the finest specimen of amphibian she had ever seen.

Skye beamed. "Can I keep him?"

"If your father says it's okay. Now come with me. I'll be driving you home instead of your Uncle Riley."

Joe met them at the carriage house door. "I figured it was getting close to time for you to leave."

To Emma's relief, Sugar was already hitched to the buggy and ready to go. "Thank you. You're very kind."

"No problem, ma'am. It's getting dark, though. Mebbe I should ride along with you."

Skye had swallowed her jovial mood the moment Joe appeared, and now clung to Emma's skirt like a baby opossum clinging to its mother.

"No, thank you. We'll be fine." The child seemed to relax at her rejection of Joe's offer.

"All right. But you should at least take a light." He removed one of the kerosene lanterns from its hook and handed it to her once they were both seated.

After thanking him again, Emma clicked to Sugar, and they headed for Skye's home, with a silent prayer that she'd be able to find it in the dark.

"You'll have to help show me the way," she told Skye when they turned out of the drive. "I'm not sure I could find it again in the daytime, and here it is, dark."

"It's easy. Just close your eyes."

"Close my eyes? I'm not sure that's a good idea, with me driving the buggy." She looked at Skye, with the lamplight flickering on her olive skin.

The girl lifted her face to the heavens and closed her eyes.

"What are you doing, honey?" Emma asked her.

"I'm feeling the way." She pointed in front of her, then moved her arm to the right just a little. "Home is there."

After a little ways, the road curved to the right before coming to what appeared to be a dead end.

"Through here." Skye pointed.

"But there's no path there. I remember there being a path."

"The path is there. Come. I'll show you." The child climbed down, and Emma secured the brake and reins, then followed, clutching the lantern as if these woods were an ocean and the light were the last buoyant thing she could find.

Sure enough, there was the path she and Riley had taken, overgrown with grass and weeds. "All right. I'll know better than to question you again."

They climbed back into the wagon. Soon they pulled to a stop in front of the cabin, but there was no sign of life. No sign of anyone waiting by the window for a little girl to come home. Emma couldn't just dump Skye here. A sharp sense of foreboding pulsed through her.

"You stay here a minute. I want to speak to your father."

Emma climbed down. Should she leave the lantern with Skye? Emma would probably need it more than the girl. "Will you be okay in the dark?"

"Yes," Skye answered, and Emma tried to inhale some of the child's bravery. Skye may not be afraid of the dark, but in this instance, Emma was.

"You know how to get back to the big house, don't you?" she asked Skye.

"Yes."

"Even in the dark?"

"Yes."

"All right. I'll...be right back." Emma ignored her shaking hands, ignored the pulse roaring in her ear, and took tenuous steps forward until she stood in front of the rough door.

She knocked three times.

No answer.

Knocked twice more.

Nothing.

"Mr. Stratton? It's Emma Monroe. I'm bringing Skye home."

Silence.

With more courage than she felt, or perhaps it was just raw nerve, she pushed the heavy planks until the door scraped open. "Mr. Stratton?"

A putrid smell assaulted her nostrils. Tenuously, she took one step inside and held up the lantern, then sucked in a scream. Donnigan Stratton lay on the floor, arms spread wide, his head turned to one side.

Was he dead?

Her answer came in the form of a deep, ragged snore. Closer examination showed several empty whiskey bottles scattered near him. *Dear, God! What do I do? I can't leave Skye here.*

As soon as the prayer formed, the answer came clear. Tonight, Skye would go home with her.

A quick examination of the chaotic quarters turned up an envelope and a stubby pencil, and she scribbled a quick note.

Dear Mr. Stratton,
I was sorry to find you...

How in the world was she supposed to word her statement to him? She couldn't very well say, *I'm sorry you're a sorry, no-good drunk. I have your child.* True as it may be, even she knew the law wouldn't side with her in a suspected kidnapping. Especially not if John Stratton were to step in. Not that he would. Still, it was best to keep things civil with Donnigan Stratton, if she wanted to continue a relationship with his daughter.

I was sorry to find you ill. Rest is often the finest nurse for
many of our ailments. I've taken Skye home with me for the

*night, in order to give you time to recuperate. I hope you're
feeling better soon.*

Sincerely,

Emma Monroe

Cautiously, Emma placed the note between the man's outstretched thumb and forefinger, then tiptoed out and shut the door behind her.

"Your pa isn't feeling well, so I told him you could stay with me tonight."

The lamplight revealed enormous brown eyes, too old for their years, as Skye nodded. She looked both sad and pleased, as if she'd been handed a great treasure, only to learn the cost was more than she wanted to pay.

Well, Emma would simply do whatever she could to bring the childhood back into those eyes. She couldn't fix everything, but hopefully she could make some parts of Skye's life a little better.

At times, Emma missed Ma in a whisper.

Other times it was conversational.

And in moments like these, the ache for her mother roared.

Yet somehow, caring for Skye both accentuated and soothed the loneliness of Emma's heart, as if by needing Ma, she drew her closer.

"You'll have to direct me out of here, Skye, or I may have us in Canada before daybreak."

The girl giggled and pointed the way.

Back on the main path, the crickets serenaded them in a loud, cheerful melody that seemed to proclaim everything would be all right. When they passed by the main house again, the Strattons had gathered around Mayor Bridges' surrey as they spoke their goodbyes. It must have been the way the wind blew, for Emma caught Clara's words to Riley.

"Isn't that Emma? Who is that child with her?"

Emma couldn't hear Riley's response. But she placed her arm around Skye's shoulder and whispered, "Someday, when I have a little girl of my own, I hope she's very much like you."

~

When Emma drove by a little while later with Skye in the wagon, headed toward the Monroe place, Riley knew he had to follow her. Skye was his niece, and he needed to check on her. Why was she going home with Emma?

Oh, who was he fooling? He hadn't checked on her much at all before Emma took an interest in her. What kind of person was he?

An awful one.

But something deep in his spirit told him he could be a better man. That he wasn't shackled to his family name, as if that alone defined him. Before Emma Monroe upset his world, he was perfectly fine with himself. But now, seeing the way she accepted difficulty with fortitude, seeing the way she lovingly cared for her own family and for strangers alike...he wanted to be better.

Aside from Mom's death, Riley's life had been easy. He never had to worry over money. School was a breeze. He never wanted for friends, male or female. Yet for all his ease, he couldn't think of one thing he'd really accomplished. Not one way his life had affected others, for the greater good. At least, not until Emma showed up in his kitchen.

He thought again to his conversation with Charlie Monroe, about talking to God. So as he saddled Medina and climbed on her back, he talked—muttered, really, in nondescript syllables that must have sounded like nonsense.

"Where are you headed?" Dad's voice pierced the darkness.

"I...feel like someone needs to make sure Emma gets home safely." He figured it best not to mention Skye.

"It's not your place." The disapproval in Dad's tone was obvious, even without being able to see his face.

Riley knew there was no point arguing, unless he could convince his father he had something at stake. "A woman out alone at night isn't safe, even in these parts. If something happens to her, it will reflect poorly on us."

A few moments of silence must mean he was considering it. "I'll send Joe."

"I'm already saddled. I'm going."

"You should let Joe handle it. He and Emma seem to enjoy one another's company." Riley could hear the veiled threat in Dad's voice. "Your time would be better spent on Clara."

Riley chose not to respond. With a flick of his spurs, he and Medina left his father in the dark.

Joe and Emma.

That was one relationship Riley couldn't figure out. Joe was too old for Emma. Wasn't he? Were they sweet on each other?

No. That was none of his business. Tonight, it was time he stepped up and showed his niece a bit of the love and concern she deserved...especially since no one else in his family planned to.

God, I've carried this idea about myself that I wasn't like my father or my brothers. That I was the good one, with the kind heart. But I'm no better than they are. Is change even possible?

Medina must have felt Riley's tension, because as soon as they got on the open road, she increased to a full run.

It wasn't fast enough, however. By the time he arrived at Emma's, her horse and buggy were already in the barn.

∽

*E*mma's brain felt like a pile of scrambled eggs, like all the parts of her life had collided, been whipped and beaten, and poured into a too-hot skillet. Try as she might to separate the things that weighed on her heart, she couldn't. It was one big mess.

Ma's death was the first domino to fall, and each day, another one collided. Pa's illness. Tonight's humiliation. Would the money hold out? What if she lost her temper with John Stratton or Allison? Because she might. But she couldn't afford to. And what of Lyndel? He just kept rolling along. He rarely complained. She worked so much, she hardly saw him. How was he holding up?

Somehow, so far, she'd managed to hold all her anxiety inside with a slim layer of will. She had to, for Skye's sake. For Pa and Lyndel's sakes. But if one more thing happened, that paper-thin veil of self-control would rip open, and who knew what would tumble out?

As usual, Pa sat by the fire when she came in, straining to read the latest copy of the Lampasas Dispatch in the dim glow.

"You'll ruin your eyes," she whispered, as she did every evening.

He grunted, as he did every evening, then folded the paper and set it aside. When he saw Skye, his brows lifted. "Well now. Who do we have here?"

Skye stepped partially behind Emma, as if that might make him un-see her.

"This is Skye." Emma moved aside and placed a reassuring hand on the child's shoulder. "She's going to stay with us tonight."

Pa's wrinkled face split into a delighted grin. "Lucky for us. This is the brilliant young lady you've told me about?" He paused to catch his breath. "You said she was pretty, but you failed to tell me she was beautiful. We're honored to have you in our home, Miss Skye."

Skye dropped her eyes, but Emma sensed the child relax a little. "Skye, this is my father, Mr. Monroe."

Down the hall, Lyndel must have heard their voices, because his bedroom door scratched open and he padded into the living room.

"And this is my brother, Lyndel."

Skye peered up for only a moment before dropping her eyes again.

"Lyndel, this is Skye."

Lyndel's eyes held questions, but he had manners enough not to ask them. "Howdy, Skye."

"Are you hungry?" Emma asked the child as she led her past the table. She noticed the dishes were all done and put away. She'd have to thank Lyndel later.

Skye's answer was a silent shake of her head.

"Well then, let me show you where you'll sleep tonight. I hope you don't mind sharing a room with me." Emma knew there'd be questions later. But for now, thankfully, both of her menfolk carried on as if they had seven-year-old guests stay overnight all the time.

In her room, Emma showed Skye the bed, the dresser, the hooks on the wall. "Let's hang your new dress here. That way it won't get wrinkled, and you can wear it again tomorrow."

She tucked the tiny girl under the covers on one side of the double bed they'd share and said a simple childhood prayer. She was turning down the lamp when she heard the clopping of a horse's hooves, accompanied by a unique snort-blow-snort she recognized immediately.

Medina.

Riley Stratton was the last person she wanted to see. Why couldn't he leave well enough alone?

"I'm going to do a few things in the kitchen, and I'll be back shortly. You close your eyes and go to sleep." With a kiss on Skye's silky forehead, Emma shut the door behind her and trekked through the front of the house without stopping. She opened the front door just as Riley lifted his hand to knock.

"What?" Even she was surprised at her own rudeness. Surprised, but at the moment, not sorry.

"I...saw you and Skye pass by the house earlier. I just wanted to check to make sure everything's all right."

Without a word, Emma grabbed the lantern on the hook by the door, stepped onto the porch, and shut the door behind her. "No. Everything is not all right, Riley Stratton," she whispered. Alarm bells sounded in her head, telling her she was on the edge of hysteria, but she didn't care.

She did care, however, about the audience she may gather if she stayed on the porch. With a lift of her chin, she pushed past Riley, down the porch steps, and headed toward the barn. Halfway there, she stopped and turned back to Riley. "Are you coming or not?"

Only then did he follow her.

In the barn, she hung the lantern on a high hook and spun around. "How dare you follow us here, as if you care one whit about me or that child. I don't know what kind of game you're trying to play with me, but whatever it is, you can just stop."

He opened his mouth as if to respond, but she didn't give him a chance. She had no desire to hear anything he had to say.

"You, with your veiled flirtations and your false compassion. If you really cared about your niece, she wouldn't be living the way she is. Do you know what I found when I took her home this evening?"

"Uh..."

"Your brother. Passed out cold on the floor, reeking of alcohol. No telling how many times that child has had to tiptoe around a drunken father. No telling what she endures when he's not unconscious."

"Now hold on a minute—"

"That's right. Go ahead and defend him. I thought you might be different from the rest of your family. But you're exactly like them. You only care about appearances, not about the truth. As long as Skye and Donnigan are tucked safely away where no one can see, you don't concern yourselves with what Skye might be going through. What are you people, some kind of monsters? I can't even stand to look at you."

Even as she said the words, her conscience pricked at her to stop. She knew Riley was at a loss to know what to do for his niece. He had shown her kindness. But then he'd had the gall to flirt with Clara tonight, after being so nice to Emma all these weeks. Was that what had really brought on her fury?

But she didn't spend more than half a second contemplating that possibility before she spewed more. Pure, unedited venom.

"There's Allison, whose main source of pleasure in life, at the moment, is humiliating me. As for that accident tonight with the tea, that was no accident. I'm sure of it. But she's not even as bad as your father. He's nothing more than a foul-mouthed, self-important tyrant who talks with his mouth full and smells of cigars. But at least he has a little bit of a brain, unlike that dimwitted, simpleton of a brother you call Colt. No wonder Allison's so mean. She's probably bored out of her skull, having to be married to him.

"The almighty Strattons. If only people really knew...you've got a bully, a tyrant, a clod, a drunk, and...and then there's you. You're the worst of them, as far as I'm concerned, Riley Stratton. You're a coward, because I can see you know right from wrong, but you refuse to stand up to any of them. You just sit by and watch all the wrongs your family heaps on others, and you don't do a thing about it. That makes you the bottom rung.

"And you have the nerve to play up to Clara Bridges? Why, she's too good for you, Riley Stratton. She's too good for all of you. I only pray she figures that out before she takes your name and it's too late. No wonder my mother didn't talk more about all of you. She had too much class. She rarely said a cross word about anyone, but with all of you, there really wasn't much nice to say."

Emma hated the wounded look on Riley's face. Hated that she had put it there. She didn't mean half the things she said. But somewhere deep within her, the dam had burst, and she felt powerless to harness the torrent of emotions she'd held in since...since...*oh, God.* Part of her soul cried out to her Maker, and she fell to her knees and sobbed. "I miss her, Riley. I miss her so much."

CHAPTER 11

*R*iley had never been in a gunfight. But what he felt at that moment was, in his imagination, a pretty good indicator of what it must be like to get shot up, beaten, and left to die on the road.

To have the worst things he'd ever thought about himself or his family confirmed, out loud, by the one person in this world he wanted to please, left him both numb and shell-shocked. When did her opinion come to matter so much to him? And why? When had he...wait. Was he in love with her?

He was. He was in love with Emma Monroe. And she couldn't stand the sight of him. At that realization, his dinner threatened to come back up the way it went down.

He tucked his feelings aside, however, and knelt in the straw next to Emma. Right now, she needed to cry. And he wasn't going to let her cry alone. Should he touch her? Just sit there? He reached a tentative hand and placed it on her back.

She recoiled from his touch, even as she sobbed. And in that moment, he felt as disgusted with himself as she was with him.

He sat there another moment, watching her shoulders convulse in emotional agony and feeling about as low as he'd ever felt, knowing he'd added to her burden by his complacence. Emma's lantern flickered on the rough wooden barn walls, and the musty smell of old hay fought against the cinnamon-vanilla smell that was all her. Well, a little vinegar, too...but the sour display she'd just showed him was truth. In a way, he'd been given a gift. He could see himself clearly through Emma's eyes.

Eventually her sobs abated, and they were left with nothing but the sound of crickets, accusing him, just as she had. *Guilty...guilty...guilty.*

Slowly, he rose to his feet and held out a steady hand. "Come on. I'll see you to your door."

With a snuffle and a sniff, she allowed him to assist her to her feet. They spoke no other words. He walked her to the porch. Watched as she cracked open the door just enough to squeeze inside. Shut it behind her, leaving him alone with nature's chorus of condemnation. Truly, it didn't shout nearly as loudly as his own heart.

He climbed back on Medina, but did little else. The horse, probably sensing his mood, ambled toward home in a relaxed pace, as if in her own way, she wanted to soothe her master. Riley used the opportunity to look at the stars, wondering if it was even worth it to ask God for help out of this mess that was his life.

Somewhere deep in his memory, a voice whispered. His mother's voice. *Riley, you can do or be anything you wish. I know your father wants you to stay on here, but you don't have to. You're free to pursue your own destiny, whatever that may be.*

Had she really said those words, or had he dreamed them? Why would she say that to a young boy?

But the further he rode, the more certain he was that yes, she had said those things to him. That she was preparing him for the day when he realized he wanted out. Encouraging him, even.

Truth was, he loved his family. He loved the way they

accepted each other, even as they looked down on everyone else. He loved their loyalty. He loved that, no matter how they bickered, they put on a united front to the community. It made him feel like someone had his back, all the time.

But as much as he loved them, he didn't *like* them very much. And he certainly didn't want to be like them. When he was around them, without realizing it, he adopted a "go along to get along" attitude, and that made him no better than they were. Emma was right. He was worse, for he knew he could do better. He just chose not to.

Not any more. Emma Monroe may hate him...and that broke his heart. But there was something even worse...Riley was pretty close to hating himself. Whoever first said that money can't buy happiness knew what he was talking about. Riley's father had made their family one of the richest this side of the Mississippi. But all the money in the world couldn't buy self-respect.

God, I don't know how or when or where, but I want to separate myself from my family. Just enough so I can be the man You want me to be. Can You help me?

There was no answer, other than Medina's slow, steady clop-clop-clop. Not that he expected the clouds to part and God in the flesh to step off His throne, in order to help Riley figure things out. Still...it would be nice if He did.

He had no idea how much time passed between leaving the Monroe's and arriving home. The place was dark when he got there. He settled Medina in the barn, made his way through the house, and lay down on his bed without even removing his clothes.

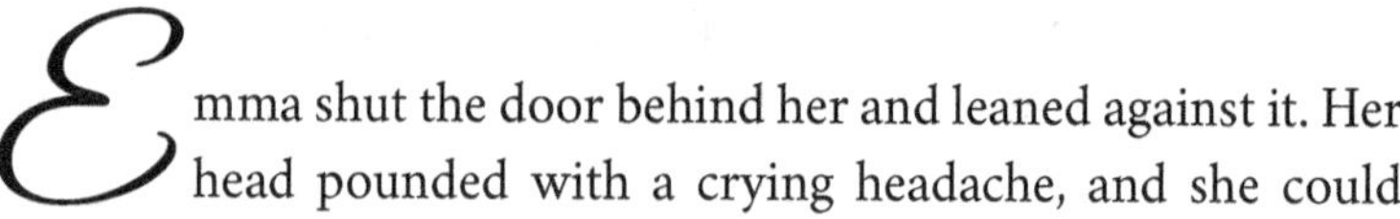

*E*mma shut the door behind her and leaned against it. Her head pounded with a crying headache, and she could feel the swelling in her eyes and nose. But her conscience ached even more than her head. Never in her life had she hurled such cruel words at another human being as she had to Riley, just now.

How many times had Ma told her the rules of polite conversation? She was to ask herself three questions, before speaking about another person.

Is it true?

Is it kind?

Is it necessary?

Unless the answers to those questions were "yes," she should remain quiet.

Well, the things she'd said to Riley tonight certainly weren't kind. And they weren't necessary.

It didn't matter if they were true or not...which, many of them weren't. Riley was a good man, and he had no control over the way his family behaved. But even if they had been true, she shouldn't have said them.

"Want to talk about it?"

Emma started at her father's voice, and shame oozed over her like pond scum. She'd assumed Pa was in bed already. "No, thank you." Right now, all she wanted was a cup of hot tea and her soft pillow. The thought of curling up next to Skye, like a live doll, offered the only solace she could find at the moment.

She walked to her father, kissed the top of his receding hairline, and left him without another word. After fixing her tea, she took her cup to her bedroom and placed it on the bedside table. Soon, she snuggled beneath the covers, one arm around the little girl who had stolen her heart.

As tired as she was, it took a long time for sleep to claim her. Instead, thoughts swirled around her mind, wrapping and squeezing like weeds in the okra patch.

Would she still have a job tomorrow?

If not, what would become of Skye?

Would Riley ever forgive her for the things she said tonight? She needed to apologize.

Would Riley marry Clara? If so, Emma would have to quit her job. As much as she loved Clara, she didn't think she could be a maid in their home. Although Ma did...she was maid to her best friend. But Ma never had feelings for John Stratton the way Emma had feelings for Riley.

She knew Riley would eventually marry someone, but it seemed to her, it would be easier if a stranger captured his love, rather than her dear friend.

Finally, in the wee hours of the morning, Emma let go. She gave the tangled ball of yarn that was her mind to God, and let Him have it. A last, single tear slipped down her temple, past her ear and onto the already-soaked pillow. A last, single thought of her mother's face drifted through her mind, and she slept.

～

Morning came too soon, and Emma lay in bed for too many minutes, in that halfway place between asleep and awake. Her sleep had been fitful, haunted by dreams of weddings with ill-fitting gowns and babies being snatched from her, and special meals cooked and burned. But then, toward the end of the dream, Ma showed up. She didn't say anything, just took Emma in her arms, held her and let her cry.

Now Emma relished the last moments of her mother's presence, not ready to say goodbye. It all felt so real. But alas, the pinky-white edges of Ma's face faded, her scent evaporated, and the dream was gone.

Emma forced leaden feet onto the cold floor, shuffled to the kitchen—it seemed only a few minutes ago she'd made that cup of tea—and started a pot of oatmeal.

And it dawned on her, this would probably be her life. Every single morning, fixing two breakfasts, a simple one for herself and an elaborate one for her employer. A black hole closed over her spirit. No light. No air. How long could she survive without hope?

But she'd keep doing it, for Pa. For Lyndel. For Skye. She'd keep doing it, to help care for the ones she loved.

Just as Ma had done for her, all those years.

$\mathcal{E}$arly Friday morning, Riley arose long before the sun. He dressed with no particular destination in mind, other than away from here, and crept out of his room. He was just about to descend the stairs when he thought he might take his Bible—the one Ma gave him for his twelfth birthday—his last birthday she was alive. He retrieved it from his night table and went about his stealthy business of saddling Medina. The Bible fit perfectly in his saddlebag.

He led the horse on foot until he got to the road so he didn't take the chance of waking anyone. He knew he was leaving early enough that he wouldn't meet Emma on the way. Where to go, he wasn't sure. So he headed for town. Rebecca's Café opened early, maybe he'd get a cup of coffee and some eggs.

Sure enough, the café lights already burned, though the "Closed" sign was still turned outward. Looping Medina's reins around a hitching post, he approached the door. Maybe the operating hours were listed somewhere. Cupping both hands around his face and pressing against the glass, he saw Rebecca Hendrix flit from table to table, straightening chairs, getting ready for the day. She caught her breath when she saw him, then hurried to the door and opened it. "Riley Stratton. Is that you? You like to scared the livin' daylights out of me, boy!"

"I'm sorry, Mrs. Hendrix. I just wondered what time you open."

"Ten more minutes. But you might as well come on in now. Can I get you some coffee?"

"If it's no trouble."

She hurried away, and soon came back with a cup and saucer, a pot of coffee, and a pitcher of creamer on a tray. "You're out early."

"Yes, ma'am. Couldn't sleep, and as I lay there in bed, I thought, 'A cup of Rebecca's coffee sure would be mighty fine right now.'"

The crinkles around the woman's eyes deepened, and her gaze sparked. "Riley Stratton, you sweet-talkin' son of a gun. You'll have to wait on your breakfast like everyone else."

Riley laughed. "Yes, ma'am."

She left him to enjoy his coffee, and he pulled out his Bible. Pulled the small table lantern close. Let the Bible fall open to a random location, hoping for some divine wisdom that might point him in the right direction. But as the pages cascaded open, something caught his eye. Were some of the verses underlined?

He flipped through and sure enough, here and there were verses, sometimes entire chapters, underlined. And in the margins were notes, written in his mother's script.

For a suspended moment in time, he couldn't breathe. He couldn't think. All he could do was turn the pages while his heart pounded and the sound of rushing blood echoed in his ears. There were dozens of passages. Dozens of encouragements from his own dear mother.

All this time, this Bible had rested on his night table, nothing more than a decoration. How much time had Mom spent writing notes and underlining passages just for him? This was obviously important to her. How could he have missed this for so many years? Her reminder to seek God. Her reminder that God was essential. How might his life be different now, if he'd bothered to crack open these pages years ago?

A few more customers entered, and soon Rebecca stood in front of him with a note pad. "You ready to order?"

"Uh...yes. What do you recommend?"

"Well, I've got flapjacks, eggs, bacon, sausage, and biscuits. You can have one or all of those things."

"Send me a little of everything, if you don't mind. And a glass of milk." Might as well settle in. It looked like he'd be here a while.

Rebecca nodded, scribbled something on her pad, and moved to the next table.

With as much care as if he were handling an ancient, gold-covered treasure, he leafed through the pages and settled on a passage in Jeremiah. Chapter 27, verses 11-14.

For I know the thoughts that I think toward you, saith the Lord, thoughts of peace, and not of evil, to give you an expected end. Then shall ye call upon me, and ye shall go and pray unto me, and I will hearken unto you. And ye shall seek me, and find me, when ye shall search for me with all your heart. And I will be found of you, saith the Lord: and I will turn away your captivity, and I will gather you from all the nations, and from all the places whither I have driven you, saith the Lord; and I will bring you again into the place whence I caused you to be carried away captive.

In the margin, his mother had written, *God has good plans for your life. That doesn't mean you won't go through hard times. But when you seek God with all your heart, you'll find Him, and He'll lead you to a good place. Always seek God with your whole heart.*

Seek God.

How long had Mom had this Bible before she gave it to him? He knew it wasn't her own personal Bible. Dad had that beside his bed, though Riley was certain it was ornamental. Perhaps sentimental, too.

She must have worked for months, preparing this for him, underlining verses and writing notes. And he'd never even opened it until today. Joy and sadness bubbled up in the same well inside his soul. He felt like, for this moment, he had her back. Like she was sitting across the table, talking to him.

Well, now that he'd found the treasure box, he'd keep mining it until he found a map to point his way out of this maze...a way to escape the choking tendrils of the Stratton dynasty.

~

*E*mma worried all the way to work about her uniform —or lack thereof. She'd gotten in so late last night, she hadn't had time to launder her two dresses. And since they were both soiled, she could either wear a dirty frock, or a clean dress that wasn't a uniform. She opted for the clean dress.

She needn't have worried. Allison didn't even come to breakfast. Riley wasn't there either, and Colt and the senior Mr. Stratton merely grabbed a couple of biscuits on their way out the door. It would have been nice if someone had alerted her before she fried a pound of bacon and scrambled a dozen eggs. But oh, well.

She saw Joe tending to something in the barn corral. Maybe she'd offer him some of it. Skye was busy with a few simple math problems, so Emma heaped eggs, bacon, and biscuits on a plate and slipped out the back door.

"Are you hungry? It seems I have enough left over to feed a small army."

"Hungry? No. I already ate. But I can always make room for food that smells this delicious." Joe took the offered plate and leaned against the fence. "Thank you."

Emma didn't know whether to stay or leave...but something about the way the wind whispered in her hair and offered a cool balm to her still-swollen eyes, made her want to linger. She leaned her elbows on a post and looked out over the landscape.

"Everything all right, Miss Monroe? You seem...pensive."

"Pensive? Yes, I suppose I am."

"Want to talk about it?"

"I'd love to talk about it, Mr. Barnes. But my mind is such a jumble, like a bunch of strings all knotted together. I don't think I could even find words. None that would make any sense, anyway."

"Why don't you just pick one of the strands and start talking?"

"Hmmm...pick a strand. All right. I miss my mother terribly."

"I know you do. And you'll always miss her. But you will learn to go on without her. The pain won't ever leave you completely, but it will dull some with time."

"You sound like someone who knows what he's talking about."

"Unfortunately, yes. I lost both my parents when I was a child. I was raised by an aunt and uncle. They were good to me, but no one could ever take my parents' place. Later, I lost my wife and child."

"Your wife and child? I didn't know. I'm so sorry."

He scooted the eggs around on his plate and took another bite. After a moment he said, "We were both young. I married her, and we went west in search of adventure. What we found was a lot of hardship. We claimed a little piece of land, built a cabin. I was gonna be a farmer. Then, when we learned a baby was on the way...well, those were the happiest days of my life. But there was no doctor or midwife close by. There were complications...a little girl...they both died."

A weight pressed on Emma's chest as Joe's story unfolded. "I don't know what to say. I really am sorry for your loss."

"After that, I lost my heart for farming. I just wanted to get away...far away. I've been traveling around, doing odd jobs, ever since. This is the longest I've stayed at any one place. I suppose it's because as long as I do my job, the Strattons leave me alone."

If only the same were true for her.

They stood in amiable silence. He finished eating, and she needed to get back to work. But her head still hurt, and something about Joe Barnes just felt...easy. Safe. Like the big brother she never had.

Not like Riley, who set everything all topsy-turvy whenever he was near.

"Next string?" Joe asked.

"We'll have to save that for another time." She took his plate and turned toward the kitchen. "Mr. Barnes?"

"Yeah?"

"Thanks for telling me. About your wife and daughter."

He didn't respond, and she didn't say more. Nothing more needed to be said. But there was a house to clean and a few items to add to the grocery list. If she hurried, she and Skye could make it to town and back in time to prepare lunch. Something about the beautiful spring day comforted her, and she wasn't ready to confine herself indoors.

A trip to town might be just what her spirit needed.

~

*R*iley had taken up the corner table at Rebecca's Café for nearly four hours now, and frankly, his backside was getting numb. He thanked Rebecca, gathered his things, and went for a stroll around town. First, he fed Medina a leftover biscuit, and she thanked him with a whicker-snort. Then he walked her to the livery, which hadn't yet been open earlier this morning, and asked old Ben if he could find a shady spot and a bucket of oats for her. He hated to leave her in town for so long, but at least at the livery she'd have other horses to keep her company. "Just a little while longer, girl."

During his amble along the walkway, his thoughts turned to the mayor's plans for the town. Why was Dad against it? Wouldn't it bring jobs to Lampasas? Surely a boon to the economy would benefit everyone. But Dad didn't care as much about *everyone* as much as he cared about himself. He liked being the richest, the most powerful, the most important.

Maybe Dad didn't like the idea because somebody else came up with it.

Riley was no more than two blocks up the boardwalk when he ran into the mayor.

"Riley. It's been too long, son." He laughed at his own joke and offered a hand.

"Yes, last night does seem like a long time ago, sir."

"What brings you into town today? Ranch business?"

"Not exactly. I...." An idea slipped in. "Could I schedule an appointment with you? I have a few questions."

"Why certainly. You free for lunch? I have a meeting in about ten minutes, but I'm available after that."

"Lunch sounds great, sir. Just tell me when and where."

"How about my house? My cook always prepares more than enough. Twelve thirty?"

"Sounds good. I'll see you then."

Mayor Bridges hurried to his meeting, and Riley wandered along, paying little attention to his surroundings. His mind still pondered the verses he'd studied that morning, along with his mother's voice, speaking as clearly in his mind as if she stood next to him.

He wandered into the mercantile, looking for a journal in which to record his thoughts and responses to the verses and his mother's counsel. He knew he was about to embark on a thunderous journey fraught with lightning and hail and heavy boulders blocking his path, and he didn't want to let a single drop of wisdom slip through his grasp.

He turned the corner to the aisle where stationery was kept and nearly ran smack-dab into Emma.

"Oh, pardon me," she said before looking up.

He watched her face transform at the realization of whom she'd bumped into, from surprise to remorse to discomfort. That was the effect he had on her, and it felt like a slap in the face. If only his presence brought joy, instead of pain, to her lovely features. Well, so be it. "My fault. I should have watched where I was going."

"No, it was entirely my fault. Please accept my apology."

He nodded and moved aside so she could pass. But she didn't pass. Instead they stood there, inches apart, a wide chasm between them. It hurt all over.

"Riley, about last night..." Emma whispered.

"There's nothing to talk about."

"I think there is. The things I said...they were deplorable. I have no excuse. I...I hope you'll forgive me."

He looked at her a moment, at the pain in her deep green eyes, as if a sad storm brewed just on the other side. The sight injured his heart even more deeply, and he looked away. "There's nothing to forgive. Everything you said was true. Good day, Miss Monroe."

He squeezed past her to his destination, hoping she wouldn't follow. Praying she wouldn't press him for more conversation. He just...couldn't.

She didn't. But around the corner, at the other end of the aisle, was Skye, cradling a miniature porcelain doll.

"Oh, hello," he told her.

She looked up at him, and her enormous brown eyes reminded him of a newborn spotted fawn, full of innocence and hope. The tiniest of smiles crept across her face.

He took that as a good sign. Maybe it wasn't too late to make things right with his niece. "What do you have there?"

She angled the doll so he could see better.

Kneeling to her level, he said, "She's beautiful. Almost as pretty as you are."

Still no words, but her smile deepened.

"Would you like that doll?"

Her eyes widened, but she didn't respond.

"I'd be honored to buy her for you. But only if you promise to name her after me."

She giggled then, and the sound offered a mild respite to the throbbing ache in his chest.

"What's so funny? I think Riley is a fine name."

The giggles turned to a chortle, and he scooped the little girl and her doll into his arms and walked to the register. He set her on the counter, where Virginia greeted them with mild shock. She looked from Skye to Riley, as if trying to figure out the relationship. Thank heavens she didn't say anything out loud. "You ready?"

"Yes. I may have some more purchases. But if the young lady agrees, I'd like to go ahead and buy this doll."

"That's a fine choice. She's one of my favorites." The woman examined the price tag without taking the doll from Skye, wrote the price once in her ledger, and again on a receipt pad.

He turned his focus back to Skye. "What else do you think Riley will need? Does she want a piece of candy? Fabric for a new dress? How about that cradle back there?" He motioned to a doll cradle, displayed behind the counter.

"I can't give her a boy name," Sky whispered, but the look of glee on her face, the delight in her quiet voice, enveloped his heart, and in that moment he was ready to buy her the whole store.

"All right, all right. How about Rilene?"

More giggles, but this time she nodded.

"Please add enough fabric to make Skye and Rilene matching dresses. Whatever she chooses. And a bag of peppermint candy."

Virginia filled a small sack with peppermints and brought

several bolts of yellow and blue and pink fabric to the counter. "Which is it gonna be?" she asked Skye.

Skye looked from Riley to the fabric, then back at Riley, as if making sure he really meant it. Then she looked over his shoulder, and he presumed Emma stood behind him. He wouldn't turn, though.

Emma must have given her a nod, for soon Skye pointed to a pretty pink dotted pattern.

"The dotted Swiss. That's the one I would choose, too." Virginia cut several yards and placed it with the candy and the cradle.

He paid for the items before lifting Skye to the floor. "I'll take the fabric to Mrs. Wesson and have her make your matching dresses." To Emma he said, "Would you mind taking Skye by there, so she can be measured?"

"I'd like to make the dresses, if you'll let me. I...would enjoy it."

"That's fine. I'll make sure you're appropriately compensated." He hadn't said that to hurt her, but a marked pain shuttered her eyes before she nodded.

Even when he tried to do the right thing, it was the wrong thing.

~

*E*mma had made a grand mess of things. Last night, it felt like a release to retch her vile rationalizations onto Riley. Today, she could see the acid of her words eating away at a life-long friendship. She had wounded Riley, and he'd never shown her anything but kindness. If only she could rewind the clock and play the whole scene over, she'd do it differently.

But she couldn't. And she didn't know if she'd ever outlive her regret.

She was about to apologize again, about to tell Riley how

she'd been out of her mind with fatigue and grief over her mother and worry about Skye, when the bell jangled behind her, signaling another customer.

"Why, Riley and Emma. Fancy meeting you both here."

Clara floated in on a cloud of peach linen and lace, with her flowered bonnet and matching parasol, which she now used as a walking stick. A dainty peach reticule hung from her wrist, and *good gravy*, she even smelled like peaches.

"Emma, I'm so glad you're not wearing that dreadful uniform. I hope you don't mind..." Clara lowered her voice conspiratorially. "I mentioned to Allison that it was the new thing to have household staff dress like members of the family. They call them assistants, or companions. It's very British. I told her a well-dressed assistant is the mark of the truly elite. I think I read that somewhere, but I may have exaggerated. But when I saw you in that black-and-white monstrosity, I just had to come to your defense. You may be getting a whole new wardrobe." She giggled as if she'd done something truly naughty.

Emma smiled. This was why she loved Clara. They were worlds apart in both status and interests, but a more loyal friend, you'd never find. "Actually, I haven't seen Mrs. Stratton this morning. Thank you for your...help, though." She wasn't sure if that was the right response, or if there *was* a right response to Clara's declaration.

Clara turned her attention to Riley. "I just came from Papa's office. He said you're joining us for lunch? I'm delighted. If you'll wait for me, I only have a few purchases to make, and you can escort me home."

Riley nodded, then turned away as if he were embarrassed. Of course he'd be embarrassed, after her tirade last night. Emma was the one who should be ashamed.

Hot liquid bit at her eyes, and she fumbled with her purchases, which she had yet to pay for. They could wait for another day, though. She set them aside. Right now, she needed to get away from this place. "Skye, are you ready?"

The child nodded, and, carrying her new cradle with her new doll and the fabric inside, she followed Emma through the store to the waiting buggy.

She had just helped Skye aboard and was climbing on when Riley called her name. But when she looked his way, he averted his eyes.

"You forgot this." He handed her the package with her discarded items, and their gaze met for the briefest of moments before Emma looked away.

"Thank you. That wasn't necessary."

He nodded and circled the wagon to stand on Skye's side. "Take care of Rilene, okay?"

Skye giggled again and held the doll to her chest. "Okay."

Emma clicked to Sugar, and soon the two girls and the doll were on their way back to the Stratton Ranch.

The world kept shifting. How could she make things right? Would things ever be right again? She looked at Skye, holding her doll, and forced herself to breathe deeply. One thing was certain—he couldn't make everything right all at once. But she could start now, and do one right thing. Make one right choice. Where that would lead, she didn't know. But for now, that was the only course of action that made sense.

CHAPTER 13

"What's on your mind, son?" Mayor Bridges leaned back in his chair and pushed his plate away.

"I'd like to hear more about how you think the natural springs can draw people to Lampasas. Do you really think you can sell this as a tourist town?"

"I know I can. I just need a few more supporters."

"People in town don't want tourists here?"

"Oh, they want them here just fine. But ranchers and farmers privately own all the land. Nobody wants to give up their ranch or their farm that they've worked so hard to grow, to build a hotel or a spa. Most of them don't even want their waters tested."

"How many healing springs do you think there are?"

"Judging from my unofficial research, five or six. Maybe more."

"And what is your unofficial research?" Riley's curiosity was full force.

The mayor laughed. "My nose. The springs that stink on a hot, windy day? Those probably have some sulphur."

Riley didn't think they had any of those on their property.

The smelly springs were closer to town. Closer to the Monroes' land.

"If we can access the mineral springs, the problem won't be getting the tourists here. The issue will be acquiring a place for them to stay once they arrive."

Riley took a long sip of the sweet iced tea. "Have you talked to all the landowners, or just a few?"

"Only a few, but so far I haven't made much progress. The Bowmans have agreed to dedicate one corner of their land, but they'd want someone else to develop it. And they want to retain ownership."

"I think I may know a farmer who'd be willing to develop his property."

The mayor leaned forward. "Really? Who?"

"I'd rather speak with him before I disclose his name. I'd also like to speak to the Bowmans, if you're not opposed to that."

"Be my guest. I'll take all the help I can get."

Clara offered Riley another piece of pie, but he declined.

"What do you have up your sleeve, Riley Stratton?" Clara did that fluttery eyelash thing. She was good at that. Could teach classes, if she wanted to.

"Just a couple of ideas. I hate to eat and run, but I have some business I need to see to, and I don't want to hold you up."

Mayor Bridges stood and offered his hand. "Nonsense. You're not holding anybody up, but by all means, go take care of business. Clara, walk Mr. Stratton to the door."

Riley stood and offered his arm to Clara, and she walked him onto the porch.

"I hope I didn't overstep my place or come across as critical to your sister-in-law about Emma's uniform. Emma and I have been friends a long time, and she's very dear to me. I can't imagine she enjoys dressing that way, but perhaps it wasn't my place."

Riley laughed. "When Allison gets something in her head, it's hard to change her mind. But you're right. The thing looks ridiculous."

Clara nodded. "I feel protective of Emma somehow. She's had enough hard knocks against her lately. I know wardrobe is a minor issue, but for a woman, it plays a big part in how we feel about life. If we look pretty, we feel more confident. If we look dowdy, it just...I don't know. It affects our mood. I'm sorry...I'm probably not making much sense to you."

Riley looked at the woman before him through a new lens. Clearly, there was more to Clara Bridges than met the eye. She had depth as well as beauty. And her protectiveness of Emma caused his respect for her to lift considerably. "No, ma'am. I think you make perfect sense. Now if you'll excuse me, I must be going."

He replaced his hat on his head, tipped it, and headed for the livery. He and Charlie Monroe had some business they needed to discuss.

~

*E*mma served lunch to Allison and little Davis by themselves. For the second time that day, nobody told her about any changes in plans for mealtime.

Oh, well. She supposed they didn't owe her an explanation.

Allison practically ignored Emma. She had a stack of newspapers and ladies' journals at her side, which she read out loud to Davis. He responded with laughter and cooing as if she were reading him a bedtime story. As much as Emma disliked her employer, she had to admit, she seemed to be a good mother.

Tension clawed through Emma's shoulders and neck as she waited for Allison to comment on her dress, or her lack of uniform. But Allison seemed not to notice. Should Emma say something, or wait for her employer to address it?

She finally decided to just take the calf by its hind legs and rope the issue herself. She placed a piece of cherry pie in front of Allison and waited for her to pick up her fork.

"Excuse me, Mrs. Stratton. I'm sorry to bother you, but I was wondering if I might have a word with you when you finish your meal."

"Certainly. I have something I'd like to discuss with you as well. I'll see you in the parlor as soon as the dishes are cleared."

"Yes, ma'am."

Skye sat on the back porch steps and hummed softly to her doll. The memory of Riley's tenderness with his niece only amplified Emma's own guilt over her outburst last night. For a moment, she'd allowed herself to lose control and unleash all the anger and frustration within her, and for a moment, it felt good.

Unfortunately, that moment had a high price. The cost of a friendship.

She pushed open the screen door. "Skye, I'll be in a meeting with Mrs. Stratton for a few minutes. Will you wait here for me?"

"Okay."

When Emma returned to the dining room, Allison and Davis were gone. Emma cleared the dishes and set them in the sink to soak, then went to the parlor. Davis sat on a quilt at Allison's feet, and alternated between shaking his rattle and chewing on it.

"Emma. Come in. Have a seat, please." Allison's tone was dangerously neutral.

Emma sat across from her employer.

"I see you're not wearing your uniform. Would you like to explain why?"

"I'm sorry about that, ma'am. I used both of them yesterday, and they were dirty. I didn't have time to wash and dry them before this morning. I'll make sure they're clean before tomorrow."

"I see. Well, that won't be necessary. I've decided you may wear your own clothes." When she said, "your own clothes," she wrinkled her nose and looked Emma over from head to toe as if disgusted by the thought.

"The problem is, from what I've seen, your clothes are little more than rags."

Emma stiffened. That wasn't true. She was an excellent seamstress. The fabrics she wore may not be imported silks and satins, but she certainly didn't dress in rags. Sure, she wore her older things to work in, because after all, she was a cook and a maid. Why would she wear her Sunday best to do this kind of work?

"I'd like to have some dresses made that are more...appropriate for a servant of your status. I'll use my personal seamstress and deduct the cost from your pay."

Emma could feel her blood pressure rising. Could feel the anger clawing at her stomach lining, as if it would surely tear through and jump all over Allison at any moment. What was it about this family? Emma had to get hold of this anger before it took over her life.

God, help me. I don't know how to respond.

Calm surrounded her like a warm blanket, fresh from the clothesline on a sunny, summer day. She couldn't control Allison. She could, however, control herself.

"That's very...kind of you, Mrs. Stratton. However, if you'll tell me what exactly you'd like me to wear, perhaps show me some pictures or something, I'll be more than happy to see to it myself."

"I'm not sure you could manage the styles I have in mind. I'll let Ingrid Wesson handle it. She makes all my dresses. I know you worked for her before you came here, but there's a reason you were only the assistant."

Emma swallowed. She knew she couldn't afford the dresses and fabrics Allison would choose for her, especially if she had to pay Mrs. Wesson to make them. But for the life of her, she couldn't think of a response that wouldn't get her fired.

"Yes, ma'am," she said, but in her mind she was saying some very uncharitable things. *God, help me.*

Emma remembered her hard-learned lesson from last night. What was it Ma used to say? *The less said, the less mended.*

And also, wasn't there something in Scripture about loving each other deeply, because love covered over sins? Well, she wasn't sure she could ever love Allison Stratton deeply. But she could at least try to be civil. Maybe even kind.

Yes. What if, every time she wanted to say something ugly, she forced herself to say something kind, instead? It was worth a try. She searched her mind for something—anything—positive to say to Allison. Nothing...nothing but blank space. Oh, wait.

"Mrs. Stratton, I'm sorry to change the subject, but I just wanted to remark on what a happy child Davis seems to be these days. I guess his teething issues are over for a while. He certainly is content when he's around his mama. You clearly have a way with him."

Allison looked at her son and smiled. *Smiled.* That was a rare occurrence, at least around Emma. "He is a delightful child, isn't he?"

"He's adorable."

Something softened in Allison, and Emma was glad she'd made the effort. Yes, that would be her new tactic with this family. Every time they made her angry, she'd say something kind. Even if it had no long-term results, it certainly did help diffuse a potentially explosive moment.

Deep breath. Emma wasn't sure what else to say or do.

Allison stiffened again, then nodded curtly. "If you'll please stop by Mrs. Wesson's next time you're in town and allow her to take your measurements, I'll choose some styles and fabrics for you. That's all."

And just like that, Emma was dismissed.

~

*R*iley rode Medina past the cutoff to the Monroe farm and circled back around four times before he finally decided he might as well go for it. He had nothing to lose, and maybe something to gain.

Still, his stomach twisted and turned into a pretzel at the thought. Did Mr. Monroe know about the confrontation last night? Would he even welcome him into his home any more?

And would it be better to do some more research before asking Mr. Monroe if he was interested?

Probably. But that could take weeks. Months, even. And the mayor had acquired someone to do the research. No use putting off the question.

This time, he rode Medina right up to the front steps and looped her reins around the porch rail. As usual, after Riley knocked, he heard Mr. Monroe's weak voice.

"Come in."

Was his voice getting weaker? What was it he had? Consumption?

"Riley. Good to see you, son. Come on in. You know the routine. You hungry? Got beans on the stove..."

A rush of relief flowed through Riley's veins at the warm reception. "No, sir. I've already eaten, thanks. Can I get you anything?"

"I'm good. What brings you here today? The ranching business not keeping you busy enough? Or did you just miss my handsome mug?"

Riley chuckled. "Well, sir, I'm actually here on business."

"On business? I'm not sellin'..."

"Oh, no sir. I don't expect you to sell your land. But since you're not able to farm right now, I wanted to share another opportunity with you. Something you could do to bring in some extra income...just until you get back on your feet."

Monroe wheezed and coughed, a weak cough that made Riley's chest hurt just hearing it. The other man took a sip of his water and set down his cup. "I must admit, you've got me curious. What is this business venture you're so fired up about?"

"Have you ever heard of Saratoga Springs?"

"Seems like I read something about it. Some kinda hot springs, isn't it? Supposed to heal people. Sounds like a bunch of nonsense to me."

"Nonsense or not, many people have given testimony to how the springs have improved their health. But they're a long way away. Mayor Bridges thinks we can make money off our own sulfurous springs. He wants to advertise Lampasas as 'The Saratoga of the South' and make this a tourist town."

"Hmmm...I'm listening."

"He feels it will be a success. Problem is, all the land with sulfur in the springs is owned by farmers and ranchers, and so far none of them wants to give up their water source as a tourist destination. I thought...under the circumstances...you might be interested."

The older man studied his wrinkled, age-spotted hands for a long time.

Riley felt for him. Farmers had a lot of pride. It would take a big dose of humility to agree to this. In a way, agreeing to do this would be admitting defeat. Admitting that in truth, he'd probably never farm again.

Finally, Mr. Monroe lifted his eyes. "You say I won't have to sell?"

"No, sir. You'd retain ownership of the land and control of the property."

"What are you proposing, exactly?"

"Well, I'd have to give it some more thought. I mainly just wanted to see if you're open to the possibility. If you're interested, I could see developing the area around your springs with a small hotel, a restaurant, maybe a spa of some sort. Of course, as owner, you'd have final say over anything that was done."

More silence.

"You think this would help pay a few bills around here?" Mr. Monroe asked after a time.

Riley weighed his words before he spoke. "I believe so, sir. No guarantees, but I think the mayor's onto something. This could help a lot of people. It will bring more jobs, for certain. Mayor Bridges even mentioned bringing a college to Lampasas. Better access to higher education is always a good thing, in my opinion."

"And what would be your involvement? Aren't you committed to your father's business?"

More silence. But nothing about it was awkward. There was something about Charlie Monroe that was just...easy.

Riley cleared his throat. "Well, sir...I'm not sure the, uh, ranching business suits me. I guess you could say I'm exploring other options. If you're interested, I suppose I'd like to be as involved as you want me to be. I'd love to oversee the development of the types of businesses I described."

Monroe coughed again. The lines etched in his face seemed deeper than they had just a few days ago. "You've given me a lot to think on. Come back next week, and we'll talk more."

"Yes, sir."

"Before you go, though, I have one more question for you."

"What's that?"

"What are your intentions toward my daughter?"

~

*E*mma walked back to the kitchen, determined not to let the concern about money for these new dresses get the better of her. Most professions had expenses associated with them. If new attire was required, it was required, and she'd just have to figure out how to scrimp and save to make ends meet.

But right now, the best therapy she could think of for her worries was Skye. That little girl had a soothing effect on Emma's soul. And at this moment, she needed to be near the one person in this place she knew was, as of yet, pure and sweet and untainted.

She opened the back door, half expecting to see the child in the same place she had been earlier, rocking and singing to her doll.

Skye was gone.

The dishes she'd used were left untouched to one side of the porch.

How odd. It wasn't like Skye to run off. "Skye! Where are you?" Emma called.

Nothing.

Emma returned to the kitchen and looked in the pantry, but it was empty.

Her heart tightened and quickened at the same time, making it hard to draw in breath. Had Skye's father taken her? Certainly, it was his right to take his own child any time he pleased...but without saying goodbye?

Or had she wandered off, perhaps stumbled into some type of danger? With shaking hands, Emma opened the back door again and rushed down the steps. "Skye! Skye, where are you? Come here, please."

No response, other than two mockingbirds taunting each other, taunting Emma with their calls.

The barn. Maybe she'd gone in search of the old tabby cat. "Skye! Are you in here?" She couldn't contain the tremor in her voice. Her own echo answered back, but still no Skye. Sugar whickered as if she wanted to tell Emma what she knew, but couldn't find the words.

"Skye!" she tried to yell again, but panic clawed her throat and blocked the sound.

"Miss Monroe? Everything all right?" Joe's voice was a welcome one. He knew these parts as well as anyone. He could help find her.

"It's Skye. She's gone. I don't know if her father came and got her or if she's lost or—"

"I believe I saw Donnigan riding this way earlier. Looked like his horse, anyway. Would you like me to ride out to his place and check?"

"Yes. As a matter of fact, I'd like to go with you."

"Suit yourself." Joe quickly saddled both Sugar and another horse. Soon, they sped toward Donnigan's place and banged on the door.

Donnigan answered, his eyes dark and droopy. He smelled like some dead thing the cat had dragged from under the porch.

Emma craned her neck to see around his shoulder, and there was Skye, inside her house, rocking her baby and humming a tune Emma wasn't familiar with. *Thank God!* She was safe. Why would Donnigan take her without telling anyone?

"What do you want?" Donnigan asked, looking back and forth between Joe and Emma.

Emma pushed back her frustration. "I just wanted to make sure Skye made it home all right. I'm sorry you were, uhm...unwell last night. I hope you're feeling better." Emma spoke with utmost care so she didn't anger this man who could, if he chose, keep Skye from her.

"Yeah, well." Donnigan cleared his throat. "I suppose I am. Thank you for looking out for her."

"It was no trouble, I assure you. Skye is a delightful child." Emma shifted her eyes to Skye, who looked up at her and smiled for just a moment before going back to her doll. "Did she show you the doll her uncle gave her?"

"Her uncle? Oh. Rilene. Yeah...I should've guessed Riley had something to do with it."

Donnigan made no move to invite them in. He gave no indication if he'd allow Skye to return to the big house or not. Emma's mind scurried for something, anything, to say that might convince the man of how important it was for Skye to spend the days with her.

Oh, God, please. I'm a mess. This is a mess. But please don't let him keep her here, like a prisoner. Please, God. Let this man see.

That's when Joe spoke up. "You know, Mr. Stratton, I've been meaning to talk to you about some things. I've noticed some discrepancies around the property lines, where some large sections of fence have come down. I need to repair them, but I'm not sure exactly where the lines are. Since you grew up here, I thought you might be able to ride out and advise me."

Something amazing happened. Donnigan's eyes actually lit up, as if a spark had just been ignited in the deepest part of him. Not a full flame, but a glimmer, and though he didn't move, he stood a little taller. "I suppose I could do that. When?"

"Now, if you feel like it. I'm sure Miss Monroe would be kind enough to watch your little girl back at the house for a while."

Donnigan looked at Emma again...was that suspicion in his eyes? Did he think she was trying to steal Skye from him?

Was she?

It was all so confusing.

Emma held her breath while silent cries went up to heaven. *Please, God, please, God, please...*

Finally, Donnigan nodded. "Skye, you wanna go back with this lady?"

She jumped to her feet, still holding Rilene, and ran to Emma.

Emma saw—even felt—Donnigan's pain in a fresh way.

The man before her wasn't a monster. He was sick. He was

sad. And he was without hope. As bad as things were for Emma, she had never been without hope.

Donnigan backed into his home and reached for his hat, and in the process, his foot bumped a liquor bottle. His hope, or lack of it, was contained in that vile bottle.

Her hope was in the Lord.

How could so much happen in her spirit, in that tiniest sliver of time? She felt simultaneously sorry for being angry at God, shame at judging this man so harshly, and a fierce determination to save Skye from following the same hopeless path as her father and his family.

Riley's face dashed through her mind. That sweet, beautiful face, with flashes of vulnerability, flashes of longing in his eyes. He was searching too. He needed saving too.

But realization didn't equal ability. She pulled Skye to her side and knew she couldn't save anybody. All she could do was love them, and point them to the One who could.

The four of them rode back to the house. Riley arrived at the same time. She wanted to avoid his eyes, but she couldn't help herself. She searched his face for any sign of forgiveness. What she saw was him looking from her to Joe and back with an unreadable expression. After Joe helped her and Skye down and took Sugar's reins, Emma led the girl to the back entrance as quickly as possible. No sense prolonging the misery that seemed to be her existence every time Riley Stratton was anywhere around.

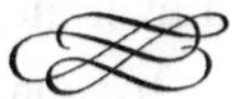

CHAPTER 14

The next Sunday morning, Riley got up early and drove to Donnigan's place. "You up?" He called after knocking several times.

The door creaked open and Skye peeked out. "Shhh. My pa is still asleep."

"Oh, okay," Riley whispered. "May I come in?"

Skye stepped back and held the door open for him.

The place was filthy, save one little corner that was meticulously arranged with the doll bed he'd bought on Friday, a child-sized blanket and pillow, and a few other toys and trinkets.

This was unacceptable. No wonder Emma had been furious.

Riley knelt down to his niece. "I'd like to take you to church with me. Go put on your prettiest dress, and bring me a hairbrush. I'll help you with your hair."

She looked at him like he'd spoken a foreign language. "Church?"

Oh, mercy. Had this child never been to church? "Yes, church. I'll explain all about it on the way. But right now, you go get ready."

She nodded and disappeared behind a curtain.

Donnigan lay passed out on the one bed in the room, snoring so loudly, Riley feared he'd suck the roof in on top of him.

Riley poked him. He flinched, but didn't move. No use trying to have any kind of conversation with him now. It would have to wait until he slept off whatever alcohol still claimed his body. But this...this was all going to change. From now on, Skye would stay with him in the big house. It was their responsibility to care for this child. Surely Dad could see that. But no...Dad felt no responsibility toward Skye, and Riley knew it.

He pushed the harsh thoughts to the side and decided, for now, to take things one step at a time.

Soon, Skye reappeared wearing a blue dress that looked new. Had Emma made that for her? She must have.

Skye handed him the brush, and his hands felt clumsy and awkward with the child's silky strands. If only he had a string or something. What did girls use to tie their hair back? "Do you have a ribbon for your hair?"

She handed him one she had folded in her tiny hand, and he fumbled with it, trying three times before making a respectable bow. It wasn't great, but it would have to do.

"Let's go," he whispered.

She ran to the corner and picked up her doll. "Can Rilene come?"

"Of course. Everyone is welcome at church." He hoped, for her sake, that was true.

~

The bags under Emma's eyes were so large, she felt certain she could pack her entire trunk in them. She hadn't slept well since Thursday night. Since then, she spent each night tossing and tangling herself in the sheets, replaying her dreaded outburst and trying to figure out a way to undo the damage. She knew her ruminations did no good, but she was like an old Jersey cow with her cud—she just couldn't stop chewing.

But it was Sunday. And despite the fact that she felt like the world's biggest hypocrite, she knew she had to go to church. More than that, she *needed* to go to church. Needed to sit in the pew where Ma sat. Needed to look at the rugged wooden cross on the back wall behind the pulpit. Needed to hear the familiar, comforting sounds of the pipe-organ as Hettie Woods missed the beat every fifth or sixth measure, and Hal Thomas's off-key tenor blared from the back row.

In this time when her whole world seemed to have shifted, where the walls of her existence seemed to be caving in on themselves, the imperfection and sameness of the little church felt somehow reassuring, though reassuring of what, she couldn't say.

So, eyes still closed, she pushed her feet off the bed. Was this what Donnigan felt like when he had a hangover?

Pancakes for breakfast. Quick and easy.

Hair in a chignon. Quick and easy.

On the way to church, the sun stood regally in the sky, directing an alleluia chorus of cardinals in a grand performance. Pa weakly whistled Amazing Grace while Lyndel pointed out every rabbit and squirrel along the way, and lamented the fact that it was Sunday and he wasn't allowed to hunt. Emma found the whole ride painfully consoling. She was glad the cocky little birds shared their song. Glad Pa felt good enough to whistle. Glad to see a glimpse of her little brother, instead of the old man he'd recently become.

At church, they offered the obligatory greetings and endured the pitying stares of neighbors who'd promised to stop by but hadn't. And Emma felt a heightened twinge of the ever-present ache when she scooted into their row, with the reminder that they now had more elbow room than they had just a couple of months ago.

But when Riley walked in, Skye at his side, Emma sucked in a breath. She watched the silent exchange between Riley and his father, as the older man refused to move in and make room. She watched Mayor Bridges come to the rescue and invite Riley and Skye to join his family on their pew. She watched others in the room, throwing eye daggers at Skye. She watched Skye, seemingly oblivious to it all. Yet Emma was familiar enough with the still surface of the child's countenance to know she didn't miss a thing. When Skye sat between Clara and Riley, she caught Emma's eye for just a moment, and Emma offered a reassuring smile, an encouraging nod.

Hettie struck the first chords of the first hymn, and the congregation stood in unison and sang a hearty rendition of *Blest Be the Tie that Binds.* Emma struggled through the chorus, trying not to watch the pretty picture they made—Riley, Skye, and Clara—trying with everything in her to be happy that her two beloved friends would surely provide a lovely home for Skye one day. Emma was happy. She really was.

But for some reason, she couldn't stop her bottom lip from quivering, or the tears that slid down her cheeks, wet her collar, and surely turned her nose a most ridiculous shade of red.

~

*R*iley knew, without a word spoken between himself and his father, that a mark had been drawn. In the coming days, he knew more lines would be etched. There was no going back. And the funny thing was, he didn't care.

No, that wasn't right. He did care. But despite the fact that he cared deeply what his father thought, he knew he couldn't continue to carry the façade his father wanted him to carry. So what if people talked about them? They'd talk, regardless.

Dad's fantasy that people only had good thoughts about the mighty Strattons needed to be challenged. For all Dad's bully and bluster, he was a coward. He was afraid of people seeing him as weak or flawed. An Indian grandchild would certainly put the Strattons in the "flawed" category, in a lot of people's minds.

As soon as the service was over, Riley took Skye by the hand and introduced her to the people around him. "Hello. Good to see you. Have you met my niece, Skye?"

Most were polite, if not sincere. Some marched past him, as if they couldn't hear his greeting. He tried to ignore the gunpowder glare coming from his father. But he couldn't ignore the jagged words, hissed in his ear as Dad passed him in the aisle. "Get home. Now."

Dad's face looked like an overripe tomato. He stalked through the crowd, not even nodding or giving the usual pleasantries.

The scent of cinnamon and vanilla alerted Riley to Emma's nearness even before he saw Skye lunge into her arms. "Look at you," she said. "You look so pretty in your new dress. Did your Uncle Riley fix your hair?"

Skye nodded.

"He did a very nice job." Emma placed a hand on Skye's shoulder and greeted Clara, to his left, before she looked at Riley. *Thank you,* she mouthed. Something in her eyes looked both relieved and sad before she followed the ebbing crowd toward the exit.

She might be relieved, but he certainly wasn't. He might have done the right thing this morning, but it wouldn't be without its price. He had the devil to pay.

Riley dropped Skye at the cabin and went straight home. Now, he sat in Dad's study and tried not to cringe under the verbal barrage.

"You sorry, good-for-nothing traitor. Do you have any idea the damage you caused by dragging that brat to church? We do business with those people, Riley. Word travels fast, and it travels far. Our livelihood depends on being able to sell cattle, to sell beef to people. Do you really think they're gonna buy beef from Indian lovers?"

Dad's eyes held a treacherous glint. Riley had to work hard to maintain eye contact.

"I have given you everything, boy. Paid for your fancy school, for those fancy clothes you wear, given you a job where you don't have to do a thing but pay a few bills. All I've asked for in return is that you honor the Stratton name. Instead, you spit in my face! I'm done being the nice guy. That little girl ought to be on a reservation. I've a good mind to send her and Donnigan away right now. One more stunt like this, and I will." Dad's eyes bulged from his head. Veins popped from his neck like they might explode, and for a moment, Riley feared his father would have a heart attack. "What were you thinking?"

Riley weighed his response carefully.

Before he could form words, Dad slammed his fist on his desk and yelled, "Answer me!"

Riley sat up as tall as he could. "What was *I* thinking? I was thinking that Skye is my brother's child. She's lost her mother. And she needs to be shown some love and consideration. What would Mom think, Dad? What would she say about the way you're treating your own granddaughter?"

In an instant, Dad was out of his chair and across the desk. The punch that landed across Riley's jaw left him stunned, though the pain of it hadn't had time to develop yet. He reached his hand to the spot, now beginning to throb, and looked at his father. How was he supposed to respond to that? Physical violence had never been their way.

Dad stood there, fists clenched, a dangerous glaze over his eyes that told Riley no response would be the correct one.

Riley stood, nose to nose with his father. After a thirty-second eternity, Riley turned and exited the office. He needed some space.

As soon as he slammed the door behind him, he saw Colt, leaning against the wall, hands stuffed into his pockets, looking like he'd just witnessed a gunfight where both parties ended up dead. Riley tried to pass, but Colt placed a firm hand on his brother's chest and let out a string of curse words. "Why would you do something like that? Bringing her to church? You knew how Dad would react."

"Do you think people don't know about Skye? Do you honestly think they're not talking already?"

"I don't care what other people are doing, Riley. You knew bringing her to church, parading her around in public would upset Dad. And it sets a precedent. If we'd just ignored the situation, eventually people would've found something else to gossip about. Now, Donnigan and Skye is *all* they'll talk about. Dad's right. We'll lose money over this. You know how it is, how many people in these parts hate Indians. It could take years for Stratton Ranch to recover. I swear, Riley. For all those brains in your head, you can be pretty stupid."

"How do you think Mom would have reacted to Skye? Do you think any of this would be happening if she were still here?"

"She's not here, Riley. Mom's dead, and she's not coming back. It's us and Dad now, and unless we play by his rules, we're going to lose everything. I won't be surprised if Dad doesn't disown you over this. "

"More for you, then?" Riley hated himself for the accusation, but he wouldn't apologize.

Colt's eyes hardened. "You know that's not what I want. If you want to mess everything up for yourself, go right ahead. But think real hard about doing things that affect the rest of us." He jammed his hands back into his pockets, turned, and stormed away.

Riley rubbed his jaw again. It was starting to swell, along with the growing knot in his stomach.

~

For the next week, the climate in the Stratton household changed. Emma saw very little of Riley, and his absence hung on her spirit in a thick shroud of regret. Colt and John Stratton ate their meals in silence and skittered away as if the house itself made them ill. And though Allison seemed all business as usual, she opted to take Davis with her into town when she went for her Temperance Society Meeting.

Emma assumed Donnigan continued to work with Joe, for each morning when she arrived, Skye sat on the back porch steps with Rilene. On Tuesday, Emma took the girl with her to town, for she still needed to see Mrs. Wesson about the measurements for her new work attire.

But the joy in Emma's heart constricted at the whispers and glares thrown their way whenever Skye was present. Not everyone, but enough people to make her wonder if she ought not save her trips to town for when she could go alone. She held her head high and smiled. She would not kowtow to public perception when that perception was wrong.

Her heart sank even more when she looked across the street and saw Riley rushing into the mayor's office holding a stack of papers and looking very much like a man on a mission. What was he doing?

She chided herself. It was none of her business what Riley

Stratton did with his time. None whatsoever. And the sooner she learned that, the better off she'd be.

~

"Why, Emma. Mrs. Stratton told me you'd be stopping by, and I've barely been able to contain myself. Come here and give me a hug." Mrs. Wesson folded Emma into her arms, and it felt like coming home to a safe place.

"I've missed you," Emma whispered with more emotion than she was prepared to deal with. "I have someone I'd like you to meet. This is Skye."

"Good day to you, Skye. What a lovely young lady you are. And who is this?" Mrs. Wesson gestured to the doll.

"Rilene," Skye answered, though her voice was barely audible.

"I love that the two of you have matching dresses. Did you make them yourself?"

Emma smiled. That was one of the things she loved about Mrs. Wesson, and one of the reasons she had such a loyal following of customers. She made every person who entered her presence feel important.

Skye shook her head. "Emma made them."

"I see. Well, I should have known. Did you know Emma used to work here in this shop? But she's gone off and left me, and I'm quite lost without her."

This time Emma laughed. "I doubt that. I was told you needed to take my measurements."

"Nonsense. I still have your measurements from the last dress we made you. I just wanted an excuse to see you. Mrs. Stratton has ordered quite a wardrobe for you. Apparently, you're no longer her maid. You're her *assistant*."

"Her assistant?"

"That's what she said. She must think very highly of you, to go to such extravagant expense."

Emma didn't comment, but her face must have clouded, for Mrs. Wesson leaned forward. "She is covering the expenses, is she not?"

Emma turned away from the woman. "My, would you look at this new fabric you have. It's lovely."

Mrs. Wesson took Emma's arm in her own and whispered, "Surely she's not making you pay for these dresses."

Emma cleared her throat, but didn't answer. How could she? She refused to be disloyal to her employer. But she wouldn't lie.

"Oh, dear. That's what I was afraid of. Now you listen to me, young lady. I won't charge you for my time, and you'll pay what I pay for the fabric. Understood?"

"I can't accept that, Mrs. Wesson. This is how you make your living. I wouldn't feel right."

"Oh, posh. I'll not hear another word about it. Surely you won't begrudge an old woman a bit of joy, dressing you up like the daughter I never had, will you?"

"Your generosity, as always, overwhelms me. But I assure you it's not necessary." The last thing Emma wanted to be known as was a charity case.

"I didn't say it was necessary. I want to do this. It will make me happy. Will you please just let an old woman have a little happiness in life?" The spark in Mrs. Wesson's eyes belied her poor, pitiful-me tone.

"Only if I can reserve the right to do something kind for you one day, when I have the chance."

"Deal." The woman pulled Emma into another sideways hug, then moved behind the counter. "Now about the fabrics Mrs. Stratton chose. Hmmm...she was in quite a hurry when she stopped in. I'm afraid I can't remember which of these she wanted...why don't you come over here and help me decide."

Emma had a strong suspicion Mrs. Wesson remembered

exactly which fabrics Allison had chosen. She just wanted Emma to select her own. But she had no way of proving such an allegation, so she just played along.

"I've always been partial to blue." Emma fingered an exquisite blue cotton toile. "And green."

"Look at this green one. It matches your eyes perfectly." The woman held up a stunning length of imported silk plaid that took Emma's breath away. Where would she ever wear such a thing?

"It's beautiful. But it's not very practical, I'm afraid."

"Remember dear. You're Mrs. Stratton's assistant. She wants you to look your best."

That was probably true. Though why on earth Allison would want her to cook and clean in a silk dress was beyond her. That she'd originally wanted to humiliate Emma in front of Riley was obvious. Now that Riley and Clara were courting, she supposed Allison didn't mind if Emma looked nice. But silk for a maid? Ridiculous. Maybe she could save this dress for the days she went to town. "All right."

"And look at these, since you're too practical for your own good. Here's a pretty pink calico I just got in yesterday afternoon. I haven't seen this shade before, but it suits you quite well. And here's a striped muslin—would you look at those tiny blue flowers between the stripes? So pretty. Oh, this will be such fun!"

Emma could see her friend really was enjoying herself, and Skye joined the excitement. "What about this one?" Skye held up a lavender checked cotton with heliotropes embroidered here and there. It had been hidden beneath some of the other bolts, but it truly was one of the prettiest things Emma had ever seen.

"That's perfect!" Mrs. Wesson cried. "Oh, dear. It's the end of a bolt. I'm afraid I don't have enough to make a dress of it, but don't worry. I'll come up with something."

"I'm afraid we've chosen enough fabric to clothe half of Texas," Emma told them, but really, she relished the moment. Her clothes had always been more serviceable than pretty, though she did try to look as attractive as possible. But having pretty dresses just for the sake of having pretty dresses—even if they were impractical—even if Allison Stratton had lost her ever-lovin' mind—well, Emma had to admit. This was fun.

∽

For the first time in Riley's life, he felt alive. *Really* alive. He had a mission. A purpose. Before, he'd viewed life through a clouded lens, but now the window was clean.

Not that everything in view was pleasant—quite the contrary. Riley had always wanted to please his father, but not any more. All those years at college trying to make Dad proud. None of it mattered, if Riley couldn't be proud of himself.

He left home early every morning and stayed out late. And truly, the thought of escaping, of creating a new life for himself, and possibly for his future family, drove him more than he'd ever felt driven in his life. All the while, a calm assurance blanketed his spirit, as if he were being both pushed from behind and pulled from ahead by God Himself.

So this was what faith felt like. It was simultaneously comforting and terrifying.

This morning, when he saw Emma and Skye park in front of Mrs. Wesson's shop, he wanted more than anything to go to them. To look into Emma's eyes and see if any of her disdain for him was gone. But the thought of seeing disappointment in her eyes was more than he could bear.

No. He'd wait until he made something of himself, apart from his family. Then he'd go to her and declare himself. The worst she could do was reject him. Again.

For now, he'd have to be content knowing that whether or not she ever looked at him with love in her eyes, he was doing his best for her. For her future. One day soon, if everything went as planned, she wouldn't have to serve his father or Allison or anybody else, all for the sake of a dollar.

If he had his way, the Monroes would have plenty of money to support them for the rest of their lives.

CHAPTER 15

Everything was coming together nicely, in Riley's estimation. Though the Bowmans had decided to hold off until after the train depot was well established, Charlie Monroe was all in. A crew was set to begin next Monday on a twelve-room hotel and spa near the springs on the Monroe's property, with a tentative plan for a restaurant and another hotel nearby.

If everything went according to plan, the hotel should be ready by the time the first train pulled into town. Mayor Bridges was so excited he could barely sit still. He had already purchased ads in newspapers around the country, inviting tourists to Lampasas come next spring.

Riley rode Medina all the way up to the front porch and looped her reins around the rail post, climbing the steps two at a time. Three knocks, but he didn't wait for an answer before he nudged open the door. "Hello? Charlie?"

"Come on in," Charlie called.

"It's all ready to go." Riley handed the older man the large brown envelope and took a seat next to him. "I have a good feeling about this."

Charlie's knotted fingers smoothed out the building plans on his lap. He adjusted his spectacles and studied the papers. "Looks pretty fancy."

"Yes. People who can afford to come to a luxury spa will expect fancy."

Charlie didn't say much else, other than an occasional, "Hmmm..." as he turned the plans this way and that. But Riley thought the man looked pleased.

"You sure you got the money to pay for all this?" Charlie set the papers aside and eyed him.

"I believe so, sir. I've worked for my father since I was fifteen, and I've invested that money. My dad's actually a pretty savvy investor, and I've followed his lead. It's taking nearly everything I have, but as I said, I have a good feeling this is going to be a success."

"I hope so. For all our sakes," Charlie said. "Did you see to the other matter we discussed?"

"My lawyer is drawing up the papers now. He said it would be another week or so."

"And Emma and Lyndel will inherit equally? I want Emma taken care of."

"Yes, sir. I made sure he understood."

"We have just a few months before the first train arrives. How long do you think it will be before we turn a profit?"

"Since the land is paid for and I'm not having to borrow to cover the building expenses, it shouldn't take long. If we can hire the staff we need and keep the hotel filled to capacity, I'd say you'll be well provided for in no time."

"I don't like Emma working as a maid. She wants to be a teacher. No offense to you or your family."

"I understand. A local university is part of the mayor's long-term plan. Maybe Emma can get her teaching certificate without leaving home."

"As long as she has the option." Charlie speared him with a

look that said more than a library of books ever could. If only Riley could make the man understand. Whether she ever returned his affections or not, nothing would make Riley happier than to see all Emma's dreams come true. Actually, nothing would make him happier than her love...but even if she never loved him, he'd do his best for the Monroes. For Emma.

Because that's the kind of man he wanted to be.

~

*I*t didn't take long in the General Store since Emma only needed a couple of things to restock the Stratton's pantry. By the time she and Skye finished, Medina was gone. Still, Emma didn't want to take a chance of meeting Riley on the road, so she decided to take a quick detour. She'd stop by and check on Pa before going back to work.

She'd ventured so deep into her thoughts, lulled almost into a trance by Skye's soft humming, that she was all the way in her yard before she noticed Medina hitched to the porch rail.

What was Riley doing here? Should she turn around and go back to work?

But it was too late. They must have heard the horse and buggy, for the front door opened and Riley stepped out. The expression on his face held a mixture of guilt and regret and something almost mischievous, as if he'd gotten caught pinching the cornbread again.

"Hello," he called.

"Uncle Riley!" Skye jumped from the wagon and ran up the stairs, lunging at his legs with the force of a young filly running for a fresh bucket of apples.

"Hey there, Sunshine." Riley scooped up his niece and held her close. "I see you're taking good care of Rilene. Has she been minding you?"

Skye giggled and nodded.

"She eating well?"

More laughter. "Yes."

"Cleaning up her room?"

Skye chortled. If Emma hadn't seen it with her own eyes, she wouldn't have believed the transformation. What had happened between these two?

She climbed from the buggy, and Riley swept down the stairs to offer his assistance, still holding Skye on one hip. Why did he have to be such a gentleman?

"Thank you," Emma whispered. "I must admit, I wasn't expecting to find you here."

"I was just leaving," he said, but offered no further explanation. He set Skye down and tipped his hat to them both. "Ladies." Then he climbed on Medina and left them on the porch in a cloud of dust.

Emma stood there, mouth agape, watching him ride off into the blue-sky-and-cedar-framed road. Then she took Skye by the hand and marched into the house.

"Hello, Pa."

"Well, hello. I certainly didn't expect you at this time of day. Hello, Skye."

"What have you been doing?"

"Oh, nothing. Nothing at all. Just sitting here, like always."

Clearly, Pa wasn't going to give Emma a clue as to why Riley was there. If they wanted to play that game, they could just play alone.

Except curiosity was about to eat her from the inside out. She swallowed back the questions that fought to get out and kissed her father on the head. "I'm glad to see you're well. Skye and I best get back to work."

"See you in a few hours." Pa picked up some papers...what were those? But she wouldn't give him the satisfaction of looking over his shoulder. She'd just have to wait until tonight when he was asleep. Maybe she could snoop then.

"All right." She used a haven't-got-a-care tone, but Pa seemed unaffected.

For now, she didn't have any choice but to take Skye by the hand, climb in her wagon, and head back to the Strattons.

It was going to be a long afternoon.

$\sim$

*R*iley had found the best crew money could buy. Or at least the best crew in these parts. He'd even paid extra to have the foreman's word that they'd keep the entire project under wraps until its completion.

Oh, word would get out long before then. But the longer Riley could avoid telling his father about his plans, the longer he'd have a place to sleep. When Dad found out what Riley had gotten himself in the middle of, he was going to detonate.

And Riley would be quite homeless.

Emma was another story, though. In a few days, men would be crawling all over her property, not to mention the enormous structure that would soon rise like a phoenix from the barren fields of what was once a beautiful farm. How would she react? Would she be angry? Would she accuse Riley of taking advantage of her father's illness, or using his influence to push the man into doing something he didn't want to do?

Knowing her opinion of him, he felt pretty sure she wouldn't be happy about his joining forces with her father. But maybe one day, she'd see that he really was trying to do the right thing.

Maybe one day she'd see he wasn't like the rest of his family. But even if she didn't, that was all right. Just knowing he was acting honorably, following God's lead, was enough for him.

At least that's what he kept telling himself.

But the thought that one day soon, he would stand alone against everyone who'd ever been important to him was more than a little unsettling. It left him feeling both excited and terrified. He'd already jumped from the boat. Whether he sank or swam was yet to be seen.

~

*J*ust when Emma was finally recovered from the Thursday evening dinner, Allison decided she wanted to throw a tea party for the Temperance Society ladies. She showed up in the kitchen Friday afternoon, Davis on her hip, a stack of recipes in her hands, and announced the party would be the following Tuesday.

Emma took the recipes and assured her employer she'd see to it, and Allison exited toward the front of the house, onto the wide front porch. The music of Davis's giggles and squeals brought a smile to Emma's heart.

Was there a third voice on the porch? Oh, dear. Where was Skye? Emma had sent her to the garden to cut some fresh rosemary. A look out the kitchen window showed Skye was nowhere to be seen.

She tiptoed to the dining room where she could peer, unnoticed, onto the porch. There was Skye, sitting cross-legged on the blanket next to Davis, playing peek-a-boo with the little boy as Allison watched, laughing.

Emma was transfixed. Never in a thousand lifetimes would she have thought Allison Stratton would show any kind of tenderness, or even tolerance, toward Skye. Yet here she was, treating the child as if she had a right to be there, playing with her cousin.

After several minutes, Emma returned to the kitchen. This family was truly an enigma. Were they good people or evil overlords?

After a time, Skye returned through the back door and said nothing of the interaction on the porch.

A short time later, Allison reappeared. Surprisingly, she sat right down at the kitchen table and asked Emma's opinions on which sandwiches and what flavor of punch sounded best for the party. She even asked Skye if she'd like to help make decorations.

Skye nodded.

Truly, this new side of Allison left Emma feeling pretty wobbly. Was it a trick? Was Emma being set up?

"I hope at least one of your dresses will be ready by then, Emma," Allison told her.

"I suppose I could stop by tomorrow and see how she's coming along."

"Splendid. You can get supplies for the party while you're in town."

Emma had never in her life had such a hard time deciding if something smelled of roses...or a rat.

When Skye whispered she had to use the necessary, Emma dismissed her to the outhouse. As soon as the door shut behind the child, Allison cleared her throat.

"I...want you to know...I think it's a good thing, what you're trying to do for that child. It's a pity...well..." Allison pulled at a thread on the tablecloth.

Allison Stratton, nervous? And at a loss for words?

She'd seen everything now.

"I don't know what will become of her," Allison continued. "But whatever happens, I'm glad you've taken an interest in her."

"You know, she's really warmed up to her Uncle Riley. I'm sure she'd welcome attention from her Aunt Allison, as well."

Allison stood, walked to the kitchen window. "You don't understand how things work in this family. It's not that easy. Riley is John Stratton's son, I'm just the daughter-in-law."

She was right. Emma didn't understand. What was Allison afraid of? John Stratton? How could anyone just stand by and watch an innocent child suffer?

But Emma knew better than to voice those questions out

loud. For now, it would have to be enough to know Allison had revealed a chip in her armor. She had a soft spot for children.

Emma wasn't quite sure what to do with that information. It was so much easier to think of Allison as the Ice Queen—cold and uncaring. She didn't know how to respond to this new version of her employer.

As if Allison sensed the disarray her revelation had caused, she sealed up the chink, stiffened her back, and turned to Emma. "There will be a lot of important ladies at this tea. I hope you won't let me down." And with an icy stare that chilled Emma from her nose to her toes, Allison left the room.

For the hundredth time since she'd been in their employ, she thanked God for not making her a part of this crazy family.

But even as the thought floated through her mind, Riley's face melted away the chill, and she felt a twinge of regret that, indeed, she never would be part of this family.

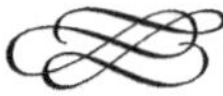

$\mathcal{R}$iley was beyond tired. Exhausted. But he couldn't sleep. Too much was on the line, and no matter how still he was or how he tried to push everything from his mind, he ended up just lying there in the dark, staring into the black.

What time was it? One a.m.? Two? He fumbled around and lit the kerosene lamp, then looked at his watch.

Four thirty. Man. He'd lost an entire night's sleep, and today was the big day. He'd instructed his crew to be at the Monroe place at seven thirty. Since Emma always showed up here by seven o'clock, he'd at least have a day to get things started before she found out. Before she had a chance to object, or to change her father's mind. Hopefully by this evening, they'd at least have some kind of skeletal structure in place.

He would have felt like a rat, except Charlie Monroe himself had suggested they do it this way. "Sometimes, when it comes to Emma, it's better to ask forgiveness than permission," he'd said, with a glint of humor in his eyes. "She's a lot like her ma that way. She'll fuss and fret about something before the fact, but once it's underway, she's as loyal and supportive as a hound dog. Don't tell her I said that."

The picture of Emma as a hound dog made Riley chuckle. He sure hoped Charlie was right, that Emma would be supportive once they got started. But even if she wasn't, what did he have to lose? She already thought he was lower than a cemetery mole in a graveyard tunnel.

Well, there was no sense wasting time, lying here stewing like a lovesick pigeon. He sat up, pulled on his Levi Strauss & Company denims, and grabbed his boots. On socked feet, he crept through the hallway, down the stairs, and through the kitchen toward the stables. He and Medina needed some riding time...and some thinking time.

"You sure have been makin' yourself scarce lately."

Riley nearly tossed his boots in the air at the sound of his father's voice from the study. "Dad. I didn't know you were up."

"Hurt my back yesterday. Keeping me awake."

"Sorry to hear that. Can I get you something?"

"You can sit down. Talk to me. Tell me what's going on in that head of yours."

That was the last thing Riley wanted to do. But he also didn't want to lie to his father. He pulled up a chair and sat. At least Dad offered a bit of civility Riley could grab onto. For that, he was grateful. "What do you mean?"

"You courting the mayor's daughter. Who do you think set you up? I like her. She's a good match for you."

"I'm...what?"

Dad laughed, then grabbed his side. "Hurts to laugh. I know it's fun to keep things a secret when you're first courtin'. But don't go sneakin' around too much. Her father finds out you're meeting her in the dark, he's liable to get a gun after you. Just declare your feelings, right out in the open, and keep things respectable."

"But, you don't..."

"No point in denying it, son. People talk. You've been goin' to town every day. You've been seen comin' and goin' from the mayor's house. Nothin' to be embarrassed about. Clara's a lovely young lady. She'll do us right proud. And it'll be good to have the mayor's alliance."

"Alliance? Dad, I..."

A low groan escaped his father's mouth. "I'm sorry, son. I thought this chair would be better for my back, but I was wrong. Can you help me back to bed?"

"Certainly." Riley supported his father to a standing position, then assisted him to his room and helped him settle in, tucking the covers around him. "Would you like anything else? Tea? Water?"

"How about some whiskey? That should numb the pain."

A picture of Donnigan, surrounded by whiskey bottles, flashed in Riley's mind. "Why don't I fetch Dr. Hutchins?"

"Good idea. He'll have morphine. Wait for daylight, though. I'm not dying or anything. I can make it 'til then."

"All right." Riley watched his father's head lean to one side and his eyes droop to half-mast.

Riley felt like the lowest sort of creeping thing. Here was Dad, trying to have a heart-to-heart, father-son talk. Trying to bridge the gap that had been present for weeks now. What would happen when Dad learned the truth?

Would he truly disown Riley?

He might. Riley had known the possibility was there from the beginning. But now, with Dad actually being nice. Heat stung Riley's eyes, clogged his throat. Why couldn't Dad keep being a jerk? For the thousandth time, Riley counted the cost and came up short.

God, this is hard.

For now, he'd avoided the issue of Clara Bridges. But one day soon, he'd have to explain himself, and his actions, to his father.

It was nearly six o'clock when he and Medina finally trotted toward the Monroe farm. He'd have to stay out of sight until

Emma left, but something pulled him that way. Exhilaration for this new venture. Anticipation, maybe. But he couldn't wait to get started.

When he approached the turn-off to the Monroe place, he heard singing in the distance.

Was that Emma?

It sure sounded like her. What was she doing out at this time of morning? Where was she?

He guided Medina off the road, into the woods, toward the sweet sound of her voice. Soon, they approached a small stream, which branched off from one of the springs. There, in the blue-gray dawn, with the first watercolor streaks of pink stretching across the horizon, was Emma, sitting on the shore, shoes beside her, singing her heart out. He'd heard her sing before in school. He remembered her voice was lovely. But here, in the quiet, worshipful birth of a new day, it seemed he wasn't in her presence alone. He felt God here, in her words, in her voice, in the sweet echo of her heart reaching out to her Savior.

> *What a friend we have in Jesus*
> *All our sins and griefs to bear*
> *And what a privilege to carry*
> *Everything to God in prayer*
> *Oh, what peace we often forfeit*
> *Oh, what needless pain we bear*
> *All because we do not carry*
> *Everything to God in prayer*

He watched from the cover of a copse of oak trees, feeling like an interloper, yet for the life of him he couldn't take his eyes from the scene. She reached up and wiped her dewy cheek, then covered her face with both hands, and he knew he had to leave. This was her moment. Hers and God's. He had no right to be here.

But Medina didn't have the good sense to display diplomacy and tact, and to remain quiet during their retreat. She snorted and whinnied, as if to say, "Encore, Emma! Sing another one."

"Hello? Who's there?" Emma called, and Riley felt every kind of terrible. Now he'd gone and frightened her, busted in and broken up this exquisite moment like a moose at a tea party.

~

*A*fter another long night of no sleep, Emma had finally decided a visit to her secret place might soothe her spirit. That place by the stream where she used to go with Ma to pick berries, back when she was very young, before Ma worked for the Strattons and didn't have time for berry picking any more.

It was more than just the berries, though Emma still went there from time to time during blackberry season. But the memories she had of this place went far deeper than the black-stained hands and apron, or the deep purple juice running down her chin, or the burst of flavor on her tongue as she popped the ripest berries into her mouth instead of the basket.

When they finished picking, she and Ma would take off their shoes and wade in the stream for a while, holding hands to keep from slipping. Then Ma would sit on the bank and sing hymns and talk to her about God's love and how He had a special plan for her life, and answer Emma's questions about where the birds went at night or why the stars didn't fall and crash into the earth.

If she closed her eyes, she could still remember Ma's singing. Such a soothing, rich alto voice she had, and she'd sing and sing and sing while Emma made mud pies and twig dams and tiny waterfalls fashioned from pebbles.

So she'd crawled out of bed and dressed in the dark. The sun wouldn't yawn over the horizon for another hour or more, but thankfully, the full moon cast enough light that she didn't need to take a lantern along. It was as if God Himself had set up a tea party at their special place and sent the invitation, and now waited for her to arrive.

When she at last broke through the overgrown path into the clearing by the bank, she felt a rush of peace she hadn't felt in oh, so long. She took off her shoes and waded in, gasping at the first shock of the cool flow. She stood in the middle of the stream and closed her eyes, and soaked in God's presence just as sure as the hem of her skirt soaked in the water.

A gentle breeze tickled her face...a hug from heaven. How long she stood there, absorbing the serenity, she didn't know. But after a while, she waded back to the shore and sat on a fallen log that seemed to be placed there just for her use.

Closing her eyes again, Emma heard Ma's voice, with its soothing, low timbre, telling her they'd never have a friend as true as Jesus. And she opened her mouth and sang from the depth of her soul, making a duet of her own voice and Ma's, loud and clear in her memory.

Something shifted in the brush, then she heard a familiar snort—Medina? "Hello? Who's there?" she called. She didn't feel afraid. Only curious about why Riley's horse would be in her woods.

"It's just me, Emma. Riley."

More crunching and movement, until Medina nosed her way into view.

"I'm sorry...I didn't mean to interrupt." Riley looked at her like he expected another verbal assault. "No worries. I'm leaving."

She swiped at the tears on her cheeks. Looked at her feet. Oh, molasses, she was barefoot. What must he think? "What are you doing here?"

"I...uh...was just out for a little morning ride. I heard singing, and thought I'd come investigate. Again, I'm sorry. I should've minded my own business." He pulled Medina's reins to turn her back toward the road.

"Riley, wait. Can...can you stay a minute?"

He looked at her like one might look at a tiger in a petting zoo. After a long pause, he said, "Sure." Then he climbed down and led Medina to the water for a drink. "Nice place."

"This is where I like to come to think. And to pray. I haven't been here for a while, though." She breathed in a prayer for the right words. "Riley, I want to say again how deeply sorry I am..."

"No need to apologize. You spoke your mind. You needed to get those things out."

"I disagree. The things I said to you were hateful and judgmental and harsh, and I had no right to say them. I feel horrible, and I don't deserve your forgiveness. But I hope you'll forgive me anyway."

She stood there, her emotions laid out on a silver platter. Would he handle them gently or toss them into the stream? In those long seconds, she didn't breathe, and her heart seemed to stop beating as she waited for his response.

"All is forgiven."

The words soaked into her spirit like warm honey on freshly baked bread.

They stood there for several minutes in the holy quiet of the morning. Nothing more was said. Nothing needed to be said. For the rest of her days, until she was old and withered and her hair was coarse and gray, she'd remember this perfect, peaceful moment when two hearts shared the most innocent kind of intimacy.

～

*R*iley was waiting on Dr. Hutchins's clinic porch when the man flipped the sign to the "Open" side. He saw Riley through the window and smiled as he unlocked the door.

"Good morning What can I do for you today?"

"My father's hurt his back again. He was hoping you might prescribe some morphine for the pain."

"That's too bad. Is he staying down? He's a stubborn one. If he'd take it easy like I told him to, this wouldn't keep happening."

"I think he's planning to stay in bed today, but with him, you never know."

"Yes, I'm quite familiar with your father's unreasonable work ethic. I'll head that way as soon as Nurse Hathaway arrives."

Riley thanked the man, then rode Medina hard all the way back to the Monroe's. The crew wasn't set to arrive for another half hour, but he wanted to be there before them. He had promised to take Charlie to the building site and let him look at the layout before they set up a single string line. He also wanted to talk to the crew foreman about a few things.

Sure enough, when he got there, Charlie waited on the porch. "I thought you'd forgotten." The man possessed that spark of humor in his eye Riley had come to appreciate.

"Had a little business in town to take care of. You ready?"

"To make my fortune? I was born ready."

"Okay. Be right back." It didn't take Riley long to hitch up the old work wagon to a couple of plow horses who looked more than anxious to go for a ride. Soon, the two men were on their way.

It took a little time to get the wagon to the top of the rise, but once there, the view was breathtaking. Far enough away from the main house to give the Monroes some privacy. Overlooking the warm, bubbling springs just below the hill. Yes, this would be the perfect place for a hotel and spa.

Charlie unrolled the blueprints again, then looked this way and that. "You say you're going to build a walkway from here to the springs?"

"Yes, and a garden with native flowers and plants, with tables and benches tucked here and there." Riley pointed in the opposite direction. "Eventually, the restaurant and a small theater could go there. But for now, the hotel will have its own kitchen and dining room."

"So everything a guest could want or need will be right here."

"That's the plan. Of course, more shops will open in town, so they can go there if they want to get away for a few hours."

Charlie looked at the land—his land—and sighed. His eyes glistened, but no tears fell. "I wish Sally were here to see this. I wish...I wish she hadn't needed to work so hard." His voice broke, and Riley placed a hand on the man's back.

"I wish that too. But Mr. Monroe—Charlie—I don't know what I would've done without your wife after my own mother died. I'm glad I got to have her as part of my life."

Charlie smiled a wobbly smile. "She thought the world of you, Riley. She really did."

Riley started to respond, but the sound of several wagons rumbled toward them. Soon, six buckboards pulled onto the rise, each one loaded with lumber and other supplies.

Ricky Green, the foreman, pulled beside them and climbed down, then offered his hand. "Riley, Charlie. Good to see you. Y'all ready to get started?"

Riley's heart pounded out a hammer tune that would have rivaled Paul Bunyan's. "Ready as I'll ever be."

CHAPTER 17

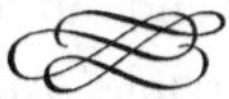

*E*mma wasn't sure what to do with herself, with Mr. Stratton hanging around all day. First, Dr. Hutchins came and administered morphine. After the doctor left, Mr. Stratton decided he'd be more comfortable in the parlor, where he could see out the large picture windows. Except the morphine was already taking effect, which left him in a groggy, half-sober state.

After getting Skye started on a copying assignment in her makeshift classroom, she and Allison got the man, one of them on either side, and helped him to the chaise lounge near the parlor window. He wasn't there five minutes before he was sound asleep.

That would have been fine, except he snored so loudly, it felt like the walls would cave in. Now she knew where Donnigan inherited his snoring patterns.

In fact, Mr. Stratton sawed logs at such an earsplitting level, he kept waking himself up, and every time he awoke, he wanted something.

"Bring me some water!"

"My blanket fell off!"

"My pillow slipped."

Emma went running every time the man called, but at least half the time, he was already asleep again by the time she arrived. The whole thing might have been comical if she hadn't needed to get ready for Allison's tea party on Tuesday.

She finally decided to address Allison about it directly. "Do you think he'll still be down and out tomorrow?"

"I don't know. This is terrible." Allison paced back and forth in the hall.

"How would you like me to proceed?"

"I suppose we'll have to cancel it."

"Why don't we postpone it? We can notify everyone that the meeting has been delayed until...Thursday? Do you think that's long enough?"

Allison nodded, then shook her head, then nodded again. "Make it Friday. But how will we notify everyone?"

"Tell Virginia at the General Store. She can get the word out as customers stop in," Emma suggested.

"But what if they don't all stop in?"

"I suppose Skye and I could go to each house, individually, and let them know."

"That would be ideal."

The bear awakened, startling them with a growl. "What are you two hens yammering about?"

Allison went to her father-in-law. "Sorry to disturb you. I was planning a tea party here for tomorrow, but we're postponing it so you'll have plenty of time to recover."

"Tea party? Why in the Sam Hill would you have a tea party?"

"It's for the Temperance Society," Allison told him.

He snorted. "Seems a little hypocritical to have a Temperance Society meeting here, don't you think?"

Allison started to respond, but Mr. Stratton interrupted her.

"Don't go getting your feathers in a ruffle. I'll be out of your way tomorrow. Is that Bridges girl coming?"

"Clara? Of course. She's one of our most active members," Allison told him.

"Good. Make sure Riley's around. We need to do what we can, and hurry things along. That boy's getting restless. He needs a wife to settle him down."

Emma took that as her cue to leave, and went back to the kitchen to check on Skye. The girl was almost finished with her lesson. She had neat, careful penmanship, and Emma commended her with a wide smile.

But the smile felt wooden and false. Riley and Clara. She tucked a loose hair behind Skye's ear even as she tucked her own hot emotions out of the way. Later, she'd likely rail at God for the unfairness of her life. Right now, she had work to do.

~

The crew worked and sweated and drove themselves to accomplish as much as possible that first day. First, they surveyed and cleared the land at the building site. They spent the remainder of the day framing and leveling the subfloor of what would end up being the largest hotel in Lampasas.

Riley worked right alongside them, enjoying the change in pace. Charlie Monroe did a fine job of supervising. About mid-morning, Riley wasn't ready to take a break, but he could see Charlie was. After a quick word with the foreman, he drove the older man in the work wagon back to his house and saw him settled in his chair.

"Come get me again at your lunch break. I just need a little nap," Charlie said.

"I'll do as you ask, sir, but if you don't mind my saying so, you'd best not overdo. Emma will never forgive me if you have a relapse of any kind. And trust me, I've seen her angry. I don't really care to face her wrath again any time soon."

Charlie laughed, but weariness framed his eyes and hung like a robe off his shoulders. "Just check back in. I'll stay put if I'm not feeling up to snuff, I promise."

"Yes, sir. Get some rest, and I'll see you in a couple of hours."

Back at the construction site, Riley caught the foreman as he took a water break. "You're sure we can rely on these fellows to keep quiet about this? Seems like a lot of folks to trust with a secret."

"I've known most of these men for several years now. The ones I haven't, some of the others vouched for. I made it clear that anyone who lets the bee out of the hive before the proper time might as well not show up to work the next day."

Riley looked around at the men working, observing each face for hints of the fellow's character. It was too late to do anything about any possible big mouths.

He picked up a hammer and some nails, ready to get back to work. This evening, he'd have to face Emma. But that wasn't his greatest concern.

He didn't want to have to explain himself to Dad one day earlier than he had to. He stood on train tracks, watching the train come at him, knowing of the coming collision. As much as Riley loved his father, he couldn't keep to the path Dad wanted him to follow. It would end their relationship, Riley was certain. But one of the verses Mom underlined in the Bible stood out to him, burned itself on his mind:

"Choose you this day whom ye will serve;...but as for me and my house, we will serve the LORD," Joshua 24:15.

Though he dreaded the consequences, Riley had already made his choice.

❧

The rest of the day was spent in a whirlwind of frosted teacakes and dainty, folded napkins and tobacco-scented complaints. By the time dinner was served—buffet-style in the kitchen, since the dining room was covered in party preparations and John Stratton was still laid up—Emma was more than ready to go home and put her feet up for a while.

She dropped Skye off, as had become their routine, and let Sugar take her home without much direction or urging from Emma. For the first time since early this morning, she let her thoughts wander back to that moment at the stream...that holy, reverent moment when everything seemed, for just an instant, peaceful.

That moment when she stood with Riley, and though they didn't touch at all, their hearts seemed to join in the awe of something special, something bigger than themselves.

The hazy essence of it covered her like a dream. Did it really happen? But yes, she knew it was real...a perfect, sweet moment when hope became fact. She would cherish it always.

But a strange sound greeted her, getting louder, the closer she got to home. Was that...hammering?

She clicked her tongue at Sugar, and the horse picked up pace. When she neared the house, she nudged Sugar off the path, toward the sound. Up, up, up the hill they went until a group of sweaty men came into view. And seated on his work wagon, watching, pointing orders to someone, was Pa.

And, was that Riley? It was. And there was Lyndel, right beside him, pounding a nail into a board.

What in the world?

Pulling Sugar to a halt beside Pa, she sat there, her mouth hanging open.

"Careful. You'll catch flies," Pa teased.

She closed her mouth, but looked at him sideways. Where to begin? "What is all this?"

"Come sit by me, and I'll tell you all about it."

She did as she was told, nearly tripping over her skirts as she climbed beside her father. At least this wasn't one of her new dresses. The first one hung in her room, ready for tomorrow's tea party.

"Several weeks ago, Riley came to me with an idea to build a fancy hotel and spa resort on our property," Pa said.

"A...what?"

"The mayor's done some research, and he feels the natural springs here in Lampasas can draw tourists. Since we've got the railroad coming, now is a perfect time to capitalize on the opportunity." He explained about the Saratoga Springs and the healing properties of the warm, sulfurous water.

"So...this is going to be a...a hotel?"

"That's the plan."

"Who will run it?"

"Riley, at first, along with whoever he hires."

"Who's paying for all this?"

"We're going in with Riley. We provide the land, he provides the funds and everything else needed to get started. We'll split the profit, fifty-fifty."

Emma shook her head, watching the men work, not a clue what to say.

Riley stopped what he was doing and looked at her. After a moment, he gave her a half-cocked grin and shrugged his shoulders, then went back to work.

"Why didn't you talk to me about this, Pa?"

"Because I knew you'd fret. I knew you'd think of every reason under the sun why this is a bad idea. And darlin', it's not your decision to make."

Only one word filled Emma's mind. One word with so many possible answers. "Why?"

Pa coughed, then leaned into the pillow he'd brought for his back. "Because I don't want you to have to work as a maid for the rest of your life."

"There's nothing wrong with being a maid. Ma was a maid."

"True. There's never any shame in good, honest work. But your ma had to work harder than I ever wanted her to, and I wish she hadn't had to. You know I can't farm this land anymore. But if I can do this, and set you and Lyndel up with a good, solid future, that will make me happier than you'll ever know."

Emma leaned toward her father and laid her head on his shoulder.

He lifted his crepe paper arm—once rippled with muscles, but now sagging with age—around her. Despite his weakened state, he sat taller than he had in months. "Your ma would have wanted this."

Emma smiled a watery smile. "Ma would have loved it."

"Then I can count on you for support?"

She reached her arm around his neck. "You can count on me for anything, Pa. I love you."

"I love you too."

There they sat, watching the men work until it was too dark to work. At long last, they loaded into the buggies and headed back toward town. All except Lyndel and Riley, who stood at the watering bucket laughing about something. All of a sudden, Riley dumped a cup of the water on Lyndel's head, sending the boy squealing and running. His laughter rang like a symphony through the fields.

Riley Stratton. He'd brought a lift to Pa's chin and joy to Lyndel's spirit. If he didn't stop being so...wonderful, so...present...she didn't know what she was going to do.

~

Riley wiped his sweat on his shirtsleeve and took a long swig of the cool water before responding to Emma's invitation to join them for dinner. "Not sure you want me at your table. I'm pretty disgusting right now."

"My father is a farmer. I've sat at the table with a sweaty man before."

"I suppose you have. I'd be honored to join you for dinner."

Emma nodded and turned back toward the house. "It'll be on the table in fifteen minutes. Come on in whenever you're ready," she called over her shoulder.

He was ready now. At least, he would be after he cleaned up a bit. In record time, he splashed his face and arms with some water and caught up with her. There were some advantages to having long legs. "So you're not angry with me?"

"Why would I be angry?"

"For setting all this up without your knowledge."

"I suppose I'd be more likely to be upset with my father...but even then, this isn't my land. I may have opinions, but it's up to Pa to make these kinds of decisions."

"So what is your opinion?"

"My opinion?"

"You said you had opinions, but this decision was up to your father. I'd like to hear your opinion about building a hotel and spa on your land."

"On my father's land." She turned to face him. "Honestly, I don't know. If I had been asked, I probably would have worried about Pa's health. This is a big undertaking, and I don't see how the stress of it can be good for him. But he seemed pretty content today, watching you all work. There was a spark in his eyes, like he had something to live for besides sitting in his chair and being waited on."

Riley nodded. "It's important for a man to feel useful."

"I suppose it is. And as long as it's what Pa wants, I'm behind it. I'm still a little baffled by the whole thing, though. I'd like to hear more about what makes the springs so special, to bring such a big tourist boom."

"I believe your father has some papers inside. After dinner, if you'd like, we can go over them, and you can ask me whatever you wish."

She smiled then and looked down at her hands, and a single dimple kissed her left cheek. Riley put his hands behind his back to keep from reaching for her.

Working this close to Emma Monroe wasn't going to be easy. What if she never saw him as more than her father's business partner?

She started toward the house again, and he loped along beside her, feeling like a puppy wanting his master's attention. And truly, he'd do just about anything to make her understand his feelings for her.

But first, he had to prove to her he wasn't like his father. Until then, he'd have to bide his time.

$\sim$

Emma commanded her heart to stop pounding so hard, so fast. But Riley Stratton was having dinner, right here in their home. She wasn't sure she could take much more, knowing his family wanted him and Clara to end up together, knowing he and Pa were now business partners. Looked like she'd be seeing a lot of him.

Best get her emotions under control.

"Would you like some more cornbread?" she asked, trying to still her shaking hands.

"I believe I would. No one makes cornbread like you do."

"I'm glad you like it. There's plenty."

He took another big hunk and passed the plate to Lyndel, who took more as well.

The way Lyndel looked at Riley and mimicked his every move, she thought her brother would volunteer to wrestle an alligator, if Riley did it first.

And then there was Pa, who talked to Riley as an equal, a partner. And he kept calling him "son." None of this did anything to help Emma's wayward feelings. *Oh, God, how am I supposed to do this? I really need your help. It would be easier if I could be angry with Riley about something...but he's done nothing wrong. He's a perfect gentleman. Can't you plant a wart on his nose or something, to make it easier for me not to love him?*

Oh, God. Did I just say that?

I love him. I do. And I know I can't have him. Help me learn to live with that.

All three men looked at her. She'd gotten so lost in her thoughts, she had no idea what they wanted. "I'm sorry, did you need something? My mind wandered for a minute."

They all laughed, and she laughed too, though she had no idea what the joke was. Finally, Pa said, "Riley asked if you were ready to become a lady of leisure."

"What? What do you mean?"

"If the hotel is successful, and Riley feels it will be, you'll be set for life."

"Set...for life?"

"Yes. You and Lyndel both. What will you do with your time?" Pa looked at her with his honey-rich eyes, love pouring out of them.

"I...guess I'll go to teacher college."

"I was hoping you'd say that. I know it's been a dream of yours," Riley said.

"Yes, it has been. I suppose I'll get my teaching certificate and go from there." Emma sighed. If only he knew there was a bigger dream in her heart. One that would most likely never be reality. She wanted, more than anything, to be Mrs. Riley Stratton.

CHAPTER 18

The next morning, Riley tried to leave early again. He dressed in the dark and crept down the stairs. He wanted to examine a couple more places on the Monroe property for possible future building sites before the crew showed up. But when he got to the door, Dad's voice startled him.

"Out early again, I see. Where you headed?"

"I...like to take Medina out for early morning rides. I enjoy the peace and quiet of this time of day." That was true.

"I don't blame you. You've been pretty scarce lately, though. You caught up on all the paperwork? Placed orders for feed? Checked the supplies?"

"Yes, sir." That was true, too.

"You bored, son? If you don't have enough to do around here, I can find more responsibility for you."

"No, sir. Not bored at all."

"I'm gonna ask you again, son. Where you spendin' all your time?"

Riley sent up a silent prayer for wisdom. He wasn't ready to tell his father about his plans to leave the ranch. Certainly wasn't ready to tell him he'd joined forces with Charlie Monroe. "Just...this and that."

Dad stared at him. *He knows something's up. Should I come clean? Get it over with?*

Dad cleared his throat, saving Riley from saying more. "Since you're not too *busy,* I want you to be around for Allison's tea party this afternoon."

"A tea party? Why?"

"You don't have to stay for the whole thing. But I'd like you to stick your head in and greet the ladies. It looks good to have a strong male presence in the house."

"I mean no disrespect, but I think my presence at a tea party might look anything but strong."

Dad snorted. "I can see why you might feel that way. But trust me. You give those ladies so much as a nod and a 'how do you do,' and you'll have them eating out of your hand. Can I count on you?"

Oh, good gravy. Really, Dad? Riley wanted to argue, but he'd better save his arguments for bigger battles to come. "All right. If it'll make you happy."

"It will. It would also make me happy if you'd escort Miss Bridges home after the tea."

Riley let out a breath. "Why?"

"She lives quite a ways from here. It's the gentlemanly thing to do."

Riley stiffened. "She doesn't live any farther than the other ladies who will attend."

"Be that as it may, I'd like you to escort Miss Bridges home." The steel in Dad's eyes let Riley know it wasn't a suggestion.

Still. "But I—"

"I don't want any arguments. Clara's a fine young lady. And you need to settle down. The sooner, the better."

Settle down? With Clara Bridges? This was going too far.

Had Dad really stooped so low as to try and arrange a marriage, just so he could bend the mayor's ear? Riley felt like a sacrificial lamb. Cold nausea oozed through his veins, and he felt sweat bead on his forehead. *God, you sacrificed your son. But not for selfish reasons.*

Sick as he felt, right now was no time to stand his ground. Not when he'd soon have higher ground to stand on. "All right." The words tasted like bile.

Dad nodded. "That's my boy."

~

*E*mma stood in front of her mirror, turning this way and that, trying to fuse the reflected image with the person she usually saw. Why, she looked every bit as...uptown?...as Clara. As Allison.

Never in her life had she worn such a lovely dress. Oh, she'd made gowns this pretty for other people. And her own dresses were always well made and serviceable. But this fabric...

It was the green silk plaid Mrs. Wesson had chosen for her. But oh, the hours it must have taken with all the detail work. Tiny folded pleats lined up perfectly, creating a fitted bodice that gently hugged her without being too tight. The full skirt was inset with panels of solid green, and each inset was topped with a puffed silken bow, and trimmed on either side with a delicate cream lace.

The same lace trimmed the neck and sleeves, and a green bow topped each shoulder. As if that weren't enough, there was a wide-brimmed hat, trimmed in a band of the same green plaid, along with a few simple white flowers.

Emma had always known Mrs. Wesson was a creative genius, but this! Emma could never have thought up such details. She knew Mrs. Wesson only used a general pattern, and added her own special touches to each dress she made. It was as if the woman had summoned all her artistic ability and poured it into the dress Emma now wore.

It was far too pretty to work in.

But Allison had told her to wear it. After all, Emma was now an *assistant,* not merely a maid. So far, her job hadn't changed at all, but today...oh, dear. Would Allison expect her to cook and serve and do dishes...in this dress?

The thought of it put such a frown on Emma's face, she finally decided to take the dress off. She'd carry it with her, and put it on before the party.

Yes. That's what she'd do. That way, if Allison truly wanted her to wear it, she could at least put it on at the last minute. She really did need to sit down with Allison and get a new job description.

She laid out the dress, then remembered the *other* garment Mrs. Wesson had sent along. Made of the same fabric—for Skye. The thought of Skye wearing this dress brought more joy to Emma's heart than her own gown did. She couldn't wait to fix her up like a doll. Wouldn't Skye be the belle of the ball today.

Emma had dawdled long enough. She changed into a simple day dress and replaced the new gown and hat in the box, and folded the tissue paper around it.

"What's all that?" Pa asked of the box when she set it on the table.

"It's...a dress. It's silly, really. I'll explain later."

"Hopefully you won't have to work for those people much longer. Do you have a minute?"

She really *didn't* have a minute. She was already late. But Pa so rarely asked anything of her besides the necessities, she hated to tell him no. "I always have time for you, Pa." She freshened his coffee and took the chair next to him at the table.

He blew on the hot liquid before taking a sip, then set the cup down. "Your ma once told me you were sweet on Riley Stratton. Years ago, when you were still in pigtails."

Emma grinned. She sure wished she could keep her face under control better. "That was a long time ago."

"She also told me that she discouraged you."

"Yes. At the time, I thought it was because the Strattons were so wealthy, and that we were in another class."

Pa gave a disgusted "Hmphhh." Took another sip of coffee. "If anything, she felt you were of a higher class. Not that she looked down on the Strattons, mind you. But she saw things that went on in that family...and she wanted to protect you."

"Now that I've been around them some, I can see why she felt that way."

"A few years before Mrs. Stratton died, she came to a new understanding of what it meant to be a Christian. She and your mother had been friends since they were girls, but while your ma had a close relationship with God, Mrs. Stratton only had a superficial knowledge of Him. By that time, Donnigan was already grown, and Colt was nearly out of school. They were both pretty set in their ways. But Riley...Riley and his mother were very close. And I think her influence on him, at the end of her life, might have had an impact on Riley's character."

Emma shifted in her chair. What was Pa getting at?

"From what I can see, Riley isn't like his father or brothers. I think he's a good egg."

"I...agree. I think Riley Stratton is a good man. But why are you telling me all this?"

"I think if you're still just a little bit sweet on Riley, it would be fine to act on those feelings."

Emma didn't know whether to laugh or cry. So she laughed. "Thank you for that, Pa. But Riley Stratton sees me as a friend. He's already set his eyes on Clara."

"Clara Bridges? Pshaw. She's a sweet girl, but a bit addle-brained and superficial for Riley. I can't see him falling for her."

"Pa! That's a terrible thing to say. Clara is my friend, and she's not addlebrained or superficial. She may be a bit...flighty at times, but she has a kind heart, and she's beautiful, and any man would be fortunate to have her as a wife."

"You're right. I'm sorry. I shouldn't have said those things about your friend. But you also have a kind heart. And you're also beautiful. And you're not flighty, by anyone's standards. Don't sell yourself short."

"You're sweet, Pa. Thank you for saying those things. I'm sure, when the time is right, I'll meet someone almost as wonderful and handsome as you, and I'll be very happy. I just don't think that someone is going to be Riley." Even as she said the words, she knew Riley had her heart in a way no one else could ever claim. She wouldn't be the first old maid, nor the last. For she was certain, if she couldn't marry Riley, she wouldn't marry.

Pa leaned back in his chair. "Fair enough. Just don't rule him out yet."

Emma kissed her father on the cheek. "Goodbye, Pa. I'll see you this evening." But his words stayed with her on her way to the Stratton home. What if Riley wasn't interested in Clara? What if he only spent time at her home because of this project? What if it was the mayor he spent his time with, not Clara?

For the first time in a long while, Emma felt hope.

~

*I*t was midmorning, and Riley wasn't near ready to leave the work site. But he had to, if he was going to buy more time. Best appease his father and go to that senseless tea party.

Clara Bridges? She was nice enough, but good gravy. He was

stuck between a rock and a hornet's nest. He'd have to pretend to court her, to please his father. For a little while, anyway. But he had no desire to lead Clara on, when his heart belonged to Emma.

That voice in his head, which was becoming more familiar every day, told him he needed to come clean with his father. Let the pieces land where they would. The longer he waited to confront Dad with the truth of his plans to leave the ranch, the bigger the explosion, when it came. *God, help us all.*

Dad and Colt would be out until late this evening, checking on a few business deals. Riley'd make an appearance at the tea party, or Allison would be a living nightmare. He'd play the game. But first thing tomorrow morning, he would sit his father down and have a long talk with him.

Best make sure Medina's shoes were in good shape for running...fast. Riley tried to make light of the situation, but there was no humor to be found. He loved his father, and he was about to break their relationship beyond repair. The only thing he could do was take the next step, and then the next. Right now, the next step was a stupid tea party.

Thankfully, he was able to sneak in the front door and upstairs without anyone noticing. He heard Allison and Emma in the parlor, talking about where to place the silverware tray or some other such nonsense. In record time, he stripped off his sweaty clothes, cleaned up, shaved and combed his hair, and dressed in clean, professional attire by the time he heard guests arrive.

No need to go downstairs yet. Give the hens time to cluck and chatter. He propped himself on his bed and took his Bible, the one his mother had given him, and continued reading in James chapter five, where he'd left off. *The effectual fervent prayer of a righteous man availeth much.*

He'd certainly been doing a lot more praying lately. But he wasn't sure he could be classified as a righteous man. Hopefully, someday he might be. What was that verse he read a couple of days ago? He flipped the pages back until he found his mother's familiar script next to a verse in chapter one.

"If any of you lacks wisdom, let him ask of God, that giveth to all men liberally, and upbraideth not; and it shall be given him."

Well, he'd certainly asked God for wisdom. And truly, he felt his present course of action was the right one. It sure would be easier if God would just put some big signs at every path, pointing the way.

After a time, he set aside the Bible and headed downstairs. Surely they'd had enough time to do whatever it was women did at these things. He'd best make his appearance before they all started home.

He stopped in the doorway and knocked on the doorjamb. "Hello, ladies. Sorry to disturb. I just thought I'd stop in and tell you all how glad we are to have you in our home today."

Much as he expected, the ladies cooed and crowed over him, offering him tea and cake, and asking him to join them. Several of the married ladies moved aside to make room for him near Clara. What was this, a conspiracy?

He'd just settled himself on one end of the sofa, with a cup of tea that was far too small for his hands, when Emma entered, carrying a tray, followed by Skye, who carried a small basket of mints. Only, this wasn't the Emma he was accustomed to seeing.

She wore a green plaid dress and matching hat that made her eyes stand out even more. Her golden waves were pinned up like one of those poster girls in the drug store. Her smile wavered only a moment when she saw Riley, then she greeted him and asked if she could get him anything.

He spilled his tea in his lap, causing the hens to cluck even more. Emma handed him extra napkins. Their fingers brushed, and a jolt flew up his arm. Did she feel it too?

He couldn't take his eyes off her. She was far and above the most beautiful woman he'd seen in his life.

And Skye wore a solid green dress that matched the green in Emma's dress, with a sash made of the same plaid fabric. The women in the room barely gave Skye or Emma notice, as if they didn't exist. Funny how Skye was perfectly acceptable to everyone present, in a *servant* role. He thought back to the cool reception when he took her to church. Could no one but him see the hypocrisy?

He smiled at Skye's attempts to walk and do exactly as Emma did. On the surface, they looked as different as could be —Skye with her dark hair and olive skin, Emma with her blonde hair and fair skin. But the looks they shared with each other showed a bond that went far deeper than being part of the same family. Why, there was more love between those two than he'd seen in a lifetime in this house.

Not that his family didn't love each other. Memories flooded Riley's mind. The rug under his feet covered countless divots made when Donnigan, Colt, and Riley play-wrestled, Dad cheering them on, Mom fussing at them to behave. Donnigan always beat Colt, but he'd always let Riley win.

There were the fishing trips every spring, the hunting trips in the fall. And there was the time Dad stood in front of a bull to protect his three sons. The Stratton men loved each other, but Mom was somehow the gravity that pulled them all together. Things hadn't been the same since she left.

His mind focused on Emma again—at her beauty, her grace, her class—and it struck him—she was destined to be a grand lady. She wasn't meant to spend her days in the background, dusting furniture, changing sheets, and cooking delicious meals —although she did those things beautifully and without complaint.

No, she was a queen with a servant's heart, which was the very best kind of queen. God had much, much greater plans for her. And He was letting Riley play a part in bringing her into a bigger purpose than she could imagine for herself. Riley wished, more than anything, she could be a part of *this* family, *this* home. She could change things with her light, her warmth, her love. But even as he thought it, he knew it would never be.

For a moment, the high-pitched chatter around him faded, and the only person he was aware of was Emma, though she paid him little mind. He watched her adding tea to the other ladies' cups. Watched her take their empty plates and place them on a tray. Watched her smile and nod and compliment this one and that one on her dress or her jewelry, or ask about a child or grandchild.

He jumped when he realized Clara was speaking to him.

"She is pretty wonderful, isn't she?" Clara said.

He jerked his gaze to her. "Oh, uh...who?"

Clara's words were kind, but annoyance clouded her tone. "You know who. The person you've been staring at for the last two minutes. Wipe your mouth. I think you're slobbering."

"I...uh."

Clara looked at her hands. "When do you plan to tell her how you feel?"

"I..."

She rolled her eyes. "Sometimes you men can be such dolts. But don't worry. Women can be clueless as well. I'm not sure Emma has any idea how you feel. So you'd better tell her."

Heat flooded Riley's face. Was he that obvious? He'd never meant to hurt Clara. How could he so offend a woman he'd never had feelings for in the first place? "Miss Bridges, I—"

"You what, Mr. Stratton?" Clara looked hurt. Confused. Resigned. "You don't owe me an explanation."

Why did he feel like the lowest sort of dog, in the rain, without a kennel? "If you'll excuse me, I must be going."

He stood, told the ladies again what a pleasure it was to have them as guests in his home, and departed. He tried to ignore the confused look Emma gave him, along with the speared look Allison sent—probably for leaving too soon. He had several important conversations to prepare for over the next couple of days. And the way his thoughts were swirling, he needed to retreat to his office for a while and write them down.

He needed to figure out how to best win Emma's heart.

And he needed to figure out how to best break his father's.

CHAPTER 19

Instead of returning to the Monroe's, Riley decided to take Medina for a ride around his own property. He did his best thinking—and lately, his best praying—on Medina's back. He didn't even bother to change out of his nice clothes.

About an hour into the ride, he didn't feel any closer to having answers, but he felt that peace he'd come to know as God's presence. And he felt a calm assurance that everything would be all right.

What he still didn't know, however, was if *all right* meant his father would accept his decision to leave the ranch, or if Riley would be all right despite his father's anger and rejection.

He also didn't know if *all right* meant Emma would eventually return his love, or if Riley would move on without her by his side.

He repeated a prayer in his mind—a single sentence. *God, I don't know what You're doing, but I know You're good, and I trust You.*

Faith, the best he could figure it, was a conscious choice. A choice to believe that no matter what, God would see him through the worst of times. No matter what, God would bring him to a good place. That's where he was now. No clue as to how the next few days might play out, but he knew at some point, God would bring him to a soft landing spot. Wasn't it kind of like the Israelites? They wandered forty years in the dessert, but they eventually ended up in the Promised Land.

He was just about to turn back toward the house when he heard voices up ahead, and decided to investigate. It was Donnigan and Joe, working together to replace an old fence with barbed wire. Donnigan looked sober, like his old self. Maybe soon, he'd find his way back from whatever dark dwelling place he'd been in.

"Well, if it isn't Uncle Riley," Donnigan said, sarcasm marring his normally pleasant features.

"Donnigan. Joe." Riley nodded to the men, but refrained from commenting on Donnigan's attitude.

"You come to check up on me?" Donnigan asked.

"Nope." What was his problem?

Donnigan snorted.

Riley decided to ignore his brother's rudeness. He probably had a hangover. He looked at Joe. "Glad to see the barbed wire I ordered came in. I've heard good reviews on it."

Joe nodded and started to speak, but Donnigan interrupted. "We're *so grateful* for your help, sir."

"Look, Donnigan. I don't know what I've done to upset you. Why don't you just come out with it?"

"You took Skye to *church*."

"Yeah. So?"

"I don't want her paraded around for everyone to point and whisper about the *little Injun girl*. She's worth more than that."

"She's also worth more than having a drunk for a father." As soon as the words were out, Riley wanted to take them back, but it was too late.

"Maybe so, but I'm what she's got. She's my daughter, you hear me? Mine. Not yours. Not your little friend's."

"No one wants to take her from you. But you've gotta get it

together."

Donnigan cursed and looked like he would have thrown a punch if Riley hadn't still been in the saddle.

"Look, Joe, I'll help you finish this tomorrow. I'm leaving." Donnigan threw down his tools and set off on foot in the direction of the cabin. After a few yards, he about faced. "Skye is not going to become some traveling side-show freak. You understand me?"

Vulnerability broke through the anger on Donnigan's face. He was scared. But at least he was out here working. Trying. He'd lost his wife. Riley never met her, but Donnigan must have loved her. Why hadn't Riley offered more comfort? Why hadn't any of them?

And Donnigan loved his daughter. Despite his dependence on alcohol, he wanted to protect her.

Riley watched his brother for a moment. "I understand."

Donnigan nodded, then turned around and continued toward the cabin.

Riley heaved a sigh, climbed down, and hooked Medina's reins around a low branch. He looked at Joe. "Sorry about that. I'll help you finish up here."

Joe handed Riley a pair of pliers and an extra set of gloves. "It won't take long to string these last couple of wires."

The two men worked in silence for several minutes. While holding the wire tight, Riley thought about whether or not he should broach another uncomfortable subject with Joe. Might as well. Couldn't get much more awkward than a family fight.

"Joe, I was wondering..." Riley wasn't sure how to phrase his question. There really wasn't a graceful way to ask. He decided to just dive in, head first. "Are you and Emma...I mean...are you courting her?"

Joe's head whipped up so fast his hat flew off. "What?"

"I...see you two talking sometimes. You're a single fellow, and she's a beautiful woman, and..."

Joe laughed a long, low chuckle.

"What's so funny?"

"I'm sorry, Mr. Stratton. It's just...sometimes folks can be dense."

"I don't know what you mean."

Joe chuckled some more, squatted back in position, and proceeded with the wiring. "The answer is no. Miss Monroe and I are not courting."

"So...if some other fellow decided to call on her, you wouldn't take offense?"

"I don't see where it would be any business of mine. But no, I wouldn't take offense. Miss Monroe is a nice lady. She deserves to find happiness. I just hope she finds someone worthy of her."

Riley was so relieved, he wanted to whoop and holler. Not that Joe's opinion mattered that much to him. But at least he knew Emma's heart wasn't committed elsewhere. Still, he wasn't sure what to make of Joe's last statement. He wasn't sure anyone, anywhere could ever be worthy of a woman like Emma Monroe.

~

The day had started out like something out of a fairy tale, at least to Emma's way of thinking. First, she got to dress like a princess. The ladies of The Temperance Society, most of whom Emma had known her entire life, treated her...differently.

Oh, they'd always been *nice* to Emma. But today, seeing her in that dress, they seemed to *see* her more. *Listen* to her more. And though she was still a servant, she was treated more like an equal.

Or maybe they didn't treat her differently. Maybe she just felt different. It was amazing what a new dress could do to one's attitude.

But then, Riley showed up. Sat right next to Clara. For several minutes, they whispered to each other in intimate tones. Emma tried to ignore them. Tried to act every inch the ladies' maid, or companion, or whatever it was Allison wanted her to be in the moment. But try as she may, every ounce of energy was tuned in to Riley and Clara, like her heart had antennae honed in to that very spot in the room.

After a while, Riley left. A few minutes after that, Clara left. Were they meeting each other? Some kind of lovers' rendezvous? It was all Emma could do to keep her composure. She smiled at Skye, whispered to the girl that she did a fabulous job. But her mind, her heart, were with Riley. She'd thought maybe when he saw her in this dress...but no. She could never compete with Clara. She was foolish to hope.

~

*R*iley couldn't stop whistling. He whistled all the way back to the house, where he changed back into his work clothes. He whistled as he went into the kitchen, hoping for a bit of leftover cake from the party, and hoping even more Emma was there to give it to him.

She was. Changed back into a normal dress, and her practicality made her all the more attractive to him.

"Got any more of that cake?" he asked.

"Mr. Stratton, I thought it was understood that this is my domain while I'm working." Her tone was cool. What had he done now?

Women.

"I'm sorry. I—"

"It's fine. Have a seat." She cut him an extra large piece of cake, along with a tall glass of milk. "Where is Clara?"

"Clara?"

"Yes. I saw her leave shortly after you did. I thought the two of you were together."

"Me and Clara?" Even Emma wanted them together? *Et tu, Bruté?* "Why does everyone keep putting me with Clara?"

She whipped her neck around. "Aren't you courting her?"

He looked at her, held her eyes. Tried to say the thousand words in his heart with that look. "No."

She met his gaze, like she had a thousand words of her own she wanted to say. Then she even gave him that smile that made the moon look like an afterthought. And, she sat right down at the table with him and asked if he'd enjoyed his ride. Which meant she'd noticed he went on a ride.

"It was very pleasant, as a matter of fact." Except for the exchange with Donnigan.

"That's nice. Medina seems like a good horse." She blushed, tinting her cheeks a lovely shade of pink.

This was turning out to be a very good day, indeed. He lowered his voice and leaned toward her. "I'm headed back to your place. Maybe I'll see you this evening?"

"I...hope so." She smiled again and looked down at her hands. Such pretty hands.

He waited for her to look at him again, and he winked at her —a move he'd seen some of the other fellows do at university, but one he'd never been bold enough to try himself.

She turned red as an overripe plum, grinned, and looked away.

Yep. Today was one of the best days he could remember. He pushed his chair back, placed his dishes in the sink, bid her good day, and began his whistling again, which he couldn't cork all the way to the Monroes' house.

He was amazed at the progress they'd made in the few hours he'd been gone. All four walls were now framed, and two of the beams were in place for the roof.

But progress that afternoon was slow, taking longer to haul the heavy beams up to the roof level. And since they weren't framing the roof on the ground like they did the walls, they had to be more careful. The last thing they needed was for someone to get hurt.

By the time the foreman called it a day, Riley was covered in sweat like the rest of them. Which made it all the sweeter when he saw Emma, waiting on her porch with a big smile and eyes that...what? He couldn't quite describe the change in her eyes, but it sure felt a lot like love.

"Good evening, Miss Monroe."

"Good evening, Mr. Stratton. Would you like to join us for dinner again?"

He wanted to say yes. Wanted to say yes more than anything. But he really needed to get home and have that talk with his father. No sense putting things off any longer. The building was framed.

But there was Emma, looking prettier than a field of flowers in the morning dew. And he was hungry. "I'd love to, if it's not too much trouble."

He'd talk to Dad when he got home.

And first thing tomorrow, he'd ask Charlie Monroe for permission to court his daughter.

～

*E*mma held Riley's gaze, waiting for an answer, and she couldn't help but wonder if there was a secret message in those deep pools of honey-gold. She hoped there was. *Oh please God. Let this be happening.* Could Riley really be interested in her?

He agreed to stay for dinner. "I'll see you at the house, then." Emma left him with a smile, but resisted the urge to look over her shoulder. For a few yards, anyway, when she gave in to temptation and looked back. He watched her, with that crazy look on his face. She blushed down to her toes and turned toward her destination, but she couldn't coax away the delight in her step, or the flushed feeling in her cheeks.

She thought about that wink he gave her back in the kitchen. Scandalous. But she couldn't stop grinning about it. Did that make her a scandalous woman?

Maybe. But for the moment, it sure was fun.

Since that wink, Emma's thoughts hadn't strayed far from the tall, broad-shouldered man with the amber-brown eyes and the cleft chin. At the house, she scrambled to make a meal fit for the man of her dreams, as quick as possible. Fortunately, they had squash. Lots of it. She made quick work of a squash-and-onion casserole, fried potatoes, fluffy buttermilk biscuits, and some smoked venison she'd been saving for a special occasion.

They ate quickly. Pa was tired, and bid them good night, and Lyndel went out to catch fireflies. She hoped Riley would stay a while, maybe sit on the porch and talk. But instead, he helped her clear the table and announced he had business at home.

"I see. Well...have a good evening." Emma fought to keep the disappointment from her voice.

"Dinner was delicious, as always."

"I'm glad you enjoyed it."

He stood there a minute, like he wanted to say more, shifting back and forth from one boot to the other and clearing his throat. But then he put his hat on his head, told her good night, and walked out the door. Just like that. It was all very odd.

She stood at the door until he got to Medina, not knowing if she should follow him onto the porch or not.

But then, before he stepped into the stirrup, he turned back around, and flashed that wide smile of his with those heart-crushing dimples. "You have sweet dreams, Miss Emma Monroe. I know I will."

And then he turned, climbed into the saddle, and rode into the sun-soaked horizon.

CHAPTER 20

Like a changing of the guard, the sun and moon had just shifted places in the sky when Riley got home. Dad wouldn't be asleep yet, and hopefully he was in a good mood. Not that it mattered. He'd surely be in a foul mood before all was said and done.

Still, Riley felt like he was on the brink of freedom, and that made his heart soar. Maybe Dad would understand. Be supportive.

Probably not.

Who was he fooling? *Definitely* not. In a moment, Riley's good mood fled, and his gut twisted and knotted like a noose trying to choke the life out of him. This would not go well. But he had to do it. It was time.

Dad was in his study smoking a cigar, just as Riley knew he would be. But he wasn't alone. Sitting across from him was Donnigan, bleary-eyed and smelling of liquor.

When Riley's shadow fell across the doorway, both men looked at him. Dad with accusation, Donnigan with an unread-able expression. Shame? Sorrow?

"Riley. Come in here, boy. Donnigan was just telling me he

heard some interesting news about you in town this evening." Dad took another puff of his cigar.

Riley looked at his brother. "Really? What kind of news?"

Donnigan leaned his elbows on his knees and looked at his feet a minute before meeting Riley's eyes. "I was sittin' there at the saloon, mindin' my own business, when a group of young men started a game of cards. One of 'em had a little too much to drink, and started talkin' real loud. He had some pretty interesting things to say."

The work crew. Blood turned to ice in Riley's veins, and he couldn't breathe. Dad wouldn't take this news well under the best of circumstances. If he'd found out through some drunk worker... Riley's mind couldn't even process the ramifications. He dropped into the chair next to Donnigan. "Keep talking."

Dad took over the conversation. "Is it true, Riley? You've gone into the hotel business with Charlie Monroe?"

Riley sat in silence for a moment that reached into eternity. He had no idea how to answer his father, other than the truth. "Yes, sir. It is."

Another long, still moment dragged before him. The heaviness in the room felt like it would crush his heart...the same heart that had felt so light less than ten minutes ago.

At last, Dad looked at Donnigan. "Leave us."

Without a word, Donnigan stood, gave Riley an *I'm sorry* look, and left Riley alone with his father, closing the door behind him.

"Why?" Dad's words were stone cold to match his eyes.

Riley squirmed under the glowering inspection. "Remember when Mayor Bridges came to dinner a few weeks ago? He talked about making Lampasas a tourist town. I became interested, and one thing led to another, and—"

"I don't care about that. Why would you join forces with Charlie Monroe, of all people? After all that man's done to us.

You're gonna help him make money off of land that should be ours?"

"What has he done? What has he ever done to you, or anyone in this family? He bought his land, fair and square, and you've let a grudge grow into a mountain of hate that's consumed you for decades. We have more money and more land than anyone in this county, yet you can't let go of the fact that you didn't get something you wanted. You didn't win, and that's eaten you up inside." Riley couldn't believe the words coming out of his mouth. Yet once they started spilling, he couldn't force them back into his thoughts where they belonged.

The skin around Dad's mouth went white, and his whole body shook. He didn't say anything, and Riley feared he'd have a heart attack. But after another slaughtering silence, Dad looked at the pipe in his hands. "Get out," he muttered.

Riley stood. Looked at his father. Watched his eyes move past anger into cold, hard hate. It was the same expression he'd held every time he mentioned Charlie Monroe, only this look, this hatred, somehow went deeper. "Dad..."

Dad didn't move. His eyes grew in rage, past hatred to seething to something akin to murder. "You are not my son."

"Let me explain—."

"I said get out. I never want to see your sorry face again." Dad's voice was tight and strained, as if one more ounce of pressure would bring the snap.

Riley swallowed back the crack that split his heart, the sob that pushed up his throat. He wanted to say something. Wanted to fix this. *Not your son? Don't say that. Dad.* "I'll need time to pack. I'll be out before sunup." He turned, left the room, and headed upstairs.

After a couple of hours, Riley went to bed certain he'd get no sleep at all. But the added manual labor of the last couple of days must have taken their toll, for when he awoke to someone pounding on his door, he couldn't remember where he was, and it took him a moment to orient himself enough to get up and open the door.

It was Colt. "What's going on?" he asked.

Riley held open the door, wiped the sleep from his eyes, and stumbled back to the bed. "What do you mean, what's going on?"

"Allison just woke me up, all in a tither, saying there's been some big argument. She said I have to stop them. She's not making any sense, and I need you to tell me what's going on."

As if on cue, Allison showed up in the doorway. "I heard them. They're making plans, and you have to stop them."

"What are you talking about, Allison?"

She took several deep breaths, her hand to her chest. "Davis woke up. He's teething. I went downstairs to find a biscuit. The study door was cracked open, and, and I heard them."

"Who?" Riley tried to make sense of her words.

"Your father and Donnigan. They said something about you and Charlie Monroe. It didn't make sense. Your father—he said he'd burn something to the ground. I hid behind the stairs when your father stormed out. Donnigan tried to stop him, told him to wait. Then they both left. Something terrible is going to happen. You have to do something!"

Burn something to the ground? *The hotel.* Riley yanked his dungarees off the hook and pulled them on, slammed his feet into his boots, and grabbed a shirt, which he buttoned— crookedly—on his way down the stairs. He didn't even bother saddling Medina, just jumped on bareback and rode her hard and fast all the way to the Monroe's place.

～

*E*mma awoke to the sensation that something wasn't right. Everything was quiet...dark...what was happening?

What was that smell?

Her eyes burned. Was that smoke?

In a flash, she went from groggy to wide-awake. Something was burning. She threw on her dressing gown and slippers and rushed into the hall, opening doors. Pa was fine, sleeping in his bed. Lyndel—the same. The kitchen and parlor looked normal, except for that haze. She darted to the front window, and there, at the building project, was an orange glow.

"Pa!" she yelled, running back down the hall. "Pa, there's a fire! I think it's the hotel."

Pa sat up in bed, then nearly tripped on his way to the front window. She steadied him on one side, and suddenly Lyndel was there too, holding his other arm. They all three looked through the picture window at the sickly glow lighting up the night sky.

Despite his weakened state, Pa took charge. "Lyndel, saddle Sugar and ride into town. Get the sheriff and tell him there's a fire. Ring the emergency bell if you have to. Bring as many men as you can back with you."

"Yes sir."

"Emma, start gathering buckets, pots, pans, anything you can find to haul water. Put them in my wagon. I'll hitch the horses."

The three of them sprang into action. But by the time Emma and Pa topped the rise and the hotel site came into view, they knew all was lost. The flames were out of control.

Still, Emma couldn't sit there and watch. Maybe she could stop the fire from spreading onto the grass around the structure. She grabbed two buckets, ran to the nearby spring and filled them, then rushed to the side of the building and tossed the liquid into the grass beside the flame. A blanket of smoke tried to smother her. The heat seemed to evaporate the liquid before it even landed. As Emma turned to refill the buckets, she heard something... Something human.

Dear God! Please, let me be wrong. Please, God. She gathered her skirts and circled the perimeter of the fire, trying to get a better view. Smoke clawed at her throat, stung her eyes. *There.*

She spotted two figures in the flames. One was lying on his back, the other crouched over him. "Get out!" she yelled, but it looked like the kneeling man was trying to drag the other one to safety. Should she go in?

Another sound drew her attention—horses' hooves. Thank God help had arrived. As the riders approached the flames, the flickering light revealed their identities—it was Colt and Riley.

"There are two men in there!" Emma yelled above the roar. Her throat raw from smoke, she could barely choke the words out.

Colt grabbed a couple of blankets from under his horse's saddle and soaked them in the springs. He gave Riley one, and the two covered themselves before running into the blaze.

God, no! Please don't let them die. Please don't let Riley die.

A loud crack sounded, and a high beam crashed somewhere inside the flames. Emma fell to her knees, sobbing, screaming a silent prayer, for her voice was no more, another victim of the lapping inferno.

Seconds before the structure collapsed on itself, Colt and Riley emerged, each one dragging a body. Emma lunged at Riley, hugging him, sobbing, then helped soothe the groaning man who now laid a safe distance from the roaring beast.

It was Donnigan. Groaning and uttering words Emma couldn't make out. Nearby, Colt knelt over the other figure, weeping like she'd never seen a grown man weep. The other man was dead.

The other man was John Stratton.

≈

*R*iley watched all his dreams collapse in the flames. With it, a part of his soul collapsed, as well. He felt empty. Hollow. Like this wasn't really happening, and any moment he'd wake up in his bed and everything would be fine.

But heat and smoke and reality slapped him, confirming he was wide awake. He cradled his brother's head in his hands, trying desperately to understand the words he spoke.

"I'm sorry," Donnigan whispered. "Please"—he gasped for air—"forgive me."

"You're forgiven. Just don't die." Riley spoke the words around the blade of terror that reached up through his gut, into his voice.

"I didn't mean to. I tried to stop...him."

"It's all right."

"He got caught—something fell on me."

"It's going to be all right. Just hang in there."

"Please...take care of Skye. Tell her I love her."

"Tell her yourself." A sob rose up in Riley's throat.

His words were too late. Donnigan's head went limp in Riley's hands. He felt the life leave his brother, and in that instant, Riley relived every sweet moment they'd shared.

Stick ball in the yard.

Hunting trips.

Fishing—Donnigan had taught him to bait a hook.

He couldn't be gone. *God! Where are you?*

Something in Riley shifted, and he moved into a haze that had nothing to do with the smoke. He laid his brother on the grass and went to Colt. Was Dad okay? Colt knelt over him, letting out a gut-yanking cry, and Riley collapsed next to him.

Oh, God. This is my fault. I thought I was doing what You wanted me to.

Riley wanted to vomit.

To scream. To beat the sky. Instead, he sat there, limp. A puppet with no strings.

No soul. No life.

Something inside him died, along with Dad and Donnigan. Two of the most important men in his life.

Guilt. Shame. Rage.

Men came, though where they came from, he didn't know. They were men from town, but he didn't look at the faces. He just watched the flames that took his father and brother.

Flames he had caused.

Deaths he had caused.

He looked up and there was Emma, standing over him, her face contorted, tears streaking ash-black cheeks. She tried to speak to him, but no sound came. After a moment, she leaned near him, and he could barely make out her words.

"Where's Skye?"

He shrugged his shoulders. Where was Skye?

She lifted her skirts and ran away.

He couldn't think. Couldn't breathe. Was his heart even beating? He wasn't sure.

~

With every strike of Sugar's hooves on the ground, Emma's heart pounded a terrified rhythm. Her mind chanted one word with every beat—a prayer.

Skye.

It was as if Sugar knew, as if the animal felt the same ache to see the child for herself, to make sure she was all right. Sugar flew through the dark, nothing more than moonlight as a guide, and didn't even slow down at the Stratton's home. She just kept right on going until they reached the little clearing in the woods that led to the cabin.

Emma jumped off the horse and ran to the door. "Skye!" she

called, forcing sound where a short time before, no sound would come. "Skye, are you here?"

She opened the door, calling for the child, her voice raspy and weak, her throat singed and dry. "It's me, Emma. Are you here?"

The dim light of a kerosene lantern lit up one corner. Skye sat up from her pallet and rubbed her eyes. "Emma?"

Emma rushed to the girl and held her, working hard to contain her emotion lest she frighten the child.

"What are you doing here?" Skye asked. "Where's my pa?"

Oh, dear God. Thank you. She's all right. What do I tell her? What do I say to her? It wasn't her place to reveal the news about her father's death. *Give me words, Lord.*

"Your...your father is at my house. So is your Uncle Riley. I'm here to take you to them."

"At your house?"

"Well, near my house. Come now. Would you like to stay the night with me again? Get Rilene. And maybe a dress for tomorrow."

Skye squealed in excitement, and Emma's heart nearly crumbled. Soon, the two were headed back through the moonlight, slower this time, toward home. Emma's home. And if she had anything to say about it, Skye's home from now on. Not that she had any right to the child. But she would certainly offer to take her. Care for her. Love her with a mother's love for as long as Emma had breath.

~

Men moved all around Riley, shouting orders, filling buckets with water and dousing the flames. He was vaguely aware of Dr. Hutchins' voice, had a hazy recollection of the doc shaking his head over Donnigan and Dad, pronouncing them both dead. Vaguely aware of Sheriff

Burnett asking him questions. He answered, but he honestly couldn't remember what he said. He thought he'd relayed his last conversation with Donnigan.

This was my fault.

Someone sat on the ground beside him, put a big hand on his back. Held a cup of water in front of his face. Riley shook his head no, but then he heard Charlie Monroe's voice. "Drink it, son. You've taken in a lot of smoke."

Riley took the cup, more because he didn't have the energy to argue than any other reason. He gulped it and tossed the cup on the ground.

"I'm sorry, son. Truly, I am."

How could Charlie Monroe be sorry for the deaths of two men who'd just vandalized his property? Yet Riley knew the man was sincere.

"This is my fault. I should have never gotten you involved…"

"Now, son, this is no more your fault than it is Emma's, or Lyndel's, or anybody else here for that matter. You didn't set this fire."

"I went against my father's wishes. I did something I knew would make him angry." He covered his face with his hands, tried to push back the tears, but they wouldn't stop coming.

Charlie reached his arm around Riley's shoulder and pulled him close. "Hush. It's gonna be all right."

Riley wanted to believe him. But right now, he wasn't sure anything would ever be all right again.

Somewhere behind him, Riley heard a man's sobs and knew it was Colt. Riley pushed to his knees and crawled over to his one remaining blood relative and wrapped his arms around his brother's shoulders. Together, without caring a whit about what anybody around them thought, the two brothers sobbed like a couple of babies.

How long they stayed that way, Riley couldn't judge. But

after a time, Reverend Jones was there, praying with them, asking if they needed anything.

Sheriff Burnett approached. "Can I talk with you both in private?"

The preacher left them.

"Best I can tell, your father got his foot stuck in a gap in the sub floor. The injuries to his ankle and scrapes on his boot match a broken spot in the floor. It seems like Donnigan tried to pull him out, and a beam fell on them both. It probably killed your father instantly. Do you have any idea why they may have been here, or what they were doing?"

Why were they here? What were they doing?

Colt answered for him. "Probably out for a moonlight ride. They did that sometimes. Saw the flames, and tried to put out the fire."

What? Dad and Donnigan didn't go for moonlight rides. That was a lie. But in that moment, Riley couldn't find the words, or the energy, to contradict his brother.

Some men lifted Dad and Donnigan and put them in the back of a wagon.

"Wait!" Colt called. "I'm going with them."

There was Emma, standing off to one side. Skye leaned against her, pale as a field of new cotton.

"Colt, wait," Riley called. "I'm coming too. Give me a minute."

He forced himself to stand, to walk on wooden legs to where Emma and Skye stood. He knelt down to the child's level, looked directly into her eyes. But for the life of him, he didn't know what to say to her. What could he say? *It's my fault your father's dead? It's my fault you're an orphan now?*

"Uncle Riley?" she stated his name like a question, as if she wanted him to fill in the answer to all this chaos. But he couldn't. He didn't have an answer that would make it all right.

"Is my pa dead?" Her voice seemed so tiny.

His lip quivered. Somehow, he had to answer her question. She deserved that much. "Yes, Sweetheart. He is."

She didn't move. Nothing about her expression changed. But big, fat tears rolled down her cheeks and dropped to the ground in front of her. He held out his finger and caught one of the tears, wishing with all that was in him he could put it back, put them all back, reverse this day and make her world better again.

Donnigan...he'd loved his daughter. Was turning a corner. *Why?*

Riley hugged his niece tight. "You stay here with Emma, all right? She'll take good care of you. I'll be here in the morning."

Skye nodded, and Emma placed her hands on Skye's shoulders.

Riley couldn't bring himself to look Emma in the eye. He kissed Skye on the cheek, stood, and walked away.

He didn't know if he'd be able to look Emma Monroe in the eye, ever again.

$\mathcal{E}$mma was at a loss for how to comfort Skye. If only she'd sob. Or scream. Or ask questions. But other than a few silent tears, Skye simply withdrew into herself. She held her doll close. She crawled in bed when Emma told her to. And she closed her eyes as if nothing were strange or odd, as if she hadn't just become an orphan in the full sense.

But Emma didn't want to push the child. Everyone grieved differently, Emma of all people knew that to be true. So she snuggled the girl close through the night. She let her sleep late, and made sure there was plenty of batter to make her hot griddlecakes as soon as she woke up.

The house was still quiet, for both Pa and Lyndel slept far past the sun. After last night's events, she probably should have stayed in bed too. But she couldn't sleep.

And she'd heard Riley say he'd be here in the morning. If he didn't come soon, it would be afternoon.

Her eyes stung. Her throat felt like it had been yanked through a thousand razor blades. But her heart...her heart was drowning. There was too much sorrow in this world.

So she did the only thing she could think of. She sat in Pa's chair, Ma's fabric box pulled close to her feet, and cut out a pattern for a new dress for Skye, and a matching one for Rilene. As if a new dress could make everything better.

Of course it wouldn't, but she needed to keep her hands busy.

She tried to pray, but her mind was so muddled she couldn't form coherent thoughts. So she just kept thinking, over and over, *God, help. Please...help.*

Hoof beats sounded outside, which must be Riley. Yet she was so weary, her body wouldn't respond when she told herself to get up and open the door.

He knocked. Then he opened the door. She knew he would.

"Come in," she croaked.

After removing his hat, he stepped inside and looked around...looked at everything in the room except at her. He looked twenty years older than he had just yesterday. "Where is everyone?" His voice was scratchy. Heavens. He must have inhaled more smoke than she did.

She lay aside the dress and went for the tea kettle. "They're all still asleep. Sit down. Let me fix you some tea with lemon and honey. That should soothe your throat some."

"Don't bother. I can't stay long. Lots of plans to make. Gotta meet with the preacher. Funeral's set for Friday. Can I see Skye?" He still hadn't looked at her.

"Certainly. Follow me." She led him down the hall to her room and opened the door. Skye lay on her side, staring at the wall.

Riley sat on the end of the bed and placed his hand where Skye's foot lay beneath the quilt. "Good morning."

She didn't respond.

"I've got to run into town to see to some things for your daddy's funeral. Would you like to come?"

Still no response.

"All right then. I'm gonna leave you here with Emma. I know

she'll take good care of you. I'll be back to check on you this afternoon."

Skye sat up then, pushed back the covers, and crawled right into Riley's lap. Rested her head against his chest. Put her arms around his neck.

Emma was afraid, from the expression on his face, that this might be his undoing. She felt like an interloper, leaning against the doorframe, watching a private family moment. As quietly as she could, she turned and padded back down the hall toward the kitchen. Now seemed like a good time to start those griddlecakes.

She was going to ask if he wanted some, but he didn't give her a chance. She heard his heavy footsteps coming up the hallway. Instead of stopping, he walked right through the dining room and out the door, without even saying goodbye.

~

*I*t all felt surreal, sitting here in the empty church house, talking to Reverend Jones about what time the funeral would start and whether or not they wanted organ music. As if that made a difference.

Riley stretched his legs under the pew in front of him and let Colt do most of the talking. Somehow Colt seemed the right person to take charge. He was the eldest surviving Stratton.

And after all, none of this was Colt's fault.

"Do you have any special stories you'd like me to mention about your father and brother?" the reverend asked.

"Actually, I do." Colt reached in his pocket and pulled out a folded up piece of paper. "I sat up most of the night, writing a speech for you to give. This should make things easy for you."

The minister took the paper and studied it. Frowned. Loosened his collar, like he couldn't get enough air. "I...uh...thank you, Mr. Stratton. I'll do my best to include as much of this as possible in my sermon on Friday."

Colt sat up, leaned forward. "I didn't ask you to include it. This is what I want you to say, word for word."

Had Colt lost his mind? He couldn't dictate what the preacher said, even at a family funeral. "May I see that?" Riley reached for the paper.

Scanning the page, he could see why it made the man uncomfortable. These were all lies. "Colt, Dad and Donnigan weren't trying to save the building from burning. They started the fire."

"Shut your mouth, Riley." The fire in Colt's eyes surpassed the hottest blaze from last night. He looked back at Reverend Jones. "Word for word."

Riley read more. "Colt, Dad didn't give half his money to the poor. He didn't give any of his money to the poor, as far as I know. Any money we gave to charity stopped when Ma died."

"I said shut your mouth." Colt stood up, leaned over the reverend and pointed his finger right in the man's face. "You'll do it, or I won't rest until you're fired."

Riley stood up and faced his brother. "You can't do that."

Colt turned, his face inches from Riley's. "Watch me." Then he stormed out of the building.

Riley watched him go. "I apologize, Reverend. The grief of it all...it must be too much for him. Say what you will at the funeral. I know you'll do a fine job."

Then Riley went after his brother, though he had no idea what he'd say once he caught him. Riding Medina full speed, chasing the cloud of dust in front of him, he caught up with Colt and cut him off in the road.

"What was all that about?" Riley asked. "You can't force the preacher to spout a bunch of lies."

"People will believe what we tell them to believe." The look on Colt's face stung. He was all the family Riley had left.

But he couldn't stand by and let Colt lie to everyone. Not about this. "You told the sheriff Dad and Donnigan always went riding at night. That's garbage."

"It's just you and me. Our reputation in this town is everything. Dad and Donnigan are dead, and we have to live with the mess they left behind."

"Colt. I won't lie."

"They'll blame us."

"They'll blame *me*."

Colt cursed. "They *should* blame you! This is *your fault*. Now do as I say, and let me fix this."

"I won't lie."

"I heard him in the study last night. I saw Donnigan leave, and I stood outside the door. He *disowned* you. That means *I'm* in charge. So shut your mouth and *do what I say!*"

He and Colt eyed each other in the road, just outside of town, like some legendary standoff in a gunfight. Only there were no guns. That might have been easier for Riley to handle.

When it was clear neither of them had anything else to say, Riley clicked to Medina and rode in the opposite direction. Where he was going, he didn't know. At the moment, he didn't feel like he had any place in the world he could call home.

～

*E*mma felt like she was living the day underwater. Everything seemed blurry as she pushed through her tasks in slow motion, and breathing didn't feel natural.

"Do you think you should check in at the Stratton's place?" Pa asked.

"Probably so...I just don't know if my presence will be welcomed or not."

Pa took a few moments to answer. "Maybe you should just go about business as usual, until you're told differently."

"I suppose you're right. And I really should return to the cabin and get some more of Skye's things." She looked out the window. Skye sat on the top porch step, holding Rilene. Lyndel sat next to her, not saying a word. The sight nearly brought tears again to Emma's worn-out eyes. Would the sorrow never end? Could they not just have a normal, happy existence?

She thought about Job at the end of his life. He went through such terrible trials...but God blessed him in his later years. *Please, God. Can you bless us too? I don't know how much more I can take.*

With weary feet and a wearier heart, Emma climbed on Sugar with a promise to Skye that she'd be back soon. No telling what kind of attitude she'd be greeted with at the Stratton home, and she didn't want to subject Skye to any more heartache.

She arrived without fanfare and entered the kitchen to find the house dark and quiet. Everything looked the same here...yet everything had changed.

Might as well get to it. She rolled up her sleeves and began washing last night's supper dishes...dishes that held John Stratton's last meal.

Chicken fried steak, mashed potatoes, and green beans. Peach cobbler for dessert.

"What are you doing here?" Colt Stratton's icy voice was edged with steel.

"I...didn't know. I thought you might...need me to—"

"My family will never need anything from you, ever again. You're not welcome in this home."

"I'm sorry." She placed the dishrag on the counter and turned toward the door. "I...have your niece. What would you like me to do with her? She's welcome to stay with me indefinitely."

"She's not my niece. As far as I'm concerned, she's an orphan."

"Colt." Allison's voice called from somewhere behind him.

"Be quiet, Allison. We're not taking that half-breed." Colt looked at Emma, his eyes piercing her with dagger-like hatred. "Do whatever you want with her."

"I'd like permission to retrieve a few of her things from the cabin, if that's all right with you."

Allison stepped beside her husband. "Yes, Emma. Get whatever she needs."

With a nod, Emma left them, letting the screen door bang shut behind her. Sugar waited in the barn, though she'd left her tethered to a rail. Joe sat on an upturned bucket in a corner of the building.

"Leaving so soon?" There was little energy in his voice.

"Yes. I doubt I'll be back."

"I was afraid of that."

"What about you, Joe? What will you do?"

"I suppose I'll stay on. For a while, anyway. Until Colt asks me to leave, or I get word of a better position somewhere."

How was it that less than twenty-four hours ago, Emma felt lighter than air? Now she carried a hundred boulders on her shoulders. "Joe...whatever happens...I'm glad our paths crossed. I hope God gives you everything you want in life."

He stood, rubbed Sugar behind the ears. "You too, Miss Monroe. You too."

He offered his hand, helped her into the saddle, and tipped his hat.

Soon she was on her way to the cabin, though everything in her wanted to go home. She could make Skye new dresses. Could provide everything the child needed.

Actually, she couldn't. She didn't have a job any more. How in the world would she feed Pa and Lyndel, much less Skye?

Nothing she could do about her job now. But it might be a comfort for Skye to have something of her father's, and some of her own clothes to wear.

Too soon, she came upon the familiar clearing. Now that she was here, she wished she'd brought the wagon. As it was, she'd only be able to take what she could carry, and she didn't know what she'd find that Skye might want. Judging from Colt's words, after today, she or Skye might not ever be allowed to return.

She pushed open the door. Someone moved inside. Her heart jumped into her throat as she let out a raspy scream.

Gracious and mercy. It was Riley. "What are you doing here?" she asked.

"I suppose I should ask you the same thing."

"I'm gathering Skye's things. Allison told me I could."

Riley nodded and stepped aside. "I've packed some of her things already. I was going to bring them by later today."

Emma nodded. "I'll just take some of her clothes then, and you can bring whatever else you want her to have later."

Riley dropped onto a chair, leaned forward, and rested his head in his palms. He looked like he'd lost his whole world.

And he had.

More than anything, she wanted to go to him. To wrap her arms around him and comfort him. But after Colt's reaction to her, she didn't know. Did Riley feel the same way as his brother?

"I'm so very sorry, Riley. I can't even imagine what you're feeling right now. Is there anything I can do?"

"You're already doing more than you should."

She knelt in front of him, her hand hanging in the air just above his shoulder, not knowing if her touch would be appropriate…or wanted. "Riley, you know no one blames you for any of this."

He sat up. Instead of warm honey, his eyes held bitter gall. "I really don't want to talk about this right now. Could you just get what you want and leave?"

Emma drew her hand back. "Oh. Yes."

What was happening? Where was the Riley who possessed

her heart? And who was this horrid man sitting in his body? She scrambled here and there, looking in drawers and on shelves, finding the essentials, trying not to cry. There was Skye's new dress. She could wear that to the funeral.

After one last look around, she walked to the door. Her better judgment told her to leave without saying anything. But her compassion got the better of her. She couldn't leave Riley here without at least trying, one more time, to reach out. "Why don't you come with me? Eat dinner with us."

He chuckled, an eerie, harsh sound. Then he looked at her with snake eyes. "Nah." He just sat in that chair, elbows on his knees. He dropped his head back into his hands, his tight fingers causing his normally-perfect hair to stand in every direction.

What could she say to that? Her heart pounded in her ears, breaking through the awkward, angry silence in the room. "Skye needs you. It's two o'clock. I'll expect you for dinner."

She closed the door behind her. But she prayed all the way home that Riley hadn't closed the door to the rest of his life.

CHAPTER 22

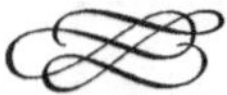

For the next few days, Riley kept to himself. He slept in the cabin, and other than the alcohol, he lived much like Donnigan had. Didn't shave. Didn't bathe.

He did stop by to check on Skye, but he didn't stay for dinner, despite Emma's insistence.

He refused to pray. Refused to open Donnigan's dusty Bible that sat on the shelf above the fireplace. Why would he? He clearly was not in God's good graces.

But that cabin was so quiet. Too quiet to drown out the voice in his mind that sounded like God. Every time he heard that voice, he'd ignore it. Push it away. Tell it to stop. Was he going a little crazy? A lot crazy?

When Riley was a little boy, he'd follow Donnigan around everywhere. He'd talk and talk and talk while Donnigan ignored him. Told him to be quiet. To leave him alone.

How annoying he must've been as a kid, That's how God was, right now. No matter how much Riley tried to snub the Lord, no matter how much he tried to pretend he didn't hear, God just kept talking and talking and talking. He wouldn't leave Riley alone.

In the silence of the day, the Almighty whispered His love. In the still of night, He soothed Riley's spirit, much like a mother might soothe a crying child.

Now, as Riley turned his pillow to the dry side, he heard a voice, clear as any audible voice he'd ever heard. *I love you. I have good plans for your life. Trust me.*

At that, Riley sat up in bed and spoke out loud. "How am I supposed to trust you, God? How? I thought I was doing what *You* wanted me to, and You killed Dad. You killed Donnigan. You took Skye's only living parent. You burned down the hotel! How am I supposed to trust You?" He spat the words, half expecting, half hoping to be struck by lightning. Or worse.

Then there was that voice again, silent yet clear. "I didn't kill them. I didn't burn anything down. Trust me."

Riley knew the voice spoke truth. God didn't do this.

His father had a mind of his own. This entire tragedy was the result of John Stratton's stubborn will. Dad caused his own death, and Donnigan's too.

That realization both relieved Riley's broken heart, and broke it even more.

~

*T*oday was the funeral. Today, Riley needed to clean up, if for no other reason than to honor Dad's and Donnigan's memories. He needed to go up to the house and get some fresh clothes. Bathe. Shave.

Colt was in the study when he entered the house. The door was open. He looked up when Riley passed by, but didn't say anything. Riley would have kept walking, even if he had.

The bath felt better than Riley wanted to admit. He laid his head back against the porcelain and let the water soak into his sweat-and-smoke-stained skin, washing away the last tangible remnants of Dad and Donnigan.

Riley would get dressed. Go to the funeral. Do what he had to do.

Tomorrow, he'd talk to Charlie Monroe. If that man was willing to give Riley another chance, they'd begin again. And he'd see about starting the paperwork to adopt Skye.

After that...well, he didn't really know what would happen after that. Had he truly been disinherited? Surely Dad hadn't had time to draw up any official paperwork. If so, maybe he'd have some money to begin again. If not, well...he supposed he'd let God lead him, one day at a time.

But he couldn't help but hope that Emma might have a place, somewhere in his future.

~

Skye clung to Emma's arm as she looked at her father's remains in the casket. Emma had questioned the wisdom of letting the child see her father this way. But Emma's own father had felt it was important for Skye to say goodbye.

"Is he with my mother now?"

Emma didn't know the right way to answer that question. She couldn't speak of Donnigan's salvation, or where he would spend eternity. And she didn't want to say anything that would cause the girl further distress.

"I'd like to think they're together, and they're happy." Which was the truth. She would like to think that. "What is your favorite memory of your parents?"

Skye brushed away tears with the back of her hand. "When I was little, he was different. Before my mother died, he would sing to us. I'd sit on Ma's lap, and Pa would sing silly songs and we'd laugh."

"That sounds like a happy memory."

Someone stepped up beside them. Riley. "Did he sing the bug song?"

Skye giggled, even through her tears. "Yes."

"He used to sing that when we were kids. He had the best bug voices."

Emma smiled. She had no idea what the bug song was, but Riley's voice, his interest in Skye, felt like a warm blanket around her heart.

The church was filling up. "Are you ready to sit down?" Emma asked Skye.

She nodded.

Emma wasn't sure if she should take Skye to the second pew —the pew normally occupied by families at a funeral—or if they should sit further back. She didn't want to cause a scene.

But Riley's hand on her back led her, directed her to the family pew. She tried to step aside and let Skye in. Emma would sit with her father. But Riley leaned close. "You're part of this family, as was your mother. At least in my mind, you are. Skye's too, and she needs you right now. Please sit with us."

Emma nodded. What would people think?

Who cares what they think?

She scooted in and took a seat, leaving a respectable gap between her and Allison. She didn't even look at Colt. Skye leaned against her other side, with Riley to Skye's left.

Organ music signaled the start of the service.

~

The two cedar boxes at the front of the church changed everything. Riley wasn't sure how to go on, how to exist in a world without his father in it...but an unexplainable peace enveloped him like a warm west wind.

The peace that surpasses understanding.

Riley tried to listen to the preacher's words. As far as he could tell, the man did a nice job of offering both comfort and wisdom in a difficult time. He didn't read Colt's speech, however. Riley couldn't help but wonder how Colt would react.

At the end of the service, Reverend Jones led them down the center aisle and outside the church so they could be first in the long line of wagons that would follow them to the cemetery. Riley could tell Colt was about to pop like a spring too tightly wound. His fists were clenched, his face was white, and his eyes held a hint of insanity, fueled by anger and pride. Riley was quite familiar with that look. It was as if Dad had taken residence in Colt's skin.

When he saw Colt speed up his steps toward Reverend Jones, Riley sped up too.

"I told you, preacher, to read the speech I wrote or you'd be out of a job. You'd better start packin' your bags." Colt's voice was low and eerily calm. That wasn't a good sign at all.

"Look, Mr. Stratton," Reverend Jones spoke in a soothing tone that Riley knew Colt would consider patronizing. "I—"

"Colt, we'll deal with this later. Let's just get through today, all right?" Riley positioned himself between the reverend and his brother.

Thankfully, Colt didn't say anything else. But Riley knew the fuse was getting closer to the cannonball. Sooner or later, it would go off.

At the cemetery, Riley couldn't even focus on his own grief. All he could think of was keeping Colt's pending explosion at bay, and keeping the shrapnel to a minimum. He was vaguely aware of Skye and Emma.

When the caskets were dropped into the ground and covered over, when the people dispersed and headed back to their house, with cakes and pies and fried chicken, when there was no one left standing at the fresh heaps of sorrow but the preacher, Colt, Allison and Davis, and Riley, the fuse ran out.

Colt lunged at Reverend Jones, knocking him to the ground,

laying a punch on the man like they were in a barroom brawl instead of a holy place.

Allison screamed and Davis cried.

Riley pulled Colt off the startled man. "Get hold of yourself! What are you thinking?" He held his brother back, putting his own body between Colt and the preacher.

Colt turned to Riley, his eyes wild and scared and full of rage that comes with a broken heart. "What am I thinking? What are *you* thinking, Riley? I don't even know you anymore. Sneaking around, doing business with the enemy?"

"Charlie Monroe was never our enemy. He's just a farmer who got some land Dad wanted. He didn't steal it. It just happened. Dad just couldn't let things go."

"Look, little brother. Make up your mind. Are you a Stratton, or not? Because we Strattons protect our own. Dead or alive, we need to protect Dad's reputation. Donnigan's too. It wouldn't have hurt anybody for that preacher to say a few kind words, to lift them up in people's memories."

"He said plenty of kind things, Colt. He just didn't lie."

"All I wanted him to do was state that Dad and Donnigan didn't cause the fire. Shut up people's rumors and gossip. Was that too much to ask? I'm telling you. Choose, Riley. Choose to be a Stratton, or walk away from the ranch and all we own and don't look back. Dad left me in charge in his will. You know I'll make a place for you, but you've gotta stand with me. Take some pride in the family name. If you can't do that, then I don't consider you my brother."

That last sentence hung between them like a guillotine blade, waiting to fall.

Movement at the far corner of the cemetery caught his eye. It was Emma. Skye's head was buried in Emma's waist, and Emma's arms were around the child. He'd thought they left already.

He looked back at Colt. Could he walk away from his brother...his only living relative? His roommate and partner in mischief? His best friend for his entire childhood? Could he walk away, knowing Dad would have condemned him for it?

In that moment, he knew the answer, though it seemed to rip out half his heart. The answer was yes.

Yes he could. He didn't want to. But if he had to make a choice between the Stratton legacy or God's, he'd choose God's.

~

Never in her life had Emma wanted to shield another person from pain as much as she wanted to shield Riley from the scene playing out before her.

In that moment, she saw clearly the reasons for her mother's hesitation, her discouragement, when she suspected Emma's feelings for Riley. She was protecting Emma with a mother's love, the way Emma now wanted to protect Skye.

But somewhere along the way, Emma had lost her heart to this man, and right now, all she could think about was how in the world she could make life better for him. How she could soothe his hurts and show him a different kind of love than he'd known before.

But she couldn't. For what he needed, more than a woman's love, was God's love.

Please, God. Let him find peace. Let him find love. I'll be all right if he doesn't choose me. Just let him choose You.

Riley backed away from his brother. He held out a hand to the reverend and helped him stand up. Then he dusted off his hands, turned, and walked straight to where Emma stood with Skye, near her own mother's grave, only a few months old.

"Are you ladies ready to go?" he asked, his voice quivering and tight.

Emma nodded. Skye nodded.

He led them to where Sugar was hitched to the wagon and

helped them climb aboard, then retrieved Medina. "Where are your father and Lyndel?"

"Back at our house. Pa couldn't make it to the cemetery. I'm sorry."

"Don't be. Do you mind if we go there? I really don't feel like going to my house right now."

"Certainly. I mean, no. I don't mind at all." She didn't plan to take Skye to the Stratton's home anyway. What a mess.

They rode away from the little graveyard, so many thoughts swirling through Emma's mind. She turned one last time and looked at Colt, Allison, and little Davis. At least Colt had his wife and child to stand with him. Riley had no one.

Well, he had her, but she wasn't sure that counted. She wasn't his wife.

At home, neither Pa nor Lyndel questioned Riley's presence. Just accepted him as if he belonged there, had every right to be there. As if there were no other logical place for him to go after the events of the last few days. Just as they'd accepted Skye. Which was so beautifully odd.

Yet she felt, somehow, that their peculiar little group made up the most perfect of families. At least, as perfect as any human family could be. They loved each other in all their wild, broken mess...just as God loved each of them, and accepted them into His family without question.

Riley didn't say much the rest of the day. He ate a little bit. Sat on the porch and drank coffee, which Emma kept filled. When the sun dipped low in the sky, he stood as if he'd go, but Pa stopped him.

"Stay the night, son."

"I couldn't."

"Sure you could," said Lyndel. "You can have my bed. I like to camp out in front of the fireplace sometimes, anyway."

Emma could have kissed her little brother right then and

there. Would have, too, if the act wouldn't disgust him to no end.

Riley looked like he'd protest. His eyes shone with unshed tears, and he looked so, so weary. After a moment, he gave one simple nod, and stayed where he was in the porch rocker.

Satisfied, Pa bid them good night.

Lyndel went inside to find some extra blankets and pillows, and Skye followed him like a puppy with a new toy.

Emma turned too, wanting to give Riley plenty of space to process all that had happened in the last few days.

"I'd like to rebuild the hotel." His voice stopped her midstride.

She turned back to face him. "I'm sure Pa would be happy to talk to you about that."

"I...I plan to adopt Skye. Donnigan asked me to take care of her, just before he died."

Emma wasn't sure how she felt about that. But she knew he would love the girl. And as much as Emma wanted to raise Skye herself, she knew the law would side with a blood relative. Not that she'd fight him on it. She nodded an ascent.

"She'll need a mother."

What was he saying?

"I don't know how I'll support a family. I'm not sure what the future holds for me right now. But I was wondering if—"

"You're exhausted, Riley. Why don't you get some rest before trying to figure out the rest of your life?" Emma couldn't listen to more. Was he going to propose? Simply because he wanted a mother for Skye? Could she live with a man, just to provide a stable home for a child?

Maybe. She did love Riley.

But she wanted him to love her back. Did he want a marriage of convenience? The thought burned a crack straight through her spirit.

Could she live with him, knowing he didn't really love her?

She wasn't sure.

"I'll make sure Lyndel's room is ready for you." She left him —and the shattered fragments of her heart—on the porch. Long before the hurricane of tears passed and she fell asleep, she made her decision. If he asked her to marry him, her answer would be no.

~

$\mathcal{R}$iley woke well before dawn. He'd tossed and tumbled in Lyndel's too-small bed. He shouldn't have stayed, but where else would he go? He didn't want to be alone, and yet, he was alone. He had no mother or father. The only home he'd ever known was occupied by a brother who'd made it clear Riley was no longer welcome there.

But it was his home, and today he would go and get his things. Some of them, anyway. The important things. He'd slept in his clothes, so he rose and straightened the bed, grabbed his boots, and crept down the hall. A low lantern burned on a small desk. He grabbed a pencil and some paper and scratched a note, then left it on the table.

Soon he and Medina were on the way home...that word didn't sound right any more. On their way to the house in which he'd grown up. But it was the place that held most of his memories and a few cherished items. He'd gather those things and try to find a small place to rent in town, big enough for him and Skye. Could he rent something on credit? He still had enough in his savings to get through a few weeks. He hoped.

He'd really bungled things last night. What must Emma think of him? He could see the discomfort, the disappointment in her eyes when he'd started to ask. She didn't want to say yes. But she didn't want to say no to a man who'd just buried two of his family members.

Great. He'd managed to take a bad situation and make it worse. He had a gift.

But there was that voice again, that urging in his spirit. *Try again.*

The house was dark and quiet. Riley crept into his office to get the papers he needed. He had no desire to take anything of Colt's, but he did have another paycheck coming. Despite his work on the hotel and spa, Riley had managed to keep up with all his business duties at the ranch. Bills were paid. Supplies were ordered.

The ranch, Colt could have. But if Riley was going to start a new life somewhere, he needed funds. Most of the inheritance Mom left him had gone up in flames. There was a little left in that account, but was it enough?

In his bedroom, he packed a suitcase with most of his clothes, his Bible, and a few toiletries. Besides his personal effects, he couldn't think of anything else he needed.

When he turned to leave, Allison stood in the doorway.

"What are you doing, Riley?" Her voice was a combination of weariness and suspicion.

"Don't worry. I'm not taking anything I don't have a right to. I'll be out of your hair soon enough."

Her expression softened. "You'll take care of the child?"

"I plan to."

The ticking of the old grandfather clock provided a heavy background for their uneasy silence. Just when he thought Allison would leave him to his business, she said, "Come with me."

He was too tired to question her. She led him into the room that had belonged to his parents. It felt cavernous in its emptiness, though it was still exactly the way his father had left it. Riley could even smell tobacco, and with the scent came a vision of Dad smoking his pipe on the front porch. Colt and Donnigan playing marbles at his feet. Mom sewing yet *another* patch on Riley's play clothes. Riley watching Dad, wanting to be tall and strong like him. He pushed back a fresh wave of tears and cleared his throat.

Allison lit the lantern, and the dim light revealed her red eyes, her splotchy cheeks. "Take what you want. You should have something of your parents'."

He didn't want anything of his parents'. He wanted *them*. But they were gone.

He looked around the room. Dad's pipe sat on the bedside table. He'd had others, so surely Colt wouldn't mind if Riley took this one. He slipped it into his pocket and turned back to the door.

"Wait. Perhaps you'd like something of your mother's, as well." Allison stood at the dresser, at Ma's jewelry box.

He walked up beside her, looked in the box, and retrieved a dainty oval necklace with a carved marble pendant. It had a lady's face on it. A cameo, he thought it was called. He remembered his mother wearing that. Skye might like to have it one day. He was about to close the lid when his mother's ring caught his eye. It had once belonged to his grandmother. Small diamonds surrounded a sapphire center, and the white gold band was carved with tiny hearts.

Ask her again.

The dainty ring looked out of place in his mammoth hand. He placed it on his pinky finger, and it didn't even fit to the first joint. In the mirror, he caught Allison looking at him, and their eyes locked for a moment.

She nodded a single, acquiescent nod. "Take it. You should have it." She pulled a thick envelope from her pocket. "And take this, too."

Riley opened the envelope to find money. A lot of it, though he didn't take time to count it. "Where did you—?"

"I didn't know your mother well. But after Colt and I married, your father shared with me that she'd always had her own allowance, to do with as she pleased. As you can see, she saved quite a bit. John told me I could have that money, since I was now the lady of the house. But I never felt right about spending it. I figured I'd know when, or how—" Her voice cracked. "I feel certain that under the circumstances, she'd want you to have it." Then she left him.

He stood there, looking at the spot she'd just occupied, not able to move or even breathe. After a million tick-ticks of the clock, he looked again at the money. Why, there was enough for...for...

There was enough.

Not for everything, but enough for a start. Enough for collateral. Enough to secure a loan.

He found it odd that, as he rode away from that place, he didn't feel as much sad as he felt free. He had chosen his heritage. It was a heritage that reached back for centuries, and would reach forward to his children and grandchildren and beyond.

It felt good.

He needed to make one more stop before he shut the door on this life. The cabin had a few more things Skye might want someday. But it also held something very important for her future. It didn't take long to pack the remainder of the child's clothes, the doll bed, and a few trinkets. But the most important thing he tucked into his bag was a thick envelope he'd discovered in the desk drawer, which quite possibly held the key to Skye's freedom and independence. To her future.

~

*E*mma was up and dressed early, and she fixed breakfast as quietly as possible. Lyndel was asleep on the floor by the hearth, and she assumed Riley still slept soundly, as well. But when the smell of steamy bacon, fried eggs, and biscuits brought Skye and Pa from their rooms, Lyndel went to check on their guest.

Riley was gone.

He probably regretted his near proposal to her last night, and now he didn't want to face her. Which was fine with Emma. She really didn't want to face him, either. If she could, she'd stay in her room all day and give her tears free rein. Instead, she moved woodenly through her tasks and tried not to think about more than the next minute, the next chore.

Lyndel finished off the last of the bacon. Could they buy more? Mrs. Wesson's niece now worked in Emma's old position. How would they live?

Someone knocked on the door, and she moved to answer it.

It was Riley, hat in hand. He shifted back and forth on his boots. Emma invited him in, but she didn't make eye contact. She couldn't. She'd cry if she did.

"Uh...I was hoping to talk with your father in private, if you don't mind."

Emma stepped aside as Pa pushed his chair back. He shuffled from the table to the front door. "Certainly, son. Step into my office." He led Riley back onto the porch—his "office" for as long as she could remember.

What could he want with Pa?

Probably something about the fire. She and Skye made quick work of the breakfast dishes while Lyndel went out back to care for the animals. When the kitchen was clean, Emma headed to her room. She and Skye could work on sewing, and she might not have to see Riley again. She knew she was taking the coward's way by ducking and hiding, but she couldn't help herself.

She had just pulled the little girl onto her lap in the old rocking chair next to the window when Pa knocked, then cracked the door open. "Emma, Riley would like to see you."

Oh dear.

Oh, God. I do love him. But I can't marry a man who doesn't really love me. I'm so afraid I'll look at him, and my resolve will fail, and I'll agree to marry him anyway. But I just can't...is it too much to ask for him to love me?

Help me say no, God.

When she walked onto the porch, Riley sat with his head in his hands, like he'd done at the cabin. She took a deep breath and exhaled, louder than she'd intended, and shut the door behind her.

He stood. "Please, sit down."

She eased down in the chair beside where he'd been sitting.

He began pacing. Poor man was miserable. She might as well go ahead and tell him she didn't hold him to any false obligations. She was about to do that when he spoke.

"Emma, I...I need you to forgive me."

"Forgive you?"

"Yes. Last night...I shouldn't have—"

"It's all right. You were distraught." She held up her hand to wave off the entire incident, but her gut felt like a stained garment, being pressed through the wringer for the fourth time. She knew he didn't love her, but to have him say it out loud was almost more than she could bear.

"No, it's not all right. I..." He knelt in front of her, and took both her hands in his. She settled her gaze into his brown eyes, and the intensity there stole her breath. "Emma, I don't recall when I fell in love with you. Looking back, it seems like it's always been there. I just didn't know it. But before all this happened—before the fire, before the funeral—I'd realized something. I love you, and I want to spend the rest of my life with you. It has nothing to do with Skye, nothing to do with anything except that I adore you. I want us to grow old together. I promise, if you'll do me the honor of becoming my wife, I'll love you more every day I have breath." He reached in his pocket. "Emma, will you marry me?"

As he spoke, she felt the wringer move from her gut to her tear ducts, and suddenly her face was soaked, and she turned into a blubbery mess.

He loved her. He really loved her! Everything was a blur, but she tried very hard to swallow back the emotion and focus on the man in front of her. She wanted to remember every detail of this moment.

When she focused again, he held a ring between his thumb and forefinger. A ring?

It was a beautiful ring, but even more beautiful was the man holding it. She nodded, but had a hard time finding her voice. Finally, in a sob she said, "Yes. Yes, Riley. I'll marry you."

She threw her arms around his shoulders and sobbed some more, soaking his shirt and neck.

He wrapped his sturdy arms around her. "Uhm...I wasn't expecting you to cry."

She laughed then, and so did he. And then, in perhaps the sweetest moment of her life, he kissed her. It was a tender, watery, salty, tear-soaked kiss.

It lasted but a moment, and then he pulled away from her and wiped her tears. "You've just made me the happiest man in the world."

"And I plan to keep on making you happy, every day for the rest of your life."

He kissed her again, only this time, the kiss lingered, both soft and strong, gentle and exciting, filling every part of her with fireworks. He deepened the kiss. She leaned into him, taking in his husky sweetness until—

Someone tapped the glass on the window behind them, and Emma jerked back as the blush sank clear to her toes.

Riley pulled her to her feet, and she placed her hand in the crook of his elbow. It was time to go inside.

They had an announcement to make.

EPILOGUE

SEPTEMBER, 1883

A brilliant blue sky shone down on the green, manicured lawn of The Big Skye Hotel and Spa. Emma sat on the shaded porch, a cool pitcher of lemonade next to her, watching Skye and Lyndel laugh over a game of croquet. To her left, Pa sat with his feet elevated, a blanket over his lap, listening to Riley give the financial report. Bills were paid. Profits were high.

For this beautiful, sun-kissed moment, everything seemed right with the world. She leaned her head back, closed her eyes, and reminded herself of all that had transpired in the past year and a half. Reminded herself of all God had brought them through, and of how far they'd come.

The hotel was flourishing.

Thanks to the fact that Donnigan had never spent his own inheritance from his mother, but had tucked it in an envelope and saved it, Skye had her own inheritance, to use as she pleased someday. She'd never have to worry over money the way Emma had just a short time ago.

Emma had even gotten her teacher's license through correspondence. She'd probably never use it now, but Riley had insisted she follow her dreams. If only he understood...she was living her dream right now.

She opened her eyes again and rested her hands on her growing belly. Come February, a baby would join their little family. Two years from the time Ma left them. She would've been so proud.

Emma still missed Ma something fierce, but she could think of her without the deep ache now. She could remember her and smile. She knew this was what Ma wanted for her.

To know peace.

To know joy.

To know the deep heritage of love Ma and Pa lived all those years.

Her gaze landed on Riley, and she realized he'd been looking at her. They shared an intimate smile that spoke an entire conversation in one glance.

And she thanked God for the great inheritance He'd left to her, full of every good thing she could imagine.

Emma's Squash Casserole

~

2 pounds squash
1 & 1/2 cups milk
2 eggs
Salt & pepper to taste
3 tablespoons butter
3 cups grated cheese
1 cup chopped onion

Preheat oven to 350 degrees. Boil squash until tender; drain. Mix all together except one cup of cheese. (Use potato masher to mix.) Pour in pan; bake until firm, about one hour. Sprinkle remaining cheese on top. Put back into oven until cheese melts.

Did you enjoy this book? We hope so!
Would you take a quick minute to leave a review where you purchased the book?
It doesn't have to be long. Just a sentence or two telling what you liked about the story!

Receive a FREE ebook and get updates when new Wild Heart books release: https://wildheartbooks.org/newsletter

ABOUT THE AUTHOR

This is the place where **Renae Brumbaugh Green** is supposed to provide impressive things for you to read. But since the most impressive thing about her is the fact that she almost won a car in one of those little fast-food scratch-off games one time, years ago, but she didn't actually scratch off the car until she found the card in her desk drawer, long after the deadline had passed, there's not much to say.

But if you really want to know about her writing stuff—she's the author of many books, made the ECPA Bestseller list twice, and has contributed to many more books. She's written hundreds of articles for national publications and has won awards for her humor.

She's married to a real hunk, and she's a mom to some amazing kids. She writes music, sings, and likes to perform on stage. She's a sometimes schoolteacher, a part-time chicken farmer, and an all-the-time wannabe superhero. Her favorite color is blue, unless you're talking about nail polish, in which case her favorite color is Bubblegum Pink.

To learn more about Renae, sign up for her newsletter or visit her website at www.RenaeBrumbaugh.com.

Lone Star Ranger (Texas Ranger Series, book 1)

Ranger to the Rescue (Texas Ranger Series, book 2)

Lassoed by the Lawman (Texas Ranger Series, book 3)

Amid the hazards of camp life, the unlikely friendship growing between the two surprises Isabelle. She's drawn to Preach's brute strength and gentle nature as he leads the ragtag crew toiling for Pollitt's Lumber. But when the ghosts from her past return to haunt her, the choices she will make change the course of her life forever—and that of the man she's come to love.

~

Katherine's Arrangement by Blossom Turner

Marrying him is her only choice to save her family, but Josiah Richardson isn't at all the man she expected.

Katherine William's family was left destitute when their home was burned to the ground by Yankee soldiers, so the ready solution presented by the prominent Mr. Josiah Richardson seems almost too good to believe. He'll provide a home, work for her pa, and a new beginning for her family...if only Katherine will accept his proposal. A marriage of convenience is the last thing she wants, but there doesn't seem to be a better option for her family or herself. Setting aside her dreams of love, Katherine agrees to the arrangement.

The gentleman in Josiah Richardson can no more force his frightened bride into his bed, than he can force her into loving him, so he sets out to gently woo her. He works hard to befriend her, to earn her trust and win her love.

Katherine is pleasantly surprised to find herself drawn to the man she thought she would never love, until an unexpected friendship tears apart all they've worked for. Where once the promise of love had budded between Josiah and Katherine, now they wonder what to do with their so-called marriage. Is love strong enough to weave its healing power through two broken hearts?

~

Waltz in the Wilderness by Kathleen Denly

She's desperate to find her missing father. His conscience demands he risk all to help.

Eliza Brooks is haunted by her role in her mother's death, so she'll do anything to find her missing pa—even if it means sneaking aboard a southbound ship. When those meant to protect her abandon and betray her instead, a family friend's unexpected assistance is a blessing she can't refuse.

Daniel Clarke came to California to make his fortune, and a stable job as a San Francisco carpenter has earned him more than most have scraped from the local goldfields. But it's been four years since he left Massachusetts and his fiancé is impatient for his return. Bound for home at last, Daniel Clarke finds his heart and plans challenged by a tenacious young woman with haunted eyes. Though every word he utters seems to offend her, he is determined to see her safely returned to her father. Even if that means risking his fragile engagement.

When disaster befalls them in the remote wilderness of the Southern California mountains, true feelings are revealed, and both must face heart-rending decisions. But how to decide when every choice before them leads to someone getting hurt?